THE

GOD®

FRANCHISE

Or

The Greatest Story Ever *Sold*!

The until-now extremely top secret
Story of the most profitable
business concept ever created.

*[As documented by impartial witnesses &
journalists randomly selected from the 13.7 billion
years of this planet's existence.]*

This Story is fiction.

by
JOHN ALEXANDER HASKETT

Also by John A. Haskett

Mike Shant Mystery series:
>> Policy Terminated
>> The Conversion
>> Lose Weight – While We Scam
>> W. I. M. P. S.

Highly controversial political satire novel:
>> The Day B.C. Quit Canada. Co-author.

Financial:
>> How to Make Money Beating Horse Races

Consumer:
>> Mexico – Your Complete Guidebook

THE

GOD®

FRANCHISE

Or

The Greatest Story Ever *Sold*!

Durango Publishing Corp.®

Dedication

To my 3 kids--Sandra, Michael, and Roger--all of whom have managed to grow into fine adults.

About the Author

John Haskett has been a freelance writer for many years. He has written hundreds of magazine articles, financial documents, promotion copy, and 7 novels. As a publisher he has published newsletters, magazines, manuals and numerous commissioned surveys.

John (center) with his sons, Roger (left) and Michael (right). Michael is the co-author of TDBCQC.

Definitions to make terms more understandable

Franchise: An exclusive right to market a product or service, granted by the creator/owner of such a right to any individual, group, or organization.

Franchisee: The group which purchases a franchise.

GOD®: The big cheese. The Group. Also known as the Big Franchisor.

GOD™: any duly authorized franchise sold by GOD®; also known as Franchisee.

SCAM: Society of Concerned [or Circumcised] Adult Males.

Story: The telling of a connected series of happenings; a hi*story*. If describing events more than 11 years in the past, always fictitious.

Sold: The selling of a product, service, or idea to the general public through various means of mass communication.

BS: Before the Group ("GOD®") sold its Story.

ASS: After the Story was Sold.

PROLOGUE
Time: 7 BS

"The word god is for me nothing more than the expression and product of human weaknesses, the Bible a collection of honorable, but still primitive legends which are nevertheless pretty childish. No interpretation no matter how subtle can (for me) change this. These subtle interpretations are highly manifold according to their nature and have almost nothing to do with the original text. For me the Jewish religion like all other religions is an incarnation of the most childish superstitions."

An abridgement of a letter from Albert Einstein to Eric Gutkind, sent from Princeton in January 1954, translated from German by Joan Stambaugh.

###

"Never mind giving out the wine right now," Mel said. "We have more important things to do."

As the other nine men fussed and then started to settle down, he poured himself a full glass from the earthenware jug on the head table near him.

"I had a dream recently," he said. "The future for our people looked pretty bad. No, not pretty bad, damned awful! So, I think we should start planning now, with a view to setting up some kind of organization that will be on-going, and which will survive even if the horrors of my dream come true."

"What kind of bad things?" asked Jack. "Did they involve losing money?"

"Yes, they did, and plenty of worse things too."

Turning to his neighbor Sam, Jack stage-whispered, "Worse things than losing money? I find that hard to believe."

"Alright, Jack, we all know your feelings on the subject of money. Just take my word that there were far worse things going on in this dream." Mel banged his hand on the table. He had forgotten he was holding the glass, and wine splattered the three nearest men.

"Can we have some quiet here already? I called this meeting, and asked you nine honchos of our most important group to come, to take some action, not sit around telling dirty jokes." He shot an irate look at David, who was infamous for his repertoire of shaggy-dog triple-entendre jokes. "So can we get started already?"

"So okay already," Hiram said. "Tell us what you have in mind."

"My dream showed that our people are in for some really bad times ahead," Mel said. "We probably can't actually change what's in the cards but we sure as hell can take steps to modify them. And as we all know—especially Jack—money can make a lot of difference. We're going to need lots, and not just on a one-time basis. So, what we need is some plan or scheme that will let us cash in over a long period of time, maybe as long as this planet sticks around. Any comments?"

"Carry on, chief," Jack said sarcastically. He was still offended by Mel's crack about his interest in money.

"Okay. We all seem to be agreed that we need money, and lots of it, and over a long time frame. Maybe forever. During the past few months I've been doing some library research. To me it looks like a franchise scheme could be just what we want. Also, it's better to get in and get a lock on the business now before others tumble to the concept. That's if we can actually be the first to set up some kind of franchise deal."

"What's a franchise?" asked Simon, the poet of the group who had not clue one about the real world.

"Well, as I understand it, it's a deal where you set up a scheme of some kind, and then charge others to duplicate what you've done. And the real sweet part is that this charging, through apparently what's called royalty and marketing fees, goes on and on. Forever!

"Of course, we all realize that for this idea—and us—to be successful, the whole scheme must be kept ultra secret. If it ever got out that our people were behind it, it would make some of the events in my dream look like the good old days."

"How can we do that?"

"Simple. We just go on record—and stay there—as being completely, totally, and irrevocably against the concept of what we're actually franchising on the quiet."

Part 1 – Chapter 1
Time: 32 ASS

"My atheism is true piety towards the universe and denies only gods fashioned by men in their own images, to be servants of their human interests."

George Santayana (1863-1952).

"It will not do to investigate the subject of religion too closely, as it is apt to lead to infidelity."

Abraham Lincoln, 16th US President (12 Feb 1809-1865).

Chairman Isaac banged his gavel. "Let's quiet down already. First, we'll go over some old notes from the initial organizational meeting in 7BS. Hard to believe that was almost 40 years ago, but as you may have heard"—he paused for the expected chuckles— "it sometimes takes our people quite a while to get an agreement on almost anything. Anyway, here we are, all set up and running, and I'm proud you chose me to be the first formal chairman of our group.

"As you all know from the memo sent out before this meeting, we've agreed on some broad guidelines. Our group will be known as "Great Official Developers", or GOD® for short. I'll briefly recap the reasons for setting up GOD®."

He cleared his throat dramatically.

"Some of us—especially Mel—have had bad feelings about the future for our people. Several even thought that the future looked cataclysmic. In a vote all ten of us agreed that we had to take steps now to avoid what could easily be one or more absolute catastrophes in the future.

"We also agreed that it was better to get in and get our scheme set up now before others got off their butts and did the same. Our consensus was that there was only room, on this planet at least, for one GOD®."

Isaac put on his serious look. "You'll all notice that our group's name is capitalized. That's only befitting for a headquarters-type organization.   But we have to have some common name that we can offer to our franchisees. You all know that those are the suck.., ah, customers, we sell our concept to. So we decided to use a lower cap 'God™' as the key brand name we'll be marketing. And this way we can sell 'God™' to a bunch of different groups, so that each in turn will be able to offer their members a 'God™' of their own.

"We'll get this brand name trademarked tighter than a virgin's pussy just as soon as Abe and the legal guys can get on it. And just to repeat, for those maybe thinking of tomorrow's inauguration party, we'll be the only GOD® allowed anywhere. Abe says he has already got a universal trademark registration certificate on the way. So, we'll be GOD®. And each accredited franchisee group will be able to lease, or franchise to be technical, the right to their own God™.

"For example, in time to come there might be a Crapolic God™ or a Buptist God™, or whatever the future groups' names might be.

"Okay, that should clear up the name situation. Without any disagreement we agreed that the people behind GOD® must be kept ultra-secret. But so that our future generations will have the true story, and be able to capitalize on it, we will keep an official top-secret confidential record. To prevent others from getting hold of and reading this, we'll have it written backwards in some old language like, say, Hebrew, so that a mirror and knowledge of that dead language will be needed to read it. And as mirrors won't even be in common use for another thousand years or so, it should stay nice and secret.

"Finally, to prevent backlashes against GOD®'s real control group—those of our people who actually make the shekels we need to cover GOD®'s expenses—the official public viewpoint of our group, and any subsequent groups it sets up, will be totally and unequivocally against everything associated with GOD®, religious groups, and other bodies of that ilk.

"To carry out our work, we'll set up a marketing division of GOD® for external usage. It will be called the Society of Concerned Adult Males. To make it simple and prevent any confusion, the acronym will be SCAM. And that's what it will be referred to, internally and externally."

The chairman poured himself a full glass of wine and downed it in a single swallow. "Now, just to reinforce our key rule, everyone remember that we can't be associated in any way with any of this GOD® franchise business. Others would never go for it if they knew we'd set it up and were making money from it.

"For now—and evermore—there must never be any written material associating us in any way with GOD® except for the official secret record. Any external involvement of any kind must be through SCAM only, and that through the external arm of SCAM only.

"In fact, our people must appear to be totally against any GOD® or big shot concept. So, when we start things running perhaps we should do so with a dramatic incident which sets out and proves beyond any doubt that point. Any ideas?"

"Maybe we could get one of us to be put on a stake or something?" Mel said.

"You mean to knock him off?" The chairman looked worried.

Mel smiled sweetly. "Maybe somebody's who's behind in his dues?"

"Hmm. How about if we just fake a, what do you call it, a stakifixtion?"

"No, I think it's called a crossifixtion," Hiram piped up.

"Whatever. Surely we can find one of our people who would like to have a crack at acting." The chairman looked around at the group.

Mel said, "Well, acting's not one of our people's strong points, but we can try to find someone."

Hymie, always a stickler for Robert's Rules of Disorder, put up his hand, waved it vigorously, was ignored, and finally spoke up anyway.

"And we should give this guy a good distinctive 'working name', something, you know, that will be catchy and easily remembered for when we start franchising."

"How about McDonald? That's pretty catchy." Mel was an anglophile.

"No. That would never grab anyone's attention. How about Windy? Or better yet, Wendy?" The chairman had once scored in Cairo with a tourist girl named Wendy.

"Too much a broad's name," Duke (aka Saul) said. "We want something to appeal to all those manly types, especially the ones who will be doing the recruiting and brain conditioning. Say, how about Joe? That's a nice short moniker."

Mel frowned. "Too communist-sounding. Jake? Jack? Say, I've got it. A southern New World friend of mine is named Jesus. That's short and sweet."

The chairman objected. "We have to be careful not to be too ethnic. That would screw up worldwide sales. But maybe Jesus isn't too ethnic. Actually, I can't even tell if it's ethnic or not. So how about a last name?"

"Cohen? Diamond? Gold? They're all nice and short." Mel was just over five feet and stuck up for shorties whenever possible.

"Christ, Mel, we just finished saying that we couldn't be associated with this scheme and..."

Mel jumped up. "That's it! Simple, catchy, and unusual enough to be remembered. It's also short enough to fit into ads without it costing an arm and a leg. Christ, Jesus Christ. It's great!"

The chairman nodded. "Okay by me. Anybody doesn't like it? No objections? Okay, motion carried. It'll be Jesus Christ for the stake boy. Now, under other old business, we have a motion from Benny to offer more than one popey. Maybe award them on a continent basis?"

Hiram, who rarely paid attention at any meeting, looked more puzzled than usual. "What's a popey?"

"Well, Hiram," Isaac said, "obviously you were asleep last meeting. We decided that one of the first titles we'd franchise and market after GOD® would be that of popey, a sort of underling stooge big-noise type who in turn would set up a bunch of flunkies beneath him. Each level, of course, would be paying us—oops, I mean GOD®— royalties and marketing fees. Having only one popey would take a lot of clerical and administrative crap off our shoulders, without affecting our net take. Sort of like an area franchise arrangement."

Benny came to life. "But having one popey on say every continent would increase our take five or six times. Perfect."

"But the downside, Benny," said Jack, "is that we might be diluting our overall receipts. A trick of all marketing is to make the suckers—the buying public—think they're getting something special, maybe even unique. If we start flooding the market with popeys, the value of each will probably decrease, and in the long run might bring in less for six, say, than one good one alone could do. So my vote is to keep just one popey, at least for the present. But make it really a profitable one, preferably able to hustle in millions, maybe even a billion, recruits."

"Your argument makes sense, Jack. Let's have a vote." The chairman looked around the room. "All in favor of more than one popey? Three. Those who buy Jack's argument for just one popey? Six, plus me to make seven. The motion is defeated. At least for now GOD® will just offer one popey, with a worldwide exclusive."

"Just remember, though, that there's no reason why we can't have more than one big cheese," Jack said. "All we have to do is make the popey a worldwide exclusive. But then we can come up with another different name for some other group, and market it also on a worldwide exclusive. So in the end, Benny, we'll actually be able to do what you suggested. End up with half a dozen different windbag big shots, each bringing in hordes of recruits under whatever organization name each area manager prefers."

The meeting started to dissolve as members looked longingly at the nearby buffet table.

The chairman quickly spoke up. "But before we break, I want to put someone in charge of getting this show on the road with some dynamite showmanship, someone who can really dazzle the dummies with fast foot work."

He looked over the members. "And there's really no one who can deliver the goods better than you, Jack. So, you're appointed in charge of the entertainment division. Come up with some good effects."

Jack pulled his notebook out. "This stuff is all under way?"

"Yeah. You want me to give you all the details?"

"That would be nice, Isaac. If you're not too busy," he added sarcastically.

"Never too busy for the members. Here's where we stand.

"First, to use the correct word, it's a crucifixion, not stakifixtion or crossifixtion, for Pete's sake." Isaac prided himself on his word knowledge. "I've lined up Saul Fellows."

"The actor who did those horrible pastry commercials for Mummy's Mellow Mouthfuls?"

"Okay, okay, Jack. I know the budget's a bitch, but it's all the committee would give us. Anyway, what's with the cross program?"

"Saul is going to use the same collapsing nails he used in his off-Broadway production of MacBill, and he's even going to throw in some fake blood free. And because he views this role as his comeback, he offered to have his cousin and brother-in-law act as a couple of crooks for free.

"They'll be on either side of Saul as JC, to add balance to the composition. They don't have to say anything, just moan a lot, and Saul said they'd like the chance to get into the entertainment business."

"How you going to cover the move of the body from the cross to the hole in the hillside? A lot of people will be still on hand for that, and it's got to look real, so that later the fantastic rebirth has a lot of pizzazz."

"No problem," Isaac said. "In that region there's a rainstorm every late afternoon, and at the height of it we'll haul Saul into his temporary tomb. It'll look real, Jack, have no fear. Saul's real good at acting dead. It's probably his best role."

"It better be. What about the walking on water event?"

"That's where most of my miserly budget went." Isaac wrung his hands to emphasize his plight. "Anyway, it has worked out pretty well. I got hold of a bankrupt stair company. They had a huge warehouse full of steps in all different shapes and sizes. So we just put together a bunch of them, spaced a stride apart, and sunk them under the waves far enough that they can't be seen, luckily they were all painted a sea blue for some woman who liked that color, and so they just disappear once they're in the water.

"I'm using Saul again—don't worry, he'll be made up to look totally different—and again the role is non-speaking, so he'll work below scale. He just walks into the river until he reaches the first step, then follows them across giving the absolute appearance of walking on water. The yokels will eat it up."

"What if they get too close and can actually see those steps?"

"Impossible. We'll have the area near the water completely fenced off—to 'protect JC from the mob'—and no one will be allowed closer than a hundred meters or so. And we have it scheduled for late evening, so all they'll see will be this bearded guy merrily walking on top of the waves. It's brilliant!"

Jack grunted. "I've heard that before. You better be right, amigo, there's a lot of shekels riding on all those performances. They're the real start of our franchising scheme, and to bring in the money they'll have to be really impressive.

"And what about the other two shows?"

"Well in hand, Jack. The feeding of the crowd with just a handful of bread and fishes is being catered by Manny's Catering. He's agreed to plant a bunch of his employees in the crowd, and they'll secretly bring out and pass around food in their areas. The overall impression will be that JC is actually feeding the mob with his own few items."

"And the big finale?"

"All ready, Jack. I've rented a couple of real powerful hovercraft from Myron's Mobiles, this is his slack season so he gave us a great deal. I've positioned them about a hundred meters apart, and on signal Myron will start them up. They'll create a swath of dry land between them, and Saul as JC can zip across the sea on dry land."

"Won't the big fans be seen?"

"I'm hiding them behind large flat bottom boats which we'll fill with our own people, who'll stand up and create a disturbance at the key moment. It'll only last for a couple of minutes, and everyone will be so engrossed in Saul's walk that no one will notice them. It'll work great."

"What if some of the prospective franchisees like our idea, but want real proof of this crappola we're feeding to the rubes?"

"They won't, Jack. These prospects are already three-quarters sold, and all they want is a little reassurance. Saul and his buddies will provide that, showing how gullible their future customers really will be. After these four acts I'll bet shekels to doughnuts that there's a waiting list of buyers who want to get in on a GOD® franchise."

Chapter 2

"There is no heaven, there is no hell; these be the dreams of baby minds; Tools of the wily Fetisheer, to fright the fools his cunning blinds."

Sir Richard Burton (1821-1890), writer.

###

"Do you really think it's a good deal, Luigi?"
He laughed.
"A good deal, Tomas? It's the deal of the century. No, of the millennium. It's our way out of this day-to-day flogging of lucky charms and amulets to superstitious peasants. If we're able to land a franchise for our country, we--and our families for ever—will have the world by the balls. You saw those four performances we were promised. Weren't they fantastic?"

Tomas hesitated, then burst into a giant grin.

"Yes, they were. I couldn't believe when that guy, what was his name, Jesus something, actually pushed aside that stone and walked out of his tomb. I'd seen him crucified just hours earlier, nails through him, blood everywhere, and yet he was then as untouched as a seven year old virgin.

"And that walk on water! I was watching the crowd, every single person had his mouth open. And when Jesus fed that huge mass of people, apparently using only a few scraps of food!

"But the best performance of all was when he walked through the sea, which parted for him. I have to say, those GOD® people are fantastic entertainers."

"That's what I mean, cousin. It's foolproof. It's the best deal we've ever been offered. If we can just get our financing in order, and get a big enough franchise area, we'll be set.

"Have you given any thought to a name for our franchise?"

Tomas pulled out a sheet of papyrus. "I came up with a whole bunch of them, but when I looked them over again most seemed pretty silly. I ended up with just three that I think you might like, Luigi: the universal group of people, or a great camaraderie..."

"Tomas. Those names sound like crap. We need something short, something simple to say and remember—we're looking for repeat business here, don't forget—and something we can trademark so other crooks can't use it. Don't you have something like that?"

Tomas frowned. "I thought those were pretty good, Luigi. But perhaps they were a little too intellectual. Well, here's my last choice, and you may find it just what you want: the Crapolic group.

Luigi sat back, massaged his temples with both hands, and then smiled. "Tomas, I think you've got it. I like it. However, I think the ending is a little weak.

"Let's tighten it up. How about club? No, too exclusive. Company? Too businessy. Church?

"Yeah, that's the word, partner. We'll call our franchise the Crapolic Church, using capital letters of course to show it's important. Agreed?"

"Agreed," nodded Tomas. "It does have a nice ring to it, Luigi. Now what about our franchise area?"

"It'd be nice if we could ask for all of what will be called Europa. But that's maybe a bridge too far. Even just the Latino areas would probably be too expensive.

"But listen, if we only ask to franchise our own country, then later sneak some friends or members or whatever we end up calling them into other areas, maybe we can actually extend our franchise area without having to pay humungous liras.

"And by then we'll know a hell of a lot more about this whole GOD® business so we should be able to rack up lots of new business at little cost. According to the GOD® biggies, once you get started the business will spread like a cold in a kid's classroom.

"People just naturally want to be part of something big, and especially something that promises—or at least appears to promise—a real payday down the road. What do you think of that plan?"

"I guess it's a good one, Luigi. As you know I'm not too strong in the business area, I'm better at meeting and greeting prospective customers. Seems like a good way to get started, though, without blowing all our capital on a huge franchise area. I was listening to a couple of GOD® guys talking in the bar—they couldn't see me behind a cigarette machine—and they were discussing the various franchise areas and what they could get for them.

"Francie was priced high, as one GOD® guy said the people there were such stupid sheep that they'd likely all join up, making it a very profitable deal for the franchisee— that's the people who buy the franchise, in case you didn't know that, Luigi—and the other guy agreed, then said that Italio would have to be almost given away, because the Italions weren't sheep like the frogs, and that whoever bought that franchise would have to work really hard to get it off the ground and profitable. So, I think we could get it for very little."

"I hope that GOD® guy's wrong about Italy. I really think our countrymen, and especially the countrywomen, will be very interested in our GOD® promotion.

"Give them some good advertising, and maybe even a few publicity stunts like the ones the GOD® people staged here, I think that down the road a few years we might really make the Crapolic Church into a goldmine, maybe even build a head office building somewhere, like Naples, where there are a lot of single broads."

"I think a more conservative area would be better, Luigi. After all, we have to maintain some semblance of propriety if we're going to tell people we can get them tickets to paradise. I think Rome would be good."

"Rome? It would never catch on, Tomas. Too old-fashioned."

Chapter 3

"We have names for people who have many beliefs for which there is no rational justification. When their beliefs are extremely common we call them 'religious'; otherwise, they are likely to be called 'mad', 'psychotic' or ' delusional'... Clearly there is sanity in numbers."

Sam Harris, (b.1967) 'The End of Faith'.

###

The London Evening Post reported the event on page 2, opposite the nude pictures of a current 16-year old girl whose latest song about the trials and tribulations of growing old had sold more than 10 million copies. It bannered the headline in 50-point type:

Hippie parts sea so he doesn't get wet!

"Yesterday an event of interest occurred at the Dead Sea, when a local hippie, well known to the authorities, and accompanied by his band of a dozen hangers-on, waved his skinny hands and appeared to part the waves. He then proceeded to run from one side to the other, choosing the very narrowest part of the watercourse, which was barely 45 meters.

"Our observer on the scene, Clayton Finch-Jones-Smyth III, said the evening light was fading fast, and he actually felt that the hippie, known as Jesus C to law officers who had previously served several ASBOs on him, had really splashed through a very little stream at the sea's head. 'It didn't appear to me that he had done much of anything,' reported F-J-S III.

In Vancouver, Canada, a quick on-the-street survey of people on the way home after work by the prestigious Vancouver Wizard daily elicited several comments, most of which are unprintable in this family newspaper.

The one woman who agreed to be quoted, a Ms Marie Smith, said "It sounds to me like another of those European practical jokes they seem to enjoy so much. If this Jesus C can really part the waves, he'd find it easy to get a job in Thailand where they seem to have continuing problems with flooding."

In Los Angeles, the Hollywood Bombshell weekly reported the incident in a paragraph on page 43, just below an obituary of a famous talk show host whose name they couldn't spell right. "Big splash in the Dead Sea," it reported. "Local man makes waves cease, then walks across to other side. Too bad Barnum is not yet born, he'd sign the man in a minute."

The Jerusalem Onguard posted a note on page 11. "Possibly more troubles developing in the Dead Sea area, as a local exhibitionist tinkers with the waters. Let us all hope this isn't the start of a water shortage scheme by unfriendlies in that area."

Chapter 4

*"This little life is all we must endure
The grave's holy peace is ever sure,
We fall asleep and never wake again;
Nothing is of us but the moldering flesh
Whose elements dissolve and merge afresh
In earth, air, water, plants, and other men."*

James Thomson (1700-1748).

###

The world public reaction was different.

In Paris, Francie, where the GOD® franchise team was hoping for a huge Euro sale, the man-in-the-street was ecstatic.

"This is wonderful news," a sexy blonde with legs right up to the top of her pantyhose said. "I have been looking for something new to get involved with ever since my last boy friend discovered he was gay.

"I tried using Ouija boards for fun, but that didn't work. Then I took up sponsoring chastity belts with no keys for prostitutes who wanted to make a life change. Unfortunately, I couldn't give any away.

"So this development at the Dead Sea—that's somewhere in Africa, isn't it? —gives me a chance to devote myself to a cause that's bigger than me, that's more meaningful, and one that doesn't really take too much time. You can say I'm all in favor of Jose, I think that's the guy's name, isn't it?"

In Malaga, Spain, the radio station 'Toda Tiempo' asked its listeners to phone in with their views.

"It's a great way to get these hippies off the street," one older man said. "Keep them busy doing constructive work like this and we'd be able to cut our welfare costs by 50 percent."

"I don't really understand why he had to walk across a lake or whatever it was," said a younger woman. "I think lakes should be kept for swimming."

"Good for him," an admitted hippy-lover said. "It didn't make much sense to do what he did, but that's the whole point of being a hippy. Like, it's doing your own thing, man, you know."

The Mexico City Macho conducted a telephone survey of a statistically-significant sample of its very large (over 4 million) readership), and reported the results on its editorial page under the heading "No more divisions needed":

"Our readers are overwhelmingly against this type of grandiose stunt. Obviously, this Sr. Jesus Christi individual is promoting some cause, some probably-secret association of people. In short, just another division, just as was his spectacular dividing of the Dead Sea stream simply a minor division, according to our expert witness, of a very small body of water.

"Not wanted, Sr. Christi, not needed. What we do need is more togetherness, not division. Our readers agree.

"We asked our readers, 'Do you agree that this Dead Sea stunt was a worthwhile expenditure of time and resources?'

"89 percent of our readers said no. Just 5 percent said yes. The other 6 percent couldn't care less."

The crucifixion performance was commented on somewhat more favorably.

In Penticton, a small wine-growing town in the interior of British Columbia, the daily Grim Reaper editorialized: "This appears to be a first-class entertainment event. While some of the audience complained that the show was far too short, and that they could hardly see the actors in the fading evening light, our correspondent reports that most in attendance at the open-air show were pleased with the authentic costumes and stage devices—the leading character was apparently nailed to a wooden beam with very large metal nails—which were well presented and skillfully used."

In the UK, the Welwyn Garden City Beaver gave it four out of five stars.

"One of our reporters was in the area, and caught the last five minutes of the performance. She thought the dying and so-called death scenes were well acted and cleverly presented. She said that most of the audience, composed mainly of middle and older aged women, were caught up in the drama, and she saw a number who were actually weeping.

'I'd recommend it to anyone who likes soap opera type shows. Any fan of East Enders (an English TV show which has been running for what seems about 80 years) would just love it.'

"We tried to get some pictures of the event but the show managers said cameras were definitely not allowed."

In Baghdad, the Iraqi Inquisitor was an exception to the generally favorable reviews.

"We do not think that pranks of this kind should be tolerated, certainly not on something as historic and important to so many peoples as the Dead Sea.

"This Jesus Krist was stated to be in his early 30s, certainly old enough to be beyond such childish nonsense.

We think the authorities should take a very firm stand against such western hooliganism."

The Montreal Canada Le Bonjour editorial was published solely in French and no one outside the French-only city could understand it.

In Hong Kong, the Entrepreneurial Entrepreneur discussed the marketing possibilities of the performance.

"We feel this type of entertainment, reasonably produced and reasonably well performed, is an excellent marriage of drama with spectacle.

"Too often performance entrepreneurs do not think about the marketing possibilities of their productions, whereas this producer—whose name unfortunately was not given—has obviously thought seriously about how this play, and future reruns, can be marketed successfully.

"Any road show company with a limited budget, and just the three main actors, could present this play almost anywhere, even in countries where a translation from English (as was used here) to another tongue was necessary.

"The play lends itself to economical, and profitable, marketing. We say well done!"

Part 2 – Chapter 5
Time: 43 ASS

"Writing for a penny a word is ridiculous. If a man really wanted to make a million dollars, the best way to do it would be to start his own religion."

L. Ron Hubbard, (1911-1986), a one-time penny a word science fiction author who came to his economic senses and who started the Church of Scientology.

"I call this meeting of GOD® to order." Benjamin smacked his gavel on the plastic table top, making a substantial dent. Damn, he thought, Morrie will probably moan and groan about that, and try to hold back the deposit we gave him for this junky furniture. "C'mon, fellows, quieten down and show a little respect for your duly elected chairman."

The hubbub died, to be replaced in several areas by muttered laughing. But it did quieten.

"I'm happy to report that matters are generally in fine shape. Later we'll hear from the various committee heads, but for now just let me say that things are definitely A-OK."

Several strangled groans were heard. Benjamin was a great believer in using pre-and post-dated expressions as often as possible.

"The main item is our franchising report. I'm actually also head of that sub-committee, so I'll carry on.

"Getting to the meat of it, I can say that franchises are going like hot cakes." More groans. "Just yesterday we closed Tanzania, and at a much higher franchise fee than we'd hoped.

"And we got them to agree to a very substantial 6 percent of overall shekel activity for sales promotion by head office—us—and that should mean a solid 3 or 4 percent left as pure profit.

"I mean, how much promotion is going to be needed in a place like Tanzania? There are only two radio stations, so we'll be able to saturate the air waves with next to zilch expenditure."

Benjamin looked very pleased, and waited for the expected round of applause. When it failed to materialize, he cleared his throat and carried on.

"Otherwise, all franchises already sold are starting to show steady gains in the gross amounts we're getting from our franchisees as ongoing royalty fees.

"The accounts haven't been audited yet, but off the cuff I can say that the picture is going to please you all. I estimate that gross will be about 7 percent higher than last quarter."

That did bring a small spattering of applause, and Benjamin blushed becomingly.

"You're doing just fine, Benny, as I knew you would when I put you up for the chairman job." David was about Benjamin's age but acted a lot older.

He felt he had to, as he had single-handedly successfully made the first franchising inroads into Latin America, a geographic region which until his move had been untouched.

Benjamin blushed again. "There is one matter which has come up, and while I had, I think, the authority to deal with it, I thought its newness might make it useful to get all your input."

"Okay, Benjie, tell us all about it. We're all ears." Jake actually had prominent ears, and loved to get a chance to use his favorite line.

"Several of our biggest Crapolic franchisees, including the frogs and the Germanos, keep asking head office about the manual we promised them."

"You mean the franchise operating manual? That's been out for several months," David said.

"No, not that, and yes, it has been published and was delivered in March," Benjamin said.

"No, they're talking about a manual the committee in 32ASS discussed. A book of some kind that each Crapolic franchisee can use to give out to its new members, sort of a club propaganda type manual which the franchisees feel will engender more feelings of 'togetherness', and thus tie the members in tighter."

"And more profitably," Saul said, to general laughter.

"Yes, that of course," Benjamin said. "So, what we have to decide is, first, are we going to produce such a manual or book, and second, what will be in it."

"Who was that bunch they used back at the start to do those tablet things?" Adam's memory for detail wasn't great, but he did remember the big points.

"You mean that quartet of freelancers that did such a good job on the stone tablets?"

"Yes. They still around?"

"Their names were Matthew, Luke, Jack, no, John, and, uh, oh yeah, Mark. Yes, they're still around, but they're not freelance writing any more.

"They've been over in Eastern Europa, and they're going like gangbusters in selling franchises to what seems like every jerkwater country over there.

"Harry was just saying before the meeting that they've been setting new sales records almost every month.

"Appears that they all have a natural gift for putting out our franchise spiel, and with their beards and all they look so impressive—so honest—that they just melt any sales resistance like an ice cube in a hooker's G string."

"So they're out for this new book thing," David said. "Anybody else floating around, Benjie?"

He hated that nickname. "Well, Dave"—how did he like it? —"there is one name that popped up. Remember that guy the '32 bunch had do those Dead Sea scroll things? What's his name?"

"Street, Woody Street, if I recall correctly, and I do." Amos was the committee's historian and took his job seriously.

"Right. Well, he's available, writing's been a little slow since he finished those scrolls, and of course they're being hidden so only his heirs will even collect any royalties. I hear he's a little maxxed out on his cards."

"That sounds good, give him some work and save us some pesos."

"Just what I thought, Saul. Even better, I thought we could have him use the famous quartet's names for some of the sections of the book.

"Those guys used to be really publicity hungry, and now that they're out of the writing spotlight, they might take a little free PR in lieu of royalty commissions."

"Great idea, Benjie. That way we can capitalize on some celebrity names and save bucks at the same time. How big is this manual or book going to be?"

"I guess that's pretty much our call, Davie." There, that should piss him off. "We can call the shots as we like.

"From what franchise sales told me, they want something long enough to look impressive to the rubes, something short enough that it won't cost an arm and a leg to produce.

"We do have a couple of contacts in the printing trade, so we may be able to get a good quantity price if we keep the size reasonable."

"Okay, enough already."

Mort had a chain of used chariot shops, and believed in cutting right to the chase.

"Let's just pick a figure, say 150 sheets of papyrus, and tell this Woody writer guy to fill that.

"That should be big enough for the end customers, small enough not to bankrupt us or the franchisees who will supply it."

"Okay, Mort, let's put it to a vote. All in favor of using Woody Street and having him fill say 150 sheets with stuff from GOD®? Seven, eight, nine, okay, with me it's unanimous. Carried."

"Hold on a sec, Bennie. We need to give him some instructions about what's on those 150 papyrus sheets. I know writers"—he didn't, actually, but he believed it added veracity to make this claim— "and if everything isn't spelled out, they're going to go crazy.

"We'd end up with some crap about how their mommy didn't love them or something."

"A good point, Davie." Would he never get the point? "From what the franchising department said, they want a lot of good solid platitudes, stuff that'll appeal to little old ladies and wealthy old farts getting close to croaking.

"You know, good stimulating tips on living the good life, being nice to people, not stealing from friends, all that kind of stuff."

"That should do it," Amos said. "No point in doing the whole job for this writer. Let him earn his pay. Just emphasize that it's for a family audience, so he should keep the cursing and hardcore sex to a minimum.

"But a little sex and mysterious stuff always goes over well. Maybe he should also throw in lots of peoples' names. Whether they're real or not doesn't matter, people just like to read about people, right?"

"I agree, Amos, there should be a lot of feel-good material, and having lists of names and places can't hurt."

Benjamin looked at his notes. "And research said we should ask the writer to underline or use red ink or something to highlight words attributed to JC. They said the promotion department got a lot of requests for stuff JC has 'said', and having it clearly marked would make their job easier."

"Another color ink? That's going to boost the printing costs. Is it worth it?" David was cost conscious when his own money was involved.

"I think one of our trade contacts will still be able to give us a good rock-bottom price," Benjamin said.

"They know we'll have lots of stuff to be printed in the years ahead, and they'll likely use a very sharp quill on this first big order."

"What about the quantity of this, what the hell are we going to call it?" Amos liked specifics.

"Doesn't really matter, but some wheel close to head office jokingly suggested we call it after him. He evidently is a big contributor to our favorite causes."

"So let's make him happy. It doesn't really matter, and it doesn't cost us a dinar. What's his name?"

Benjamin looked at his notes again. "Ible. Barry Ible."

"That's a hell of a name. Let's combine the initial and his name, sounds a lot more pronounceable. And it's short, good for cheap classified ads."

Benjamin wrote the name down. "You're right, Saul. It's simple and recognizable. We'll call it a Bible. One easily pronounceable word, no initials. No other business? Okay, meeting adjourned."

The sales promotion department was working on contests. The manager, a hotshot marketing expert named Morriss—two ss's to make his name memorable—loved contests, and aimed for one new one every week.

This week was devoted to developing a contest under which all Crapolic franchises could win free gifts. The details were a little vague at the moment, so he called in his chief assistant Ira.

Only 22 years old, Ira had found his perfect niche, operating with hardly any authority, and thus no responsibility, as underling to a basically stupid jerk who thought he was a gift to the marketing world.

Ira figured he could handle the stupidity and misplaced arrogance of Morriss for at least another year or two, long enough to get hooked up with some of the real shakers in SCAM and/or maybe even GOD®.

"Ira, my buddy and assistant, lend an ear." Morriss felt he had to continually stress Ira's inferior role in the sales promotion department hierarchy, just in case he entertained any delusions of grandeur.

"In fact, lend two." He chuckled at his joke which Ira had not heard before more than three thousand times.

"I have a situation, my colleague and friend"—he treated Ira as neither— "and we have to put our collective brains to work."

That will make a total of one, Ira thought.

"Okay, exalted leader." Morriss took the title at face value. Ira realized he'd have to be far more basic if he wanted a rise from his boss. "What's the problemo?"

"The head office boys in SCAM want us to keep up the good work in goosing the franchisees to increase their gross sales volumes. One of them, a Lenny something, you don't know him, said that over the past quarter sales have increased by about 12 percent.

"Now he wants that increased, so we have to tickle the little brain cells, just like that frog Porot would say."

Morriss was a fan of late night preplays of TV shows scheduled for eons in the future.

"I was thinking of some kind of a bonus plan, where individual franchisees could win some points, and maybe later use them to buy some cheapo gimcrack junk that we can get for almost zilch from a friend of mine who buys the stuff from Chinese rip-off guys."

"Sounds like a real winner, exalted ruler." If you were planning something for kindergarteners. "Any thoughts on the specific kind of contest?"

Morriss scratched his Elvis-style sideburns. Another contribution of those eons-early music tapes.

"Well, not really, my assistant. I was hoping that maybe you'd be able to come up with something for a change."

For a change? The last time Morriss had conceived an actual idea was before Ira's time in the department.

"You know, industry captain, (would his asshole boss never tumble to his broad-brush sarcasm?) I read an internal memo from the SCAM assistant vice-president in charge of recruitment. Did you happen to see it?"

Morriss had never read a memo. He felt that ignorance was truly bliss.

"No? Well, anyway, the substance was that SCAM big shots wanted real efforts made to lower the ages when new recruits were properly and fully integrated into their various God™ franchises."

Morriss made a point of sharpening a quill pen. He hadn't understood a word Ira said, and he knew he'd only look more foolish than usual if he said anything.

Ira waited the standard 60 seconds.

"Anyway, what they want, that's SCAM, I think, is for members from the various franchises to be conditioned at an earlier age. That way the big shot figures they can be roped in for life."

"That's an excellent idea, my assistant." So what the hell does it all mean?

As if he had read Morriss's thoughts, what few there were, Ira cleared it all up.

"SCAM wants the younger people in the various franchise countries to be indoctrinated earlier. They feel if they are, there's an excellent chance that they'll stay that way forever."

"Why didn't you say that before?"

As always poor Morriss had to do everything. "So how can we do that?"

"We can't, all by ourselves, chief executive, but we could make a tiny start."

Morriss didn't like that word tiny. Had his former girl friend been shooting off her mouth again? And everyone knew that there were more important things than size, like, well...

"So, big boss, how about we set up a contest to reward franchisees who do a better job of brainwashing their little customers?"

"Brainwashing? I don't think that's a word that SCAM, or GOD® either, would want us to be using here in the important sales promotion department, my assistant."

"It was just a joke, chief chief. But the contest could award points, based on how each franchisee set up his indoctrination programs. The younger ages he caught and converted, the more points."

"Caught and converted. I like that, Ira." In his enthusiasm, Morriss forgot to use a demeaning title.

"Caught and converted. We can use that as the overall contest slogan. I think it will really fly."

Just like a bird, Ira thought, because even the eons-early tapes hadn't shown much of the advanced aircraft that were still not invented.

"Sure, Morriss, we could tie it all together under that banner. Like all stuff we do for franchisees, however, we'd need to mark all papyrus we send out as 'Confidential Level 12-A', because I'm pretty sure the SCAM honchos might not take to that 'caught' word for general public distribution."

"Good point there, my helper. What's Level 12-A again?"

Ira knew Morriss didn't know what Level 1 was, let alone 12-A.

"That level means it can be circulated to all franchisee offices and individuals, but is not cleared for any further distribution.

"In short, it can't be used in any external advertising, certainly not on those limp blimps that the frogs tried to use last month. Luckily for them, and us as well, I guess, they were so limp they couldn't even get them off the ground."

Morriss, who had been semi-dozing now that he'd solved all the contest problems, jerked awake. Limp! Had that ex-girlfriend bitch really been shooting off her mouth?

"As to details, exalted pharaoh, I jotted down a few specifics. Want to hear them?"

Limp indeed. Well, he'd set her straight later.

"Details, my second? Of course."

"Keeping to the points, which could be redeemed later for free junk, courtesy your oriental contact, I thought that maybe 10 points could be awarded for each kid brainwashed by the local God™ franchise by age 6. If they caught and converted by age 5, then 15 points, and 25 for 4s.

"And just to tie in with SCAM's stated goals, a grand bonus of 50 points for every kid 3 and under who's added to the franchisee customer list."

Morriss had lost track at age 5 but he knew from experience that Ira was a mathematical whiz; he could actually do percentages in his head without using a quill or papyrus, or even a slate.

"That makes a whole lotta sense to me, my junior colleague." He stood and stretched.

"Okay, you have my official blessing to do all that stuff you were talking about. Just write it down, use the permanent ink for it, and add my initials and official seal."

Morriss's official seal existed only in his imagination. Management in SCAM only got personal corporate seals to use on papyrus scrolls when they reached vice-president level. Morriss was a long way from that.

"And then have it copied—tell those Assyrians to get the lead out, we'll need what, 100 copies?"

"137 actually, leader."

Morriss had lost track of franchisee sales last September.

"And probably a couple more before we get this out. The sales department is going great guns."

"Probably largely due to this department's clever and effective contests," Morriss said. "Carry on up the Nile with this, junior."

Ira nodded. That Peter Principle which would be formulated much later —people get promoted at least one level beyond their competence—was already hard at work in this department.

In the franchise sales department Clio had just received one of those infamous SCAM memos: "Getting complaints not sufficient distinction between different major God™ franchises. Fix it."

Clio had been in charge of franchise sales support for almost four years and had posted some impressive figures. She wanted to move up in GOD®, but she knew she was sexually incapable of doing that in SCAM. The last letter of the acronym was her undoing.

Nevertheless, she had high hopes for her upward mobility in GOD®, and the way it was growing verified that it was a good wagon to hitch her star to. So she tried very hard to do what Head Office requested, and fast, and on time.

The "fix it" instructions in the memo didn't indicate any dates or times, but she knew the implied deadline was "now or even sooner".

She hit her intercom switch, a string with a bell hooked on, threaded through the wall to her assistant's desk. How nice it would be when they got around to inventing real, electronic intercoms. But that was way off in the future.

"You rang, Clio?"

Her assistant Sam was 25, about her own age if she was honest, usually she said 22—she liked double digits—very tall, slightly stooped, and very much in lust with Clio.

She knew that, and like most females encouraged it when it was to their advantage, but normally she just ignored the hot eyes that Samuel threw her way.

"Yeah, come here."

When he was by her desk, "What are you working on, Sam?"

"That tabulation of expected franchise needs in the area of additional limp blimps for next quarter. You asked me to have it done by this afternoon, and I'm almost..."

"Never mind that for now. We just got a request—read order—for fixing the lack of differentiation between the various GOD® franchises.

"We'll need to get right on this. I want it finished by Saturday."

"Isn't that some kind of holy day for somebody?"

"Only for that one small God™ franchise group off the Red Sea. And they have so few members that it hardly matters what they choose to do for weekend fun. My deadline is Saturday."

Sam straightened, then immediately slipped back into his slumped posture.

"Okay, Clio. What's the plan of attack?"

Sam was a fan of the WW2 future-time movie reels, and often pictured himself single-handedly leading a platoon on patrol deep in enemy territory.

Clio sighed, then took a really deep breath to flaunt her 36Bs. That'd teach Sam to use military jargon.

"What we need to do is first make a list of what the major GOD® franchises are doing. Then we can see if there's some way, simple enough to put into practice ASAP, that we can add a little spice to the key ones to make them different.

"You do that list, Sam. Because of time constraints just pick the top two or three God™ franchises, ignore all the rest for now. If H.O. demands them, we can add in the small ones later."

Should she take another deep breath? No, she had to get Sam working, not mentally ravishing her.

"And meanwhile, I'll try to come up with a couple of differences we can accentuate."

She glanced at her wrist sundial—she really wished that the inventions department would get on the ball, wearing that damned sundial was a pain, how much better a nice slim watch would be, but they weren't due for arrival for hundreds of years, even after those ditzy alarm clocks were scheduled.

"Let's say we get together in the morning, around half way between the marks of 10 and 11. Then we can put all our info together, and aim for a final report to H.O. by the end of the day."

Taking one last look at her chest area, hoping she would fill her lungs, Sam nodded and headed back to his little walled-off area.

The next day Clio, wearing a very sedate dress which stretched from neck to toes, and didn't even indicate she was female, she wanted Sam's attention on the report, not her, plunked her papyrus sheets down on the makeshift board she used as a desk. Head Office did not believe in spoiling employees with unnecessary comforts.

She pulled the intercom string and next door she heard the little cowbell ring. Sam appeared in her doorway a few seconds later.

"What you got, Sam?"

"There is a whole raft of small GOD® franchises, Clio. Most of them have pretty small memberships, anywhere from a few thousand up to a million or so.

"That's understandable, of course, GOD® has only been flogging the franchises for 42 years, and such a new concept takes quite a while..."

"Sam. I was here before you. I have read all the historical texts on GOD®. And SCAM, too, for that matter. I'm well aware of how splendidly we've come along in less than half a century. You don't need to give me a refresher course.

"Now, what do you have on the assignment I give you?"

Such a female. How domineering. Sam could picture her, clad in a short—very short—skirt, and wielding a leather whip... "Uh, yes, I have the skirt, I mean the notes, right here, Clio.

"There are just two really big GOD® franchises: the Crapolics, mostly in the Eye Tie and frogy areas, and the Hindooos, in the Far East."

"Just two?"

"Yeah, those two have really mushroomed since they got exclusive God™ franchises.

"And of course the protestors and the mueslims haven't even been thought of yet. The Crapolics really seized on the demonstrations our founding members put on to get things started.

"They've apparently got a sort of lock on that crucifixion brainstorm, and because so many of the population in their areas are highly superstitious, their growth has been phenomenal.

"I checked with sales, and the Crapolics are racking up a compound income growth rate of over 32 percent.

"That's compounded since about 33 ASS, and Abraham in sales says it looks like that figure may even be increased.

"In fact, there's a rumor that some of the GOD® honchos are sorry they gave so much area as an exclusive to the Crapolics.

"But the growth in royalties is taking the edge of most of the grumbling."

"All right, what's the second?"

"The Hindooos. They're also growing, but not as fast as the Crapolics.

"Evidently their market is economically very poor, and so their prospects are more limited. But they are growing, and their base pop is very large, so perhaps in time they'll catch up with the craps."

He checked out Clio but couldn't see even a hint of boobs.

"That makes it simple, just having two entities. Now here's what I came up with.

"We should get each group to start promoting one key item, so that prospects, wherever they live, can make a choice between two product options.

"For example, with the Crapolics hooking on to the cross concept, and death and sins and all that, it would make sense for them to offer a sort of built in option to members.

"How about if they could offer their members a periodic cleanup of their sins? Say once a month or even once a week their key salesmen, what do they call them, pervies?, could offer to write off whatever sins the customer had incurred since his last clean up.

"That would probably really appeal to people who are basically superstitious anyway.

Sam grinned. "And when the mafia takes hold in that area, as we know it's scheduled to do some time later, then I'm sure superstitious mobsters would make excellent customers, and probably very affluent contributors at that."

"Great idea, Sam. That will sway H.O. because they'll be able to visualize the great gains in our franchise fees. What about the Hindooos?"

"Their prospects are even worse off than many in the Crapolic areas."

"Their existence now is pretty grim, so their field sales people could start stressing that while life this time around is the pits, if they stay paid-up Hindooo members, some life in the future they'll really see a great payoff for all the crap they had to take this time," Sam concluded.

"Perfect. That's smashing, Sam. Those two ideas let each of these two main GOD® franchises sell the same basic idea, pay up now for some kind of grand payoff a whole lot later, but each franchise can claim to offer a unique proposition.

"So prospects can choose either having their sin slates regularly erased—as long as they stay paying members—or be looking forward to a life of paradise after all the shit they take here on earth. Really great."

To reward Sam for his kind, albeit well deserved, comments, Clio first bent over to pick up an imaginary papyrus clip, then inhaled so strongly that even in her non-sexual attire her chest undergarment was sorely threatened.

Chapter 6

"Happiness is the only good, reason the only torch, justice the only worship, humanity the only religion, and love the only priest."

R.G. Ingersoll, (1833-1899), in a tribute to his father.

###

"A Dominic Roma from the Crapolic God™ franchise is here for his half slash two appointment, Saul. He's a little early but he said he has a lot to discuss with you."

"Okay, Rose. Get Abe from Client Public Relations in here, will you? And you'd better lay on some light refreshments. Got any red wine handy?"

A few minutes later Roma was ushered into Saul's office. He was medium height and had a little goatee, with more hair in it than on his head. He crossed his arms in the Italiano style of greeting.

"Nice to meet you, Dom. I'm Saul, and this is Abe from our client PR department. You've had a long trip, and those damned camel trains leave a lot to be desired in the comfort area. Would you like a container of wine?"

"That would be very nice indeed. And it is a pleasure to meet both of you, although I understood from your last quill mail that it would be just you and me for this meeting."

"It was originally, Dom, but the head office boys thought we should also have Abe's department represented, just in case you had any questions about our future PR plans which affect the Crapolic franchise."

Rose entered, in response to Saul's shout, and served the three men small earthenware containers of red wine.

"Very nice. A new flavor for me," Dominic said. "Does it come from the frog-area vineyards?"

"No, we stopped dealing with them a couple of years ago after they'd had another round of strikes and work stoppages. Their wines weren't bad—although we felt were far from the best—but their delivery system was a complete mess.

"This wine is from one of the new world provinces, although it won't be settled or even named for over a millennium.

"We call the region B.C., and their wines are really good, and getting better. Now, to business. What can we do for you, Dom?"

Roma reached inside his tunic and fumbled with an inside pocket.

"I wish they'd make these tunics with pocket-things on the outside, my papyrus always gets messed up with the inside things. Ah, finally."

He pulled out several sheets, carefully folded and now badly creased. He took another sip of the B.C. wine, smiled, and began.

"It's not that we're unhappy with our God™ franchise, Saul. In fact, at our most recent board meeting, we unanimously passed a resolution to let your head office know how appreciative we were of the franchise in general.

"It's just that there are a couple of minor irritations we'd like to clear up."

Abe looked at Saul, received a slight nod, and cleared his throat.

"Glad to hear that you Crapolics are so pleased in general, Dom. And minor problems are a perfectly natural part of any relationship—that's what I say when my wife complains about me passing wind—and my, our, job is to clear them up if at all possible.

"So, what's the matter, no batter in your hatta?"

Abe had been a stand-up comedian before he joined the SCAM organization, and he still felt his type of humor went over well.

Saul thought he was a jerk. But he did have the right executives' ears, so Saul bit his tongue.

"First, it's the main manual."

"You mean the operations manual? What could possibly be wrong with that, it was written at the express orders of GOD®."

Abe felt it was sacrilegious to even question the accuracy of the Ops Manual.

"No, no, not the operations manual. It's fine, fine. I was talking about the other manual, the one we use with our customers and prospects.

"We call it El bible, but I know that each main franchise sometimes refers to it by their own name."

Saul spoke up, that manual was clearly in his area of expertise.

"So what's the problem, Dom? Too long? Too short?"

"Or as the hooker said to her customer, 'Just right!'" Abe laughed to indicate he'd told a joke.

Dom looked puzzled. "Hooker? Is that a head office term?"

"It's not important, Dom."

Saul shot Abe a warning glance.

It had probably been a mistake to include him in this meeting with the sober and staid, and undoubtedly tight-assed—in more ways than one, he grinned to himself-- Crapolic emissary.

"Well, anyway, what I wanted to say, was that this book is causing some problems, especially along our franchise borders with the Germano bunch.

"Apparently at least some of them are using a shorter version of this manual.

"When we talk to prospects, or even customers, they often wonder why the Germans have what appears to be a different manual, then they realize it's the same, just shorter.

"That brings up all kinds of unfortunate questions from them, especially the prospects who haven't yet been properly brain-scrubbed to make them accept our word as absolute truth."

He paused to finish his wine, then he looked inquiringly at Saul.

"A refill, Dom? Rose, get your pretty little bum in here with the wine jug."

After all containers had been topped up, Dominic continued.

"It just makes it more difficult on our salesmen, or prests as we call them, you know, when they have to try and give answers that they don't really even understand themselves."

Saul wasn't sure what the Crapolic wanted. So he asked, "What exactly do you want, Dom?"

"Well, we—that means our board of directors, of course, not me personally, I'm just the messenger—know that it may be asking quite a lot, but what we—again, that's our board—hoped might be possible, was a sort of revised manual, one that we could honestly claim belonged solely to the Crapolics, and thus couldn't be questioned by any prospects—or even, can you believe it, by some of our established customers?—because we had the only copy of this manual."

Saul finally figured what Dom wanted.

A unique copy of the manual named at head office after the legendary B. Ible. "You want a specially written version of the bible manual, Dom?"

Dominic's face lit up like a string of lights used in the slow winter season by marketing experts to stimulate sales.

"Yes, yes, that's it exactly! If we had our own Crapolic bible then no one else could say that their manual was the true story.

"I mean, our book in time, say a few generations, would acquire the patina of truth and respectability.

"Think how much easier it would be for us to get prospects signed up, when we Crapolics had the only true copy of the main manual."

Saul drained his wine and got to his feet.

"Okay, Dominic, I see now what you're saying. You want an original revised version of the bible manual. Right?"

"Exactly, Saul. I have a couple of other very minor matters but the big thing is the main manual.

"Off the record"—Dom glanced around to make sure no one was quilling his comments onto some permanent piece of papyrus— "I can tell you, Saul, that my instructions were 'get the manual revised, Dominic, and don't worry about the other stuff. If we have our own original revision, we can increase gross member sales by 30 percent.'

"And that right from the mouth of a key board member, one whose name I won't even mention off the record, but he is highly placed on the board."

"That's a pretty big request, Dom."

Abe didn't want to be left out of this conversation, but neither did he want to be too closely associated with

Saul's answer, in case it wasn't what head office wanted to hear.

Saul motioned to him to sit down. He did.

"Dom, I'm going to have to run this very complex request by the GOD® vice-president in charge of franchise materials," Saul said.

"I can't honestly say what his reaction will be.

"This is the first time, that I know about, that a franchisee has asked head office to drastically change one of our main franchise publications.

"He may say it's impossible."

Dom's face dropped.

"Or he might offer some kind of arrangement we'd both find satisfactory."

Dom smiled again.

"Anyway, let me get together with him." He checked his wrist sundial.

"It's too late today to see him and then meet you again. So why don't you check into our franchise cocoons. These are hospitality rooms we keep for visitors just like you.

"There's a maxi bar in each cocoon, with a good selection of B. C. wines and wodkies from our ruskie franchise, and should you desire some company just pull the desk clerk cord in your cocoon and he'll send up a wench for your pleasure.

"Then we can get together tomorrow, let's say around one hour before midday siesta, and I'll let you have his decision."

After Dom had left, Abe said, "What do you think Morrie will say about this?" frowning in case Saul thought it would be unfavorable, to Dom, or worse, to him personally.

"Haven't thought about that yet, Abe. But I do think I can make a good case for doing it, not only for the Crapolics now, but as a special franchise deal in eons ahead for a wide variety of God™ franchisees.

"This main manual, let's call it the bible, I can see that it could be a potent sales weapon for any franchise, and at very little cost we can offer it as a very special franchise option.

"And by incorporating our standard GOD® royalty fees on top of regular extra franchise fees the revision could increase head office revenues substantially."

"Good thinking, Saul. Just what I was thinking.

"Also it would help us to tie up our franchisees even more.

"They'd be using a specially written, or at least a revised, version of our manual. Once they got their customers and even prospects to view it as containing the 'truth', whatever that was to the individual God™ franchise, then they'd be bound even tighter to GOD®.

"Yeah, I think it would be a good deal, certainly for the franchises, and most certainly for us at GOD®."

At the appointed time, or close to it, sundial watches weren't all that specific, Dominic was again ushered into Saul's office.

It was a little early in the day for wine, so Rose had prepared a new non-alcoholic beverage. Called hotcafe by the natives in the new world—as yet undiscovered—who had been sipping it for centuries, it tasted a little bitter to Dom, but he didn't want to come on too negative, so he smiled and said it was delicious.

But it tasted much better, he thought, with a couple of mini-spooners of that also new sweetener from somewhere in the tropical regions, called, he thought, schoogar.

"How did the vice-president react to your idea, Saul?"

Dom had his toes crossed for luck, he knew if he had successfully sold the idea he'd be due for a major type bonus next shortest-day-of-the-year.

"He took a lot of convincing, Dom."

What camel dung. As soon as he'd heard the idea Morrie had grasped the tremendous revenue and loyalty-building potential of it.

Saul had been promised a second secretary, a young one who would be ordered to fulfill his every wish, both during and after business hours.

He felt his prospects expanding as he thought about her.

"But I worked on him hard."

Yeah, for about 15 of the smallest marks on his sundial watch.

"In the end he agreed to the basic concept. Here's what he specified."

Saul wanted to drag it out a bit, he was still enjoying his prospect expanding. He waited until his prospects had receded in size somewhat, then crossed his legs now that he could.

"First, Dom, GOD® will prepare a special version of what we call the bible manual.

"You people can make some editorial suggestions, provided that these cover no more than a dozen standard papyrus sheets.

"We will put a top rewrite man on the job, and the first draft will be completed by the fourth moon after the initial contract is signed.

"In blood, of course, just as you Eye Ties do for your own contracts.

"You can then make any necessary corrections, again limited to ten changes, and the final bound edition will be ready by the end of Juno."

"That's wonderful!" Dominic could already taste the tasty wenches his bonus would buy.

"There's more, Dom. Your Crapolic franchise agrees to buy 16 millos of the first edition at a price we'll work out shortly.

"On each edition you give or sell to your customers or prospects you will also pay a nine percent royalty.

"Once every generation the bible manual will, if you Crapolics desire, be updated to reflect changes in how you're promoting your God™ franchise.

"These changes will be billed to you at our normal rates. Plus a modest overhead fee, of course.

"Conversely, if you wish to continue on with the same version, just a nominal royalty fee increase will be levied and payable in advance of future book shipments. No returns, of course, will be permitted.

"And most importantly, Dominic, old buddy, we guarantee that your Crapolic God™ franchise will have exclusive rights to the bible version we prepare for you.

"No one else will have that exact version. So you'll be able tell your customers and prospects that what they're getting in their bible manual is unique.

"Obviously you can jazz that up to your collective hearts' content, and if you people are as good businessmen as I expect, you'll be able to make a mint from this book alone.

"And no one will be able to contradict whatever you say or however you want to interpret what's in the bible manual. You'll have a totally free hand!"

Dominic was overwhelmed. He could just see the plaudits and accolades he would get on his return.

A unique bible manual, to be the sole property of the Crapolic franchise. A tremendous coup! He wondered how many young virgins he should request as his just due.

Chapter 7

"What is history but a fable agreed upon?"

Napoleon Bonaparte (1769-1821).

The Supreme Old-world Research Institute (SORI) was located just a few doors down from SCAM's headquarters.

While jealously maintaining its total independence, and thus the firm's impartial surveys, its board of directors was a duplicate of GOD®'s.

But rarely did the directors get involved in its activities.

It was effectively and unobtrusively managed by Ephraim, a nephew by third-marriage of one of GOD®'s directors, and as long as he didn't screw up—which in a decade and a half he hadn't—the directors were content to leave SORI alone.

Most of its surveys, conducted by an individual named Rorre in a small cubicle with barely room for a stack of papyrus and several quill pens, posed and asked uncomplicated questions about the public's reaction to GOD® activities.

Sometimes ORI did contract work for different God™ franchises, but the overall procedures were very similar.

In an average seven-day week slice Rorre "surveyed" anywhere from four hundred to as many as 12 or 14 millos.

Not quite as impressive as it sounds; he merely thought up half a dozen questions, and then entered the appropriate numerals as answers to total 100 percent.

Today Rorre was planning to do a survey of the pedestrian public in the city area fairly close to the office. He wanted the final survey to be based on five millos of respondents.

That would take ten interviewers at least 25-week slices, and cost far more than SORI's annual budget. So Rorre would actually personally meet and greet and interview five people on the street.

Then he'd multiply those results by a millo, and presto, the survey would be finished.

Perhaps lacking slightly in authenticity, accuracy, and aptness, but it certainly made up for those liabilities in its economical cost.

So, what questions did GOD®, or even SCAM, currently have an interest in getting asked?

Rorre knew the answer to that without even thinking about it. Nothing. They—either group—had no interest in asking anyone anything.

They'd been operating now for a 50 year period, from 7 BS to the current 42 ASS, and in that time the respective boards of directors had learned there was absolutely no need to question anyone anywhere about anything.

The original founders of GOD®, and SCAM too, had done a superb job of creating not only a very workable and practical business plan, but a plan which appeared to be on the mark for a long, long time.

Maybe, as one SCAM director had said, for ever.

So there was really no need for SORI, and Rorre knew that, as did everyone at head office.

But its year-period cost of operation was minuscule, and if any politician or other busybody ever queried what GOD® or SCAM actually did to justify the multi-billyuns it pulled in every year, they were fed an eloquent line of double talk by one of the directors, then shunted over to SORI where Rorre, or even Ephraim, if he was sober and available, would further triple-talk the poor sod until he didn't know down from way down or even up.

That meant that all of SORI's surveys, scrupulously fabricated by Rorre, very occasionally by Ephraim who didn't really understand scientific survey methodology, were just so much camel effusions from the rear door.

But Rorre didn't mind.

He had grown up wanting to be a writer of fiction, stories about heroes and villains, and of course their respective bosomy colleagues.

The market for fiction, however, was slimmer than some of the models he saw limping around the rag district, trying to stimulate buyers with their emaciated torsos which looked as sexy as a broom handle.

He had persevered with his writing, until, like in all good stories, one day he had planned to commit suicide if he didn't break through.

Just as he fixed the string noose around his neck the postman rang. Twice. This was it. He could feel it in his bones.

He shed the noose and raced down to the front door, where the postie handed him an official looking envelope from Paradise Plots, one of the biggest—and almost the only—publishers of fiction.

He tore open the envelope and unfolded the letter written on firm papyrus. It was a rejection.

He figured he'd already made good on his threat to his agent—who hadn't returned his carrier pigeon calls for almost three year-periods—to kill himself if he didn't succeed in selling a story, so he said to hell with it, and answered the ad posted on a nearby massage parlor window for "an enthusiastic and creative personality to serve as second-in-command in a bustling and booming media concern".

That turned out to be SORI, and the second-in-command meant he was the second employee after Ephraim.

In the two year-periods since he hadn't noticed any bustling or booming but neither had he felt the need to put a noose around his neck.

In fact, he rather enjoyed creating his surveys and plugging in the responses.

It actually gave him more creative satisfaction than writing schlock stories about Ames Cond and his wild adventures in the jungles of some as-yet-undiscovered New World jungle.

Today. What would it be?

A survey on why GOD® was such a beneficent organization?

Questions about the ongoing financial and social successes of SCAM?

The philosophy behind the various God™ franchises?

Or something a little more mundane, like Do you prefer red or white wine? Is it best served cold or at room temp? How much a day do you swig?

Well, maybe something a little less esoteric. Rorre stood up to reduce the cramp in his right leg from having to keep it bent to fit under his very compact desk.

Yes, something more practical. He pulled a ragged quill pen, using the new erasable ink, from its holder.

Okay, here we go.

He pictured himself riding a wild camel chasing down desperados who broke into happy-ending massage parlors and threatened the customers with blackmail.

Back on planet earth, Question one: Are you in favor of GOD® granting (that really meant selling at fantastic prices) franchises to the newly emerging countries of the darkest continent? (He wasn't too sure of where that was, but none of his five respondents would know either.)

Two: Should these new franchisees, if they are granted one, be allowed to have their own bible manuals, or should they first be forced to learn our language and use our manual?

Question three: Do you really think that your opinions on this stuff matter in the least to anyone? No, he'd better modify three. Maybe: Has GOD® made your life better, much better, absolutely much better?

That would do. No one at head office could object to those questions, in the very long shot that they ever saw or heard about them. A definite long shot. That made him remember.

He had to get a wager down at Sol's Olde Bookee Shop on the 4.15 camel race at Scarred Downs.

He'd had a tip from Ephraim, and he usually got the info right from Aloysius, the manager of the track, and he always knew who the winner would be.

Otherwise the track would make only its 28 percent net on gross revenue.

With the winners known in advance, and only non-winner bets actively hustled, the track showed a healthy 86.4 percent net, and that made Aloysius, SCAM, and in this case Ephraim and Rorre, very happy.

Rorre pulled off the tattered papyrus sheet with his three revised questions and another sheet as well.

He needed something on which to write down the responses, even though with only five required for his scientific verisimilitude he could probably remember them.

He replaced the quill pen—Ephraim was very careful about making pens last as long as possible; he received a substantial bonus if year-period expenses came in less than the previous year-period, so that meant that new purchases, and even replacements, were almost non-existent.

Rorre was still using a wall calder from two year-periods ago, and that made getting his dates correct on his wage-request sheets something of a chore—and he noticed that he had accidently blown out his light-source. How wonderful it would be when they had old Edison invent that light thing.

He poked his head into Ephraim's cubbyhole, but as expected it was empty.

So, he left the hovel, using his body-structure key to secure the outside door—although why anyone would want to loot the place was beyond comprehension. What would their haul be? Two badly-used quills? —and headed to the town square to nail his five respondents.

Then he remembered that camel bet. To hell with finding five actual respondents. He'd creatively improvise them as well. After all, his official job description papyrus sheet claimed he as a creative writer.

He walked towards Sol's Olde Bookee Shop.

Tomorrow was another day, another scientific survey, another peso earned laboring in the creative heart of the SORI media empire.

Chapter 8

"It was fear that first made gods in the world."

Statius, (61-c.96).

###

The London Tattler prided itself on its breaking news, on its scoop-everyone journalistic philosophy.

Embedded in its star-studded celebrity news staff were a number of glittering lights.

Adam Black, fresh from triumphs as a foreign correspondent located in Welwyn Garden City, far to the north of the Big Smoke, was the lead reporter on all stories requiring a mature worldly appraisal.

As he often said, "There ain't no excuse for not doing your homework when a really big story comes along." Grammar was among several subjects in which he was somewhat less than 100% competent.

"After all, there is many people out there who depend on me, well, the Tattler, I guess, to tell them what they should be thinking. And why, cause that's also a important part of this newspaper business, ain't it?

"Not everyone has the really good fortune to have been to as many foreign postings as me.

"Not only did I cover Welwyn Garden City for over three year-periods, but one time I even trekked into the wilderness way, way north, and ended up as special freelance staff guy for the renowned Manchester Bucket,

'All the news that fits in', and you can't get no further in than that.

"And once I gets discovered, I'm thinking of applying for a top spot on some rag in the New World, like maybe the Halifax Hooter or the New York Dustbin."

Black was far from the sole shining lamplight in The Tattler's retinue.

On the economics desk was Jerry Justenough.

He had arrived shortly after being convicted for massive money laundering and quill-mail fraud, but his sentence under the somewhat myopic and self-serving U.K. judges was two hours hard labor each week for one summer mowing the sentencing judge's home lawn.

Tattler management felt that his background would give him a unique perspective on money-making goings on in the City, where various financial skulduggeries were carried on continuously by almost everyone.

The piece de resistance, however, was the religion beat, where a defrocked Crapolic named Willie Wongo headed the extensive one-man team.

He'd even had the colorful 'Bell, Book, and Candle' ceremony, which was introduced by a group of bored Crapolic bishits in 69 ASS.

Following one of their mob reading the sentence of excommunication another bishit rung a large noisy bell, then closed a book—title didn't matter—and finally put his fleshy lips together to blow out a candle, which unfortunately threw the room into darkness, and prevented any of the onlookers, all of whom had paid 200 pesetas to watch the event, from seeing its grand finish.

No matter, a third bishit then formally told the lucky excommunicatee that he was henceforth excluded from all the religion's colorful affairs, but that if he wanted, he could continue to donate his 10 percent into the Crapolic treasury.

Wongo had thought it over and decided he'd sooner use the gelt to pay for his classified ads for young boys interested in unique religious experiences; orphans and others with no close relatives preferred.

Now he was comfortably ensconced in the Tattler's bosom, the only bosom he had been close to for a great many years.

On the weekly third day, normally a quiet day for the Tattler religious staff, Willie was summoned to the editor's lair, a closet hard by the men's urinal.

It was felt this posting gave the ed the opportunity to keep a close eye on his miscreant staff—all of them male, as women's rights were eons away—and make sure they weren't literally pissing away their time.

"Come in, Wongo, just make sure your don't do any of that wind passing I hear your somewhat famous for in Jake's Jovial Bar and Grilled Suspects. What have you on your plate today?"

Like most days Willie's plate was as empty of activity as a whorehouse that didn't accept the newfangled credito cardos.

But he didn't feel it propitious to say that, so he pulled out several sheets of papyrus, covered with jottings of naked young boys leaping and bending, but quickly covered those figures with his two flabby hands.

"Let me just check here on my pocket secretary-thing, chief."

The editor took umbrage.

"Do I look like a red Indian to you? My title is Superior Editorial Being, but you can call me Superior for short."

"Ah, yes, Ch…, ah, Superior.

"It looks like I could make time (as long as it required less than a 12-month period, Willie thought) for whatever juicy assignment you might have for my religion department."

"Juicy I can't say, Wongo, but it is an assignment right up your alley."

He had heard rumors about Wongo's alley taste in young boys but he couldn't believe that a Crapolic bishit, defrocked or not, could ever be accused of playing around with...No, it was just not possible.

"It involves GOD®, that giant benefactor of our advertising pages, Wongo, so don't start getting crazy ideas about some major expose.

"That would be as stupid as your earlier idea to do a piece on corruption in the Crapolic group.

"Trying to write that the Crapolic presipopey had been involved with Attila the Hun's marauders, and then was promoted into being the cover-up fixer for wayward bishits caught, somewhat literally I seem to remember you claiming, with their pantaloons down.

"What crappola, Wongo. So none of that."

Willie nodded his head.

"Of course, Supe."

But that would have been a Pulatzo-winning article, if only he'd been allowed to write it.

He had the facts down cold, verified by several ex-communicatees like him who had been bounced for gross indecency, which apparently amounted to not kicking in to head orifice half the bribes they received from churchy customers to ensure that they received a good seat in Paradise.

"All I want, Wongo, is a straightforward piece of about fifteen score words on the wonderful GOD® group, all the good they do, how they improve our country's trade balance, that kind of stuff. Can you handle it?"

"Oh yes, Superior. Of course I can, I'm a fully qualified journalisto, a graduate of the William Dunn two-week School of Journalism and Taxidermy. How soon do you need it?"

The Superior Editorial Being pulled up the cuffs of his robe and peered at his sundial watch. It was either shortly before midnight or about two strokes before mid-day. He figured the latter, as it seemed too light for midnight.

"I want it the day before today."

He'd read that command in a book on how to be a successful dictator and had lusted ever since to use it. Wongo the cretin was a prime audience. He was so stupid he'd think it was original.

Wongo gulped, his Adam's apple bobbing like a beginner giving head for the first time.

"That's almost impossible, Supe, I mean how can I turn the sundial back? We won't be into time travel excursions for a long time yet."

Superior groaned. He should have taken his mother's advice and taken up beekeeping.

"It was a jest, Wongo.

"I want it the day following today, by," he tried to calculate an unreasonable time to demand it, but got mixed up subtracting hours from the current sundial time, then adding hours for the day following, and... "I want it as soon as possible. First thing. No excuses.

"You are to have it in my hands"—knowing those Wongo rumors was that a dangerous statement? — "by the very earliest time. Is that clear?"

Wongo was tempted to say no but didn't.

"Perfectly, Supe. Do you want me to actually talk to someone at GOD®, or should I just do as usual, make up the whole thing, so long as it makes them look good?"

The veins on the editor's head threatened to burst.

"Make it up? Are you retarded? I said this was about GOD®, not some fly-by-night Crapolic charity.

"Of course you'll talk to them. In person, no messenger pigeons or can-with-wire-and-shouting conversations.

"My assistant boy has already made an appointment for you.

"You are to proceed immediately, you can even hire a camel, just make sure to get a receipt that's not blurred as usual so I can't make out the digits.

"Contact when you get to the GOD® headquarters a Solly in Press Relations. He knows you're coming"—again perhaps a dangerous phraseology? — "and will have a special pass for you at the heavily guarded gate number two and a half score.

"He has graciously allowed you a tenth of an hour-unit for your extensive interview so use it wisely.

"Mainly ask the questions on this sheet of papyrus"—he shoved a folded sheet across his desk— "and let him answer those he wants to.

"Don't bother him any more than you usually do, and make damned sure you leave when he yawns the first time.

"Remember, these fine folks keep our advertising profitable, so not a single defamatory—that means bad, Wongo—word.

"And also remember that this Solly has to see a copy of your final article, so either do it right on the spot or make arrangements to have it expressed to him by fast camel before the day is out."

Good, using that terminology saved him the problem of dealing with those annoying sundial times.

"Any questions, Wongo?"

"None, Ch, ah, Superior. You have made the assignment very clear, and it's obvious why you have reached the pinnacle of your profession. Having such a command of the language is a tremendous achievement...."

Even Superior Editorial Beings can sometimes sniff out camel dung when it's ladled out by incompetents like Willie Wongo.

"Enough. Do you have Irish relatives? Never mind. Just leave and get busy on this story.

"Do a good job and maybe I'll consider your request to pad out your religion department with a part-time flunky, maybe we could get some out-of-work celebrity to come in for a few 60 minute-units over a 24 hour-period.

"But that's not a promise," he said quickly as Wongo's eyes lit up like three cherries on a to-be-invented slot machine, "it's just a maybe."

Wongo moved, tried to get feeling back into his legs where they had been pinned down by the confines of the closet, saluted, and headed out to create journalistic history.

At the specified GOD® gate, where several battalions of heavily armed soldiers kept the peace—and all peasants out—there was a pass for Willie.

He paid off the camel driver, got his receipt for 10 drachmas more than the actual cost, but he had to return two of them as a bribe, and passed through a battery of metal, cloth, and even papyrus detectors.

He had to strip down completely, and felt somewhat embarrassed as he was wearing boxers that were seeing their eleventh straight day of duty, but eventually he was cleared to enter.

A guard with more armament on his back than in many future adventure rolling-rolls-of-filmy-stuff told Willie where to go.

Then, after laughing uproariously, he actually showed him where Solly's office was.

Another guard was stationed at the door. GOD® certainly took no chances with the peasants rising up.

The entrance covering was parted, and there sat what Willie assumed was his interviewee.

"Solly? How nice to meet you. I'm Willie Wongo, and I'm here to interview you for a major article in the Tattler. I assume you know all about it?"

Solly stood up from his heavily cushioned armchair.

"Yes, Willie, I know all about it. You have several questions to ask me. So, let's get started already, I have a meeting with the bimbo entertainment committee in just two-tenths of an hour-unit."

Willie pulled out his papyrus cheat sheet, found a seat on the huge seat-thing—the entire editorial department of the Tattler would fit into Solly's office, there was evidently a little more profit in the GOD® business than the journalism profession—and cleared his throat.

"Okay. Question one. What exactly is GOD®?"

Solly smiled, lounged back in his very comfortable looking chair, and said, "That isn't one of the questions we agreed to answer.

"Even if we had, it's far too complex for any of your readers to understand, so it would just confuse and then irritate them. Next."

"Well, okay, I guess. Question two: what does GOD® actually do?"

"Just about everything good there is to do, my friend. We are literally all things to all people, helping the poor, the oppressed, as well as the rich and bored.

"GOD® knows everything, sees everything…" and owns everything, Willie thought, "…and therefore does everything that can be done.

"It is number one, and yet greater than one. It is made up of many parts, yet it can't be subdivided.

"Unlike mere mortals it lives forever, even longer, and like fine B.C. wine it improves with age."

Solly lit up a cigar that looked like it cost Willie's annual wages. "Got that, old boy?"

"I guess, sort of. Maybe our editor will be able to clear up my notes a little."

"That's about all that editors are for. Next question?"

Willie's papyrus sheet looked like a failed entry in a massive crossword contest. He couldn't read one word of what Solly had spewed out, and he could barely make out what appeared to be question four.

Where was three? Well, never mind, who'd know the difference.

"Right. Here's the question: How much does GOD® make each twelve month period?"

"Just enough to perform its amazing works. Not a peso more, not a farthing less. Exactly the amount needed to barely sustain our few workers."

Willie knew the employment roll was in the thousands.

"So the actual amount is not relevant, it's just not an issue.

"What is important is all the good GOD® does with the meager income it earns, earns, that is, not just takes like some of these parasitic taxing groups. But that's another story. Our income is not a factor in this story, Wallie."

Couldn't he even remember my name?

"What is the key factor, Wily, is GOD®'s importance, to everyone, everywhere, every time.

"Does that answer it simply enough for your readers?"

Willie nodded. No point in mentioning that he hadn't understood one word himself.

Obviously this interview was a joke, set up to tell a probably fictitious story of GOD®. So his editor must be in on the plant. Let him worry about the scrawls Willie was going to turn in as his copy.

"Fine. You certainly have a way with words, Solly. Did you study journalism by any chance?"

Solly burst out laughing.

"Why in the world would I waste time on a useless subject like that? No, I took business admin, of course, as most of GOD®'s people do.

"We find there is a far greater need for accountants and advertising experts than for those that scribble for daily rags."

He certainly hadn't taken any courses in tact, Willie thought. He's sitting right here and continually insulting me.

On the other hand, maybe I could make use of this contact.

"I agree wholeheartedly, Solly. By any chance, are there any openings at GOD® that I might be suited for?"

Solly's eyes opened wide. He looked at Willie as an alien might look at a fat stripper. "Openings? What kind of openings?"

"Oh, you know, for people who are experienced in dealing with all kinds of situations."

And with assholes like you.

"I've interviewed everyone from bankrupts to, well, I guess non-bankrupts." He laughed to show he'd made a joke.

Solly frowned.

"Do you have anything else, Wilbur? I think you've used up the time I allocated. I have an important appointment" -- opposed to this time-wasting, useless piece of crap, was definitely implied—"so let's wrap it up.

"If you need more, I'll have my assistant-girl give you some P.R. handouts we give out to anyone who asks for them, they'll give you a lot of generalized, non-confidential copy you can add on to whatever your editor leaves of your copy."

He stood up, sort of waved his hand in Willie's direction, then used it to pick up and ring a camel bell he had on his desk.

Immediately a vision of female pulchritude shot into the room, dressed in what looked like an extremely short piece of gauze.

Solly smiled, smacked her on her bottom, which put a smile on her lips and a blush on her cheeks—obviously at least some of GOD®'s meager income was spent hiring angels like this; Willie wondered just how much ministering this angel did on or to or with Solly after the work day ended—and she turned to Willie.

Immediately her girlish charms evaporated and she became Willie's fifth grade teacher.

"This way out, Walter. Solly says he's happy you completed your assignment."

As far as Willie could see Solly had said sweet bugger all, so this vision was not only built like every young man's wet dream, but she could read minds.

She led the way and he followed like a bee to its hive. But there was no hive, and certainly no honey.

In the outer office she reclined in a chair much like Solly's, and pointed with her 15-inch fingernails at the door.

"Just turn left when you leave, and keep on following the blue line, it'll take you to the nearest armed guard station, and one of the soldiers stationed there will get you out of the building."

When he got back to the Tattler's offices, he handed in his papyrus sheet.

"Here, I can't read it either.

"This was some kind of set-up so you don't need my notes anyway. And I'm giving notice as well.

"I've decided to pursue a career as a peasant-shack to peasant-shack salesman of GOD® authorized verses for meditation when things look black. Maybe if I can sell a bunch, I'll be able to get a toehold on a real job with GOD®."

Chapter 9

"All great truths begin as blasphemies."

George Bernard Shaw, writer, Nobel laureate (1856-1950).

###

Communications in 43 ASS weren't quite as effective as later, but as GOD®'s ambassadors—aka franchisees—started to cover the globe like a quickie paint job, people in various locations became aware in varying degrees of what GOD® was up to, although why remained one of those tantalizing mysteries that was never to be unraveled.

Luis Durango on Spain's sunny and pre-tourist – ridden Costa del Sol was perhaps typical of younger men.

"Si, I have heard about this GOD® thing, and I think it's a pretty good thing," he said over a friendly glass of Mexican tequila served by a buxomy waitress in an outdoor café in picturesque Malaga.

"To be honest, I don't know all that much about it, but my girl friend—Maria of the plentiful breasts, not to be confused with her cousin Maria of the very long legs—said to me that she was sure GOD® was doing a bunch of good stuff, muy bueno, you know.

"I can't remember whether she said they were helping orphans, or old and out-of-work prostitutes, but it was something pretty damn good, I'm sure. Another tequila?"

Across the Mediterranean, in Morocco, Sebastian and his wife Socorro were having a light lunch in Maxine's Dining Emporium in Casablanca just up the street from where much later Bogie would peddle expensive drinks to actors pretending to be cowardly frogys fleeing the Nazis.

"Yes, I have knowledge of this GOD®," said Socorro.

"My mother-in-law's first cousin on her father's side had an experience with the local God™ group, it's run by a Hiram or Hymie, I can't remember which, and they have a pretty big office down near the shore.

"My mother-in-law's first cousin said that one day she applied for a cleaning lady job at those offices, and while unfortunately she didn't get the position, evidently they needed someone with a little more English ability—she doesn't know much more than Yes and No and How much will you pay? —but she was quite impressed with the courtesy they treated her with.

"They even offered her a cup of coffee—imagine that!—and then told her to come back after she had practiced her English a little.

"She plans to do that, and she is already up to the Ds, and she knows doughnuts and D-cup size already.

"So you could say that we"—she looked at Sebastian who nodded— "are very much on the side of GOD®, whatever they are doing.

"I just wish there were more like them people around, it doesn't cost anything after all to be polite, even to prospective cleaning ladies."

In Phoenix, Arizona, in what would later be called the American west, Percy Wagner was having a late morning breakfast at Smokey's Salacious Sandwiches.

"GOD®? Is that the bunch that annoys you at the airport, trying to hustle donations or sell flowers or some crap like that? No? Oh, yeah, you must mean that new outfit, I've seen their ads on TV.

"They seem to be a very reputable organization, and with a name like that you'd sorta think they would be, wouldn't you?

"I can't recall too much really from the commercial, but I think they were just promoting goodness and decency, and of course we're all in favor of those things, right?"

He paused to take a large bite from his underground (aka subway) sandwich.

"Just a minute. I think they're the company that a good buddy of mine is considering getting a franchise from.

"He just sold out his home reno business for twice what it was worth, and he's sitting on a fat pile of greenies, and he got interested when a friend of his in Florida mentioned he had purchased a franchise and was really coining it.

"He didn't tell me too much about the deal—I think he was a little nervous about telling me too much, we once had a sort of a misunderstanding when I deeked him out of a deal he thought he had sewed up, but it just proves, the early bird gets the worm, don't it? Well, that deal was a money spinner, so I guess he had reason to feel pissed off, but what the fu.., eh, heck, that's business, isn't it?

"Anyway, he seemed real hot to trot on this GOD® thing, but I seem to remember that he said the actual franchise was in lower caps—God™—not like the main GOD® company."

He finished his sandwich in one giant bite.

"In fact, I think I'm going to check in with old Stanley, just to see how he's coming along.

"Maybe I should take a crack at this GOD® franchise thing, I've learned that old Stan's a pretty shrewd judge of business potential."

In Paris, France, Pierre was sitting at a table set up outside the American Bistro. He was reading a day-old copy of the New York Nugget and smoking a Lucky Ball cigarette.

"Why am I so hot on American stuff? What do you mean? The truth is I can't really stand them.

"Just because they have all the money, and drive cars bigger than small cities, and finish the wars we start, they think they can come over here and… GOD®? What do you mean?

"I am an atheist, can't stand all the Crapolic crap.

"If those guys aren't molesting little kids, they're trying to stop females from getting rid of unwanteds, like it was any of their Eye Tie business.

"No, I can't say I know too much about this GOD®, but I do know there's an office here in town somewhere, I've seen that name mentioned in the paper. In the business section, I think, which is a little odd.

"Anyway, their financial results were pretty vague, but the newspaper columnist seemed to feel they had a great concept, whatever it is.

"If they ever get listed on an exchange I'll probably buy a few shares, with a name like that it should go over well here where 99 percent of the women spend at least part of every day moaning and bitching to some queer in a dress."

In the Guadalajara, Mexico God® office, the local PR manager was just finishing reading an email from Head Office.

"We're happy to report that for the past quarter gross revenue worldwide is up 38 percent over the previous quarter, and year-to-date figures show an increase of 31 percent.

"GOD® has opened 48 new country offices, and expanded 82 existing offices. All of this has been accomplished with just a 3 percent increase in employees.

"We continue to seek new locations, and both country and area franchisees, but we are getting considerably more particular about who qualifies for such franchises.

"We now absolutely exclude any former religious person, any convicted criminals, and females—although we will consider them for employment in modelling positions— and anyone who has ever been elected to any political office within the past decade.

"Former presidents, prime ministers, and others of that ilk are permanently excluded.

"Otherwise, a pat on the back to all loyal employees everywhere.

"We expect that there will be substantial bonuses this year end, probably considerably higher than those received by the various stock and option exchange cowboys."

Part 3 – Chapter 10
Many, many years later

"If you tell a lie big enough and keep repeating it, people will eventually come to believe it. The lie can be maintained only for such time as the State can shield the people from the political, economic and/or military consequences of the lie. It thus becomes vitally important for the State to use all of its powers to repress dissent, for the truth is the mortal enemy of the lie, and thus by extension, the truth is the greatest enemy of the State."

Joseph Goebbels, (1897-1945) chief Nazi propagandist.

"We have a great deal to cover, so before we get interrupted again by contentious crusaders, greedy Goths, or even hungry Huns, let's get this meeting started.

"First, do we have any old business?"

Abe looked at Samuel, who was busy talking animatedly to Seth, probably telling him the latest nun joke.

"Samuel?"

He looked up, smirked at Seth, and grabbed a handful of stiff papyrus materials which were on the little table in front of him.

"Yes, we do have some old business to discuss.

"Some of it goes back just a few twelve-month periods, others much farther. But I've tried to have my female helper-assistant compile things as much as possible, so we should be able to get through it all before David dozes off."

Chairman David frowned, then decided to ignore the jibe. Otherwise Sammie would have them here all night.

"First, I want to talk a little about our custom manual division.

"Ever since GOD® decided to offer a specially written version of our original bible manual, sales have been consistently strong, and consistently growing.

"Our first sale, you'll all probably remember from our own confidential internal History Book, was to some Crapolics in the frog and Eye Tie areas. That sale was dynamite.

"Ever since we've had record 12-month period sales to those same Crapolics, who by now of course have greatly expanded their franchise areas.

"Record sales of both the bible manuals themselves, and the gross sales volume totaled by the Crapolics, on which we earn a very healthy royalty income."

He paused to shuffle some paper-type sheets.

"I don't have the actual figures here, my female helper-assistant is not perfect, as none of them are, but I know they are substantial, very substantial indeed.

"And since that first custom book sale, this division has adopted the same strategy for other GOD® franchisees.

"Every one of them, from Crapolics to the newest protest groups, most of whom don't even have official religion names as yet, but that's no problem, we just refer to them in our internal records as Protest Group One, and so on.

"Once they get better organized, I'm sure we'll sell them even more of the custom bible manuals because each group really wants to be able to claim that their version is the real version."

Norman, the unofficial--and unpaid—moralist of the group, interrupted.

"Isn't that kind of selling, giving a whole bunch of franchisees the right to call their custom book the real version, a little immoral?"

Oh shit. Why does that schmuck always pop off during my presentations?

"No, Normie, I don't think it's at all immoral."

Samuel cleared his throat.

"We don't say any of the manuals are better than any other.

"All we do say, Norman, is that each franchisee who signs up to purchase the rights to a specific version, will have the exclusive use of that version.

"And each franchisee can say what he wants about it.

"The Crapolics, for example, perhaps because they've been doing business with GOD® for the longest time, like to really rant and rave about the accuracy of their bible version. And they seem to be pretty successful in convincing their customers that that's so.

"Why should we care?

"As long as they keep on ordering great quantities of the custom bible manual, and paying their bills on time, it's basically of no interest to GOD® at all."

He turned one of his "don't screw with me" looks on Norman, who was easily intimidated. "Any further thoughts, Normie?"

As expected, Norman shook his head.

"Okay, so that division is doing great.

"Next, our franchise contest department advises me that the brainwashing contests continue to generate interest among franchises. And nice healthy income.

"We've been using these contests now for hundreds of years, and still they work. The various franchises change positions over the years, but just for your interest I can say that the recent contest, started in 1187 ASS, has the newcomer budd-hism in the lead, especially in the brainwashing of kids under three.

"As always, the Eye Tie Crapolics are close behind, and then behind these two habitual leaders, there's a whole bunch of franchises, confuskows, musliz, and so on.

"A nice, simple marketing scheme and a nice simple, profitable payoff."

A waiter moved up and filled Samuel's empty receptacle with a rich dark wine. He smiled, drank it down, and motioned for another refill.

"That's not bad stuff. Still getting it from B.C., Oscar?"

Supply manager Oscar nodded. "Yes, their prices are good and the quality stays high. Only problem is it takes so long to get here. If only those yet-to-be flying machine things were invented, it'd speed things up a lot."

"Everything in due course. Now, just a few words about our new franchise sales in the orient.

"Even though we've had to reduce royalty fees to these new franchisees, they just don't yet have the bread the Crapolics do, we make up for it with reduced expenses.

"We can hire office labor and sales reps at very low sweatshop wages, so our royalty fees are almost all net profit; we require franchise fees to be paid in our sheilings, of course.

"And our legal teams were very careful to get both trademark and even service mark protection on GOD™, GOD®, and all the other derivatives, so over time I expect that those areas will start paying us very big buckos."

He saw Norman mustering his courage, obviously to object to the sweatshop situation, so Samuel simply ignored him and moved ahead.

"There is one interesting development in franchise sales activities.

"A couple of the older franchise operations have complained that their revenue from donations and bequests has tailed off as the economy slumps periodically, so our promotion geniuses came up with a cool idea.

"Each franchise that's meeting all of its sales quotas, and paying all its bills on the nose, can create—for a fee—a new special named individual every five twelve-month periods.

"Some franchisees have even coined special names for these.

"For instance, the frog Crapolics call theirs a santa, the Germanos call theirs a sayentadolphus (they always seem to go for really long names), and the Eye Ties call their guys olyaints.

"Then each franchise can promote these things, and they develop a completely new revenue source, as there are always customers of theirs who want a new face on the GOD® scene."

"Why just every five twelve-months, Samuel? Wouldn't we increase royalty revenue if we did it every, say, three, or even four, twelve-month periods?"

Sol was in charge of franchise marketing, and the more specialties he could offer made his job easier and more profitable.

"It would, Sol, except that too much of a good thing would probably in time work against us.

"As it is, the Crapolics, for example, already have about 30 or 40 of these special individuals, and from what I hear their customers are starting to have problems remembering all of them.

"No, I think it's best to keep it as is."

Sol seemed satisfied.

Samuel motioned to that lazy waiter again. He'd see if he couldn't get him shifted from head office to somewhere more suitable for his lethargic work habits. Maybe the new sales office in Alabama?

"As always, gentlemen, we continue to get complaints from almost all the franchisees. 'Your royalties and marketing fees are too high. We just can't afford them.' You know what I mean."

Several members burst into laughter. This was a historic complaint, the first one going all the way back to the founding meetings in the first century ASS.

"I know, it gets boring," Samuel said. "And there's really only one way to handle them.

"Josiah in Franchise Relations has it down pat. When a franchisee starts to bitch and moan, he simply says, 'Well, if things are that bad, maybe you should just renounce your exclusive franchise agreement. We'll let you out without any penalties, and then we'll find a new franchisee.'

"That shuts them up immediately.

"Every one of the franchisees knows that they've got a private goldmine with our GOD® franchise.

"Without it, most of them would be on the streets begging.

"Few of the franchisees have any marketable skills. A few could make livings as auctioneers or used car salesmen, but most would be SOL."

Norman looked puzzled.

"That's shit outa luck, Norman."

Norm blushed and averted his eyes.

"All they really have is our trademarked GOD® name, and an ability to convince very gullible people that they need what the franchisee is offering, a sort of peace of mind if you don't examine the proposal too closely.

"So let's move on, there's no real need to waste time on this old complaint chestnut."

Samuel checked his bulky wrist sundial. When would Hong King start mass producing those compact el cheapo watches he'd read about in Advance History III, or maybe it was IV?

He had to speed things up, he had a full-body special scheduled at Miriam's Moaning Massages and Happy Endings in just over a 60 minute period.

"Okay, men. One final bit of business.

"Some of the newer southern franchises have inquired about getting their own popey.

"The problem, as always, is that these groups— you've probably heard of some of them, episscos, prezzies, metodits, buptirs, and a bunch of barely organized franchisees like free willy bubytists and murmanns—can hardly get their initial franchise fee up, let alone cough up another bundle for a popey exclusive in their area.

"The earlier franchisees like the Crapolics have really capitalized on their popeys, but these newer bunches will have to wait until their regular customers kick in enough to cover the extra costs.

"There's no real problem here, these southerners aren't really causing a scene, but I wanted you all to be aware of their complaints, just in case you get cornered at a franchisee party by some of these guys."

He found himself hardening just thinking about his forthcoming massage.

"Okay, that's all I have. We've covered all the old business.

"Seeing that the sun is definitely over the yardarm"—he had no idea what a yardarm was, but thought it had a nice ring to it— "I propose we close this meeting, and hold over new business until next mid-week day."

He glanced at Abe, who was already dozing in the chairman's seat. Obviously no problem there.

"All in favor?"

He counted hands quickly.

"Okay, it's carried, and meeting adjourned."

Bring on the baby oil, Miriam!

Chapter 11

Radiocarbon dating of the so-called shroud of Turin has revealed that it does not date to the time of a man named Jesus Christ but instead to the 14th century, more than 1,300 years later; coincidentally, that's when it first appeared in the historical record.

In a document written in 1390, catholic bishop Pierre d'Arcis of France claimed the image of Jesus on the cloth was "cunningly painted," a fact "attested by the artist who painted it."

###

"Why can't we have it? We're your oldest—and probably biggest and best, too—franchise, and we think we deserve it."

Harry slid his coffee container towards himself, and fiddled with the handle.

This damned question was a giant pain, and he was tired answering it. But Pierre LePieu was a big shot in the frog Crapolics, and so he had to go through the whole schmear again.

"Pierre, if I personally could I wouldn't hesitate to let you Crapolics have exclusive rights to GOD™.

"From the very start you guys have done a great job of pushing your stuff, and you've really built up a very loyal and dedicated bunch of customers.

"And now that you're getting them brain-patterned right after birth, wow! You have them for life. Even beyond, according to your claims. Really impressive."

Harry paused to sip some coffee. Certainly not as good as the coffee from what would be named Turkey. But this swill from some place in Africa was cheap.

"The problem, my friend, is that each and every franchisee wants the same thing, and there's just no simple way to satisfy everybody.

"But our top people have been working on this, and they've come up with a plan which is fair to everyone."

LePieu grimaced. Since when was fairness to others a part of his country's concern?

"Here's what the brass has decided, Pierre. GOD® is going to have a secret write-in-only worldwide auction. It's a one-time deal.

"Each franchisee can submit one bid for the exclusive rights to use GOD® as a master licensee. The high bid winner would get a lower override royalty on all existing franchisee sales, and a higher royalty on all new franchises it actively set up.

"Great, huh?"

LePieu frowned. This wasn't what he had been ordered to do by his boss in Parie. "Get the exclusive, LePieu, I don't care how many backs you have to stab."

"C'mon, Harry. We're old friends," LePieu added.

Personally, LePieu hated his guts but this was business.

"Surely we can reach some kind of agreement on this without having to involve all those other jerks.

"Maybe a little bonus for you personally, Harry? In gold coin, of course."

Harry moistened his lips.

Gold coins? He could get that new broad in accounting to take a little vacation with him, some place nice and warm, maybe that soon–to-be-discovered place way down south in what-will-be the new world, Brazzie or Brazear or something.

But no, they spoke that ugly language portageezie that no one else could even understand.

Better stick to some place nearer and more civilized like Morocco, where they'd eventually make that famous movie with Boget or whatever his name would be. Yeah, Sadie would be impressed with that.

LePieu burped to bring Harry back. "So what do you think, old pal?"

Old pal indeed, Harry thought. He must pour that stinking after shave stuff on with a pitcher.

Anything closer to the froggie than five meter-units and you'd pass out from the pollution.

"Sounds good, Pierre, but just can't do.

"The execs have already decided, and getting them to change their minds is harder than getting your major myth-figure to walk on water across that creek without a concealed underwater platform.

"But listen, good buddy."

What absolute shit he had to dish out in this job. But the perks were good.

"All is not lost," Harry continued.

"It's going to be a very simple auction. Each existing franchisee can submit the one written bid. When closing time comes, that's it.

"The highest bid takes the cigar. And with your huge list of customers, Pierre, you Crapolics should be able to top everyone else easily.

"Except the Eye Ties might give you a run for your money.

"Ever since they made that big show of digging up their own copy of our bible manual, and saying it was obviously the only true copy—actually it was number 11 of our 613th print run—they've increased their membership, and the fees they collect, really dramatically."

There, that should give this Froggie a little heartburn. And a lotta envy besides.

Chapter 12

"One by one, like leaves from a tree,
All my faiths have forsaken me."

Sara Teasdale (1884-1933), poet.

###

Two 30-day periods later all the bids were in and had been inspected by exec v-p Hymie, his assistant Sharon, and Harry, in charge of special promotions.

"A good response rate, Harry," Hymie said.

"That 'Act before midnight tonight or lose out forever' special carrier pigeon mailing really goosed all the franchisees.

"We ended up with 97% of the suckers responding.

"And that stick-on note in hot pink color really did the job of making sure all the franchisees remembered that Miami was our new franchise head office.

"What a difference for us! No more bombs exploding everywhere like they were in Jerusalem.

"We lost three good papyrus clerks in one week. Cost a small fortune to hire and train new ones. Here in Miami all we have to worry about is not stumbling over all the old farts sitting around in cheap lawn chairs."

"Those carrier pigeon specials cost a lot, Hymie, but they usually show a profit," Harry said. "And they make any message they carry seem real important.

"What do you think of the bids?"

"Not too bad overall, Harry.

"But getting money from these people is like turning water into wine. Looks easy but it's a real bitch."

"And without the secret compartment on the water bottle that turns water into wine just about impossible."

Sharon wasn't impressed with most of the hocus pocus tricks used by the franchisees to gull their customers.

One she did like was the man nailed to a cross. She thought the collapsing nails which also contained and oozed out the fake blood were pretty neat.

Hymie didn't appreciate the way Sharon so freely criticized GOD®'s customers and the sales tricks they used.

But she really gave good head so he made allowances.

"The executive committee has gone over the bids carefully," Hymie said. "A couple were approaching reasonable.

"Both the Eye Ties and the frogs were in the ball park. But then Saul in Revenue Projections showed us some figures.

"First he totaled up our anticipated income from 12-month periods from franchisee royalty and license fees. Then he projected those over the next one millennium period.

"Next he listed our revenue from popeys, even though we've decided to severely limit the number of these. And what we get from the Eye Ties alone for their popey is really impressive. By now all of us on the committee were going cross-eyed from all the numbers. But Saul kept going.

"Then he used his abacus—it'll sure save time when they get those fucking computing things invented—to list total net markups, and they are really healthy, averaging about 65%, on our complete line of plastic gimcracks we first created for the Froggies, but now most franchisees peddle a lot of them too.

"Their customers seem to really go for that kind of junk, you know, little statues, crappy pictures, and clothing items that look like they were designed for that Dracula group that springs up every October-month.

"And by now we're all dying of thirst so the chairman declared a recess."

Hymie himself took a break, and got up to take a bathroom break. As he passed Sharon he stumbled and had to break his fall by grabbing on to both her sizeable breasts.

As he returned, he stumbled again, saving himself for the second time by clutching her mammaries.

"Okay, let's get this finished. Where was I?"

"Before or after you got in your free feels?" Sharon was not shy in calling attention to her natural assets.

Free, hell, Hymie thought. For what this broad costs me in hotel rooms alone I could have bought one of those great cars from our future enemies, a Merkedies he believed they'd be called.

He decided to ignore her comment. He'd get even later by being especially slow in coming.

"Finally, Saul listed projected incomes from our specialty products, the really big sellers: beads, candles, and that smelly incense. The warehouse guys told me they can't even keep this stuff in stock.

"As soon as we get a shipment from our KongHong or Chinee suppliers they have to use it just to fill backorders.

"You'd think even our franchisees' most brain-washed fanatics would get tired of this junk but apparently not."

Hymie shook his head in amazement.

"And then Saul showed us the grand totals. Incredible! Almost beyond comprehension how much money this franchise set-up by SCAM well over a millennium-period ago still generates.

"In 7 BS who could have guessed how powerful those guys' simple idea would turn out?"

"So, what's the verdict, Hymie? Who gets the goodies?" Harry wanted to get this meeting completed.

He had a hot tip on the third race at Aqueduct—since the Eye Ties and other Romaners started using that name, various tracks had tried to cash in on its respectable allure—and the nearest off-track betting parlor was over two clicks away.

"The general consensus was that the totals shown us by Saul were so much greater than even the Eye Ties or Froggies combined bids that we would be foolish to even consider selling the GOD® franchise."

Hymie motioned to Sharon to write down his comments on her papyrus.

"Officially, at the order of the executive council, you, Harry, as head of the sales promotion department, are hereby instructed to notify by regular scrolls—not those expensive carrier pigeons—all the respondents in the bid auction.

"Jazz it up as you see fit, Harry, these franchisees aren't the sharpest people, but make it clear the auction is terminated, and GOD® has decided it's in the best interests of all to maintain and continue to run as capably as we have for over a millennium-period the master franchise GOD® and its licensing branch GOD™."

Hymie paused to scratch his scraggly beard.

"And to make your job even easier, my boy, we added a nice little fillip that you can promote when you send them that bad news.

"At the moment there's very little sales activity between that Day of the Dead stuff at the end of October-month and what the Crapolics call ester in the spring.

"That's a lot of time being wasted with no one selling nothing.

"We want to change that, so that our income goes up, as will the franchisees' volume. It'll also give them some extra work to do, and take their pea-sized minds off that scrubbed auction."

"What you got planned, Hymie?"

"We haven't really gone much further than the idea, Harry. But there are several months in there that should be put to good commercial use.

"Seems to us that some big event, maybe right at the end of the year, when it's cold and dark almost everywhere, could be 'discovered' and have our franchisees promote the hell out of it.

"You could create a snazzy promo, Harry, asking franchisees for ideas on the new event and a name for it.

"Maybe say that the first franchise to come up with a really marketable idea and a good advertising slogan will get some kind of exclusive on pushing the event before we offer it to all our franchisees.

"That's besides getting the honor"—Hymie wiggled his fingers in the air to signify quotation marks— "of going down in franchise history as the discoverer of X event and name."

"Great idea, Hymie."

Yeah, like he thought it up. He was probably dozing when some other light bulb on that council had a brain wave. But regardless it meant more work, and more shekels and prestige, for Harry's department.

"Anyway, Harry, Head Office is drafting a memo explaining in more detail what I have just outlined here, but

I wanted to give you a little advance notice so you'd be prepared for that memo."

"Consider it done, Hymie," Harry said.

"I can get Marcy, the smartest broad in my department, to crap up a good letter," and I can still make the third race, he thought.

Harry stood up, smiled at and admired Sharon, a girl he'd really like to have in his bed but he realistically realized that Hymie had far more shekels than he did, and like most females that was the determining factor for her.

He sweet talked Marcy into creating a promo letter and left the office smiling, his day's complicated administration work safely underway.

"Adios" (where the hell had he picked up that term, sounded like something that yet-to-be-born Zorro would say) "and goodbye and shalom to all, fellow workers in GOD®'s interest.

"See you all later."

Harry got his hot tip bet down. When the mile race finished, and the other nine horses had crossed the finish line and been pulled up, his hop tip was still running, so the next morning his mood was black.

His secretary frowned at him, just like she did to everyone, and passed him a Head Office memo.

Harry read it quickly.

"After considering our decision to keep the GOD® master franchise, our alert petty cash manager has suggested we at least offer some secondary (Harry knew that meant basically worthless) properties to assuage the feelings of all those who entered the bid auction.

"So, to help sustain the interests of all our franchisees, we have decided to have a second bid auction. In it, same terms as before, high bidder gets the gravy, we will offer these valuable sub-franchises.

"Most franchisees now have relatively dead sales periods between 'Day of the dead' or 'Halloween' or 'Let's remember the deadies', or whatever the individual franchisees call it, and 'Nail him on a cross', sometimes 'ester', or whatever term they use.

"To us that seems like quite a bit of wasted sales time.

"To rectify that, of course for our franchisees, and even perhaps for GOD®, we are going to reactivate another medieval myth involving a birth.

"While this myth most often involves just a normal human birth, it sometimes involves, to give it that desired and necessary magical component for all enduring myths, a virgin mother.

"Now we all know that it is not unusual for many first-time mothers, especially younger girls still living at home, to claim they were virgins.

"This myth has been around for quite some time, and has even acquired a life of its own. This makes it a natural for a sales event.

"GOD® will leave it up to individual franchisees to name this sales event.

"Four quick but intelligent suggestions from Head Office" (undoubtedly after three martoonies, Harry figured) "are: Virgin baby day, Never-done-it and look what happened Day, Where did that come from? Day, and Jesus Christ!-Mas kids! Day. (The latter from Pedro, one of our non-circumcised employees.)

"Sales promotion will get underway immediately", the memo continued.

"We suggest splitting the time difference between Halloween and that Crapolics sales day called ester, and having it towards end of the dead-sales period before the New Year gets customers buying again.

"As before, a written auction, all franchisees eligible, highest bid gets to name the sales event (whether that benefit lasts beyond that franchisee's territory is beyond our control).

"And to add a few rubles, the winner also gets a 10% reduced rate on sales during the two weeks before and the week after the sales event day. For the first 50 years only, of course."

There was a PS appended.

"For some of our Eye Tie and Froggie Crapolic franchisees, we need a dependable supplier of one-day old bread, and cheap house-brand wine.

"We will expect the delivered prices to be low enough that GOD® can add on its usual 65% markup. Quantities will be supplied later when Future Sales Forecasts has worked out some estimates."

"That sure is a hell of a lot different than that bullshit Hymie gave me. Maybe the same basic 'new sales event day', but nothing else the same. And that means more fucking work for me," Harry groaned.

He immediately pulled the string which was connected to the can in Marcy's cubicle.

As he waited for her to appear in his office, Harry thought about Marcy's reaction.

'I just know she'll love having to completely change the promo letter I'm sure she's already finished after sweating on it until late last night, she's such a dedicated employee.

'Well, maybe' he added realistically.

'But whatever, she can get started on this new assignment, and later I'll exercise my executive privilege by okaying or vetoing her suggestions.'

He pulled out his stiff canvas attaché case and removed its only occupant, a copy of 'Here are the winners today at Aqueduct'. If only, he thought.

Chapter 13

"The old faiths light their candles all about,
But burley Truth comes by and puts them out."

Lizette W. Reese (1856-1935), poet.

###

The Glasgow Cheapskater trumpeted the news flash (aka press release) on its front page, just below its motto: "The world (mostly just Uropa, a lot is yet to be discovered) news and still just two uros, the bargain of the 12th century ASS."

"From sources we consider highly reliable, or at least sometimes almost accurate, we have learned via today's pigeon-mail that GOD®, that wonderfully successful and tremendously rich company of intelligent and charitable individuals [note to GOD®: our advertising rates are very thrifty for the value they give] was seriously considering offering a sort-of universal opportunity to their current franchise holders to make an auction bid on the very GOD® name.

"It is hard to believe that this wonderful organization would even consider letting others share in what must "be the most profitable concern in our known world (i.e.-mostly just Uropa; see our slogan above.)

"If that rumor proves to be true, we will again have scooped the world [see motto above] press on this shattering news story.

We will continue to follow it closely and update it in next month-period's issue.

In London, the Limey Ledger was more restrained.

"Latest flash from our roving informants, just in by canoe ferry from Frogland, confirms our earlier rumor (see Issue 1215, No. 28) that GOD® was considering serious changes in how it runs its franchise businesses.

"It now appears that GOD® is definitely looking into possible major changes in its corporate structure.

"One reporter, whose news was delayed while we translated it from dying frog to universal inglis, noted that several key GOD® executives were seen huddled together and talking animatedly in that current hot spot, the Guy Fawkes nightclub, whose memorable motto 'Treat yourself to the best; go Fawkes yourself' is heard everywhere.

"The gist of those conversations could not be overheard by our source, but by sign language he assures us that they looked serious.

"Latest news flashes will be reported to you just as soon as we can get them translated."

Even more disturbing was the lead article below the fold from the Barcelona Bugle, "All the news our current dictator thinks you should have".

"As is known to our regular readers, we avidly follow the giant GOD® company, and in fact many of our subscribers (at just three centavos a week a bargain indeed) have lifetime memberships in the local God™ franchise run by a group of gay men who say that their franchise lets them feel better than ever.

"Their franchise, technically owned by Vida-LongerLife SA de CV, is affiliated with the EyeTie God™ franchise, and uses the Crapolics brand name under special license.

"The gays operate under the motto 'Vida is good for you', and say they have special discounted memberships for all young Crapolics under the age of 12.

"But boys only, they add. At the present they have no good way of handling females.

"They have recently had to increase their lifetime fees from nine to ten percent of members' total incomes, but in a recent ad in this fine periodical they pointed out that they now offer six more holydays than before the fee increase.

"Seems to us that the fee boost is definitely justified.

"Anyway, our extensive staff of two reporters will keep at it, and we will report the latest about GOD® and its interesting doings just as soon as our benevolent dictator gives us the okay."

Chapter 14

"The greatest tragedy in mankind's entire history may be the hijacking of morality by religion."

Arthur C Clarke, 1917-2008, science fiction writer, inventor, futurist.

\#\#\#

The local chapter of the "Crapolic Chicks: Enjoy yourself 6 days. On the 7th we wipe your slate clean" was in an uproar as President Angelina DeMarco entered the glitzy junior section of saint mark's God™ emporium.

"OK, everybuddy siddown and shut up!"

Angie had spent her vacation in what will be the New World, and was so captivated by it that she had adopted several expressions favored by the natives there.

"Now, what's all dis commotion?"

Sweet little Patsy Falvo piped up.

"Miss DeMarco, have you heard? My poppy, who as you know is a senior level hit man in the local mafia, just heard from one of his hookers, the one who specializes in working only on Crapolics holydays when her jims—or is it johns?—are spending like crazy, and she heard from her God™-licensed pimper, that we're going to get a wonderful new holyday. In the wintery-season, she thought."

"Anyone else hear that?"

From the very last row Deborah, developed well beyond her 12 years, and already as tall as DeMarco, stood up.

First she stretched; she enjoyed giving the acne-ridden boys something to think about.

"Yeah, my mama is a special (she underlined the word) friend of pappy Guillermo, and he's one of the most important pervies in this area."

This area was GOD® franchise number 286 in EyeTie, one of 57 alone in the city of Roma.

The entire country, and even here in this decrepit old burg, had proven to be a goldmine for the GOD® franchisees.

It seemed like everyone wanted the benefits of a Crapolic lifetime membership: "Enjoy yourself 6 days. On the 7th we wipe your slate clean".

DeMarco frowned. That Deborah kept getting bigger boobs every time she saw her. What the hell was she eating? Or, more likely, what exercises was she giving those twin dumplings.

DeMarco was no slouch herself, 36Cs were nothing to be ashamed of. She just hated seeing these kids constantly getting more attractive.

"Yeah, I alreddy hoid that, Debbie." She knew the girl hated the abbreviation.

"So I guess it's de troot. It'll be nice to have some time off in that rotten winter-period.

"I tink I'll head back to the NW. That's Noo Woild for those who don't travel much." (All her kids had heard that abbreviation enough; DeMarco was the only person from the entire area who had made the arduous galley ship voyage.)

The rest of the class jumped up and shouted with glee. Now that their teacher had confirmed it, they were positive: another big holyday was in de woiks in the crappy, low-income winter-period.

Part 4 – Chapter 15
Time: Even more years later

Before marriage, Charles Darwin had confessed everything to his future wife: that he was in the process of rewriting the history of life. That, according to his convictions, all living things descended from a common ancestor. And that all species were not to be attributed to a god's endless creativity, but were the product of a blind, mechanical process that altered them over the course of millions of years. This alone was pure heresy. Darwin even nursed doubts about the very survival of human beings.
And this man, who had gone around the world once, and was going to marry Emma Wedgwood, did not believe a single word of the biblical story of creation.

Editor's Note: This news note originally appeared in Spektrum, and has been translated from German. It was published as part of a tribute to Charles Darwin on his 200th birthday.

###

"I called this special emergency meeting because GOD® is facing a crisis. A real crisis," Chairman Abe Diamond looked at David Stein, who was obviously working on a crossword puzzle. Stein looked up and stuffed the paper into his 3-button suit pocket.

"What's the crisis, Abe?" Sol Goldberg didn't like to waste time. He was VP of Future Planning and was used to problems.

"At last count, Sol, the Crapolics are being sued in various courts in more than 250 lawsuits. Some individual, some class action. And the Crapolics, especially those in EteTie, Francie, and now even in Latin America, are being hammered.

"It appears that the old days of being able to buy off any legal problems are no more."

"What are the suits about?"

"Sol, they cover just about everything, though mostly child molestation, child abuse through unauthorized brainwashing, general perversion, fondling choir members, and extortion.

"And we all know that those same Crapolic franchises are our biggest single customer group.

"This is the worst franchise problem we've faced since our start in 32 ASS. We need to come up with a plan. And right now."

Stein, VP of Marketing, and a sound strategy planner as well as a creative genius, cleared his throat.

"We've got another problem, fellows," he said.

"And actually bigger than the lawsuits. We've had those before. Because the suits are heaviest in the areas where we have the strongest franchises, they can just continue to fix juries, buy off judges, threaten witnesses.

"Where that doesn't work as well anymore, our franchisees can go back to the tried and true intimidations the Crapolics have learned how to use for hundreds of years: assaults, kidnappings, family shootings, 'disappearances', even simple murder.

"I don't really think, Abe, that we have to worry too much."

"Easy for you to say, Dave, you're somewhat removed from the daily battle scenes. But these lawsuits now are a lot tougher than they used to be.

"The people filing them have some top lawyers, and they know to have their kids' oral evidence corroborated, so those sneaky bastards are even using body mikes on nine-year-old kids to get the idiot pervies on tape.

"It's pretty hard to defend a lawsuit when they have hard evidence of the moron prest panting and slobbering right before he grabs the kid's dick in his mouth."

Stein jotted a few notes on the pad he always carried.

"I agree, Abe. Times have changed. But we can show those loony Crapolics how to counter much of that electronic evidence.

"For one thing, insist that all the pervies inclined toward perversion—and that would take in almost all of them, certainly everyone at their HQ in Roma, where that's Requirement One for just getting a job there—are wearing body interference units."

Sydney, head of Transport Services and a little behind in current scientific advances, waved his hand.

"What are they, David? Some tricky suit, sort of like body armor? Wouldn't that be conspicuous?"

"No, nothing like that, Syd. Newer interference units are literally the size of a postage stamp, much smaller than the smallest cell phones due to be invented in about a 100-year period. The prest can even hide it in the crack of his ass..."

"...Except that's the first place liable to be in use," Sol Goldberg burst out laughing."

"...True." David Cohen smiled. "But anywhere on the body.

"Even in one of those hollowed-out bible books many of the pervies use for liquor bottles.

"No little kid is going to catch on, and he'll report back to his parents happily thinking he's caught the fat prest, except that when they turn on the recorder they'll get nothing but garbage sound.

"Those cases wouldn't even get to the formal lawsuit stage."

Abe frowned. "That sounds good, David. But surely in time the parents and their lawyers will come up with some way to counter the interference machines and..."

"And then our guys will come up with something better, Abe. Let's face it. Any people—us-- that can come up with a guy who's now telling us just about everything we want to know about this world can devise a way to beat the opposition with technical tools."

"You mean that guy Al something, working in Switzerland."

"Yeah, I think it's Albert, last name is Weinstein or something."

The meeting paused for a few moments, while most of the members wondered if Albert whatever could really be correct in his theories about the world and how it started.

"Okay", Abe said. "Assuming for the moment that David is right, and that in the field of technical research we don't really have to worry about the problems our number-one franchisee brings on itself by the sheer ignorance and lust of most of its members, what is the other problem you mentioned before, David?"

"That first problem can be basically resolved by one of our smart guys, but this even bigger problem won't be handled so smoothly." Cohen paused.

"Anyone hear of a guy in Europa named Darwin?"

"He's the guy that wrote a scroll about revolution or something, right?" Sydney might not be fully abreast of tech innovations but he was a charter member of the Scroll-of-the-Month club.

"Close, Syd. It's about what he calls evolution. And it has a lot of unpleasant features in that scroll that may seriously affect our franchise business.

Sydney frowned. "Like revolution, how a wheel goes around in order…"

"No, quite different. Darwin's evolution purports to explain how we have been descended from apes, how they in turn came from sea critters, who in turn were descendants of pieces of star or meteor material that somehow ended up on this planet."

Sydney, and the rest of the group, were silent.

Only a couple had other than 'what the fuck?' looks on their faces. Goldberg the future whiz was one of those.

"Yeah, I read his scroll last end of week. Pretty strong stuff. I can see what's bothering you, Dave. You think if this scientific info gets around, people may start wising up to the god BS."

Cohen nodded.

"Exactly. Once printing presses, never mind the incredible communication devices due not that far ahead, get into full swing, the great unwashed masses may get a little pissed off giving their local pervert prest a tithe of all they make, and realize such payoffs are simply a scam."

He looked at chairman Abe.

"No sweat, guys," Abe replied. "I had my personal helper read Darwin's scroll and quill me a short resume.

"Sure, the guy makes sense, and his conclusions are based on scientific data, but who's really going to believe him or it?

"You think the average tithe payer to one of our franchisees prefers to think of himself as a descendant of a sea slug, or as the embodiment of some god figure who is here temporarily before he returns to heaven and rolls around all day with a clutch of virgins?"

"Where would they get that inexhaustible supply of virgins anyway?" Sydney looked genuinely puzzled. "They'd have to make them out of moulds or something to always have new ones..."

"Interesting point, Syd, but one we can discuss in the tavern later. For now, I propose that we do as we've always done, just ignore anything, no matter how scientific, accurate, correct, or whatever.

"Rest assured our franchisees will, just as they've done now for centuries, because they know that their customers, the vast majority of the population, will always pick the virgins over sea worms."

"I have to agree with you, Abe. How anyone could read that scroll of Darwin and not give the finger to any and all prests, but they won't. So, I make the motion that we just table this info for now."

"OK, a seconder? Thanks, Syd. Hands up who vote for the motion. It's carried unanimously. Now let's adjourn to ye olde tavern and discuss the virgins problem."

The report on the Oriental franchises was prepared by Oleg Cooperman and delivered to chairman Diamond promptly. As a former telegraph operator on the newly incorporated Canadian Western Ocean Railroad, claimed to be the longest railroad ever, Oleg's reports were short and sweet.

"This report updates our previous report No.75-015.

"Overall the data is excellent. GOD® has operating franchises in all the eastern areas, including regions where the local franchisees use gods such as buddham, musleem, and hindoise, as well as thought systems like confusin.

"All 22 main franchises, and their related sub-franchisees, are doing very well, and their gross receipts are growing at an overall average rate of 13.74% per year. Our gross is also up, averaging more than 21% per year.

"In addition to the excellent marketing assistance we furnish (and require franchisees to follow religiously)", Oleg liked his little puns, "the main factor in our franchisee continued growth rates is their low labor costs.

"In almost all these geographic regions a traditional 'sweatshop' approach to employees is part of the culture.

"Employee benefits, such as we have to contend with in many of the 'developed' areas, are either unknown or ignored.

"If an employee complains about the excessive work hours--14-hour days are common—he or she is summarily fired. Repeated such complaints, even at different employers, often result in 'disappeared' people.

"Door to door sales people, proselytizing for the franchisee's particular god, are effectively used to inform, persuade, and if necessary coerce and threaten, people to join and/or maintain their tithing obligations. Forever.

"Once enrolled in the franchisee's plan, exits and turnovers are practically non-existent.

"When overall labor costs are negligible, much of the gross return becomes net. That makes for happy and successful franchisees. It also makes for a happy and successful GOD®."

Chairman Diamond smiled approvingly as he closed the report. He told his secretary helper to send Cooperman Form 362-B, the 'Good job' memo.

On the 17th floor, New Franchises Manager Saul Westman was reading a scroll letter. It was from a current sub-franchisee of one of the Goth franchises in the Aleman region. He turned to his assistant, a fairly intelligent young woman named Deidre, who was stacked like an inflation-pile of marks.

"This is interesting, Dee." He kept hoping that his familiar shortening of her name might also lead to a shortening of the usual and boring boss-employee relationship time and thus to a BJ.

As he hoped, she swiveled in her new chair on wheels, tightening the pressure on her blouse already threatening with boob explosion.

"This guy is now active for one of our Goth franchises. Not the most spectacular successful but a steady profit performer.

"Now he says he has been screwed"—he liked to use suggestive words as much as possible, he figured they might smooth the path— "by one of the major Crapolic organizations. Says they keep upping the minimum sales quota he needs to produce to maintain his sub franchise."

Deidre nodded to show she was listening closely to his words of wisdom. What an idiot, she thought. People will be flying like birds before he gets his clammy paws on these babies.

"He says he's so disillusioned with the whole Crapolic setup that he's thinking of starting a new god system, and wants to know his chances of getting a new master franchise if he succeeds."

Deidre nodded again. What was the problem? "So how are you going to respond to him, Saul?"

He stroked his chin, he'd heard that it impressed young females.

"Send him the usual scroll letter, Dee. You know, 'We can't possibly commit to any even future agreement while you are with a current sub franchisee of ours.

"If you are serious, you would first have to sever current connections, then establish and successfully promote your new god system. At that time you could apply on our standard Form1008-J, which is the 'Request to be considered as a possible Franchisee'.

"Then sign my name" --another form of intimacy he hoped— "and send it off to," he glanced down at the printed name, "a Herr Martin Luther. Keep a copy in our files, although I doubt we'll ever hear from him again."

Deidre's best friend Janice was just then doing some future planning with her boss, Special Promotions Director Sam Wainstein.

Unlike her buddy Dee, Janice had high hopes that some day, not today, probably, but some day soon, Sam would not only enjoy the goodies in her blouse, but the one down below.

Unlike Dee, she found it hard to say pussy, although when together she used it frequently, often unconsciously caressing that region as she named it.

"I've been thinking of a miracles special, Janice. We haven't had one for a long time and according to our scroll records they always goose sales nicely."

Janice had a sort of hobby, reading historical scrolls. Like most, she found it impossible to separate the fiction versions from their more highly regarded so-called factual accounts.

"Great idea, Sam. I've been reading some scrolls on those early days when the christians were just getting their business going. You know, there are a lot of references in them to miracles and other superstitious stuff. Maybe we could crib an idea or two."

Sam had had good input from Janice before.

"Not a bad idea. Wasn't there some Jew around then who apparently created a nice little fuss when he claimed to do miracles?"

"Sure, a failed fisherman by the name of Christo or something."

"Then let's follow up your good idea, Jan, with a concise report on that guy and what he actually was.

"You know, was he trying to set up a new offshoot of the Jewish religion, or start a completely new sect, or what? Can you do some reading and let me have just the high points by, say, four day-periods hence?"

"I'm on it, Sam." (And I wish you were in a similar position with me, sweetheart.) "I'll have it on your bench by the end of the week period."

And she did.

Her report, 'Brief Sketch for Special Promotions Director Samuel Wainstein', was short and succinct.

Was there actually a man named Jesus Christ? The following description, combined from the scrolls that eventually came to be grouped together under the name bible, would be affirmed by most impartial history scholars, a noted biblical scholar affirmed.

Jesus was born to an ordinary woman, who already had older children, sometime just before 4 BC/BS and grew up in Nazareth, a small village in Galilee, as part of the peasant class. His father was a carpenter and he became one, too, meaning that they had likely lost their agricultural land at some point. He was raised Jewish and he remained deeply Jewish all of his life; he never intended to create a new religion.

After an unsuccessful fishing career, he left Nazareth as an adult and met a prophet named John, sort of a forerunner of the later TV preachers, who baptized him by dunking him in water. During his baptism, like many people easily hypnotized, JC possibly experienced some sort of vision. Shortly afterwards, he began his public preaching with the slogan that the world could be transformed into a 'Kingdom of God.'

He became a teacher and prophet within the Jewish region. No mention of him is ever made in non-Jewish materials which have lasted to this day.

After a formal trial for treason he was executed by Roman imperial authority. His band of close followers, sort of an early Manson-family without the murders, claimed they experienced him after his death.

It is clear, a biblical scholar said, that any visions of JC they claimed were merely dreams of him as they had known him during his historical life. Only after his death did they declare him to be "lord" or "the son of god," not the first, and certainly not the last, such claim by self-appointed religious zealots in a wide variety of cults, continuing even to the present day.

––––––––––––––––––

Sam read the scroll during morning leisure period, with Janice close by.

"Interesting, Jan. But I don't see how we can use anything from JC.

"He appears to have been a guy who was only promoted by his dozen fellow travelers after he was executed, and once they realized they might have to start working for a living.

"And it was several hundred-year periods later before that preposterous idea really started to kick into gear, after some smart marketing men realized the goldmine they could develop.

"Nice job, Jan, but I guess it's back to the drawing surfaces to come up with a new slant on promotable miracles."

"OK, Sam, how about a special promo: offering a bunch of different miracles to the highest secret bidder? That hasn't been done since about 1722 ASS, and from our records it looks like it was a big success."

Her versatility continued to impress her boss.

Through her often-direct help he had racked up four consecutive bonus periods, and they had both enjoyed—in separate rooms, to Janice's chagrin—four week-close periods at one of Miami's fanciest spas, where only rich gangsters and top GOD® officials normally went.

"Great! Any ideas on the types of miracles we'll put up for auction?"

Hell, he could retire full time to the spa and let Janice run the department. He just hoped his bosses didn't find out.

"I made up a quick list last night-period" (when I was actually thinking of your hot hands caressing my...) "and here it is." She thrust a one page scroll at him.

"Miracles" Used by Religious Scams

Saints seen in mud puddles and verified by adolescent kids who neither read nor write.

Virgins in any franchisee sect over the age of 10—and that's a miracle in itself—who have had misty bodies appear in their bedrooms.

Angels seen floating below the clouds by spinsters over 70.

Mysterious pieces of bone firmly sworn to by whatever the franchisee sect calls its prests as being part of the anatomy of one of the sect's earliest promoters.

A fragment of a scroll found buried in some desert somewhere which has been 'authenticated' by a sect expert as being a section of the sect's founder's personal diary, even though every known such founder was totally illiterate and only able to even make an X for a signature.

———————————————

"Good ideas, Janice. Let's start working on all them. I think we should be able to do very well if we secret auction them all, maybe in one group or over a period of time. Let's have dinner tonight and discuss the framework."

"Love to, Sam." (And maybe we could even turn it into a break the fast session?)

In the executive suites on the top floor Franchisee Problems top gun Aaron Highman read the short memo again.

"We're still getting some competition from non-franchisee groups. Nothing serious but annoying. See if you can fix it."

The shorter the memo the more work it caused, Aaron knew. This problem had been around for hundreds of year-periods and was mostly just a nuisance.

But because the memo had come from the Chairman, he felt some tangible result was needed.

The current problem apparently arose when a group that was an offshoot descendant of an earlier sect had begun to make noises in, of all places, a part of territory that just recently had merged into a country called Canada, an Indian name of some kind.

And the area involved seemed about halfway between the country's southern borders and the North Pole. This was a matter he had best resolve from the comfort and warmth of his Florida office; let some flunky on the scene do the legwork.

And immediately Ben Grazer popped into his mind.

A former co-worker, he had disgraced himself by trying to peddle a book scroll about the inner workings of GOD®.

Good thing he had foolishly approached a scroll publisher who just happened to be indirectly owned by the Chairman.

Grazer had been demoted, lost all his accrued bonuses—and that was a lot, because he had been a great idea man—and was banished to the new northern country where he was put in charge of promoting scrolls on 'Improving your mind' to the locals, many of whom apparently couldn't even read.

Grazer would love the opportunity to get into something a little more active, and maybe even earn a few HQ brownie points again.

When Grazer received Highman's perfect copy of the Chairman's original copy some month-periods later— those damned dogsled delivery firms weren't the fastest— he immediately thought of Joe Smith.

Smith had tried to get his idea of multiple wives for each man—an easy way to be sure of a pussy supply— accepted in the eastern and Midwest parts of the Untied States.

But the puritan ethic was still too strong and although most male pilgrims gave the idea enthusiastic acceptance, their large and formidable wives kyboshed the idea, and Smith was forced into the wilderness of that country's western frontier.

He had seized upon some land west of a large mountain range. It was sparsely populated, mostly by former buffalo hunters and their large families and a few natives who didn't appear to bother anybody, especially if they were slipped a little moonshine.

Most importantly, there were no existing government parasites or bounty hunter wild men to care about whatever Smith wanted to do, so he set up shop there and dreamed up the name morons for his sect.

He later thought about that name and decided to throw in a consonant somewhere to make it less laugh getting.

The locals quickly adapted to one man having any number of 'wives', especially if most of those wives were young, gullible, and nubile. A few older ones were always added to get the work done.

Smith's sect had prospered for quite a while until government deadbeats had run out of tax possibilities east of the mountains and needed more revenue. Simple: just levy a stiff tax on more than one 'wife'.

This worked, until the men decided to be like men everywhere else, so they got rid of the harem legally, and relied on prosties and mistresses to meet other than washing and cleaning needs.

Another government money-grabbing plot foiled!

Grazer felt sure he could use the basic plot of Smith's attempts to satisfy Aaron Highman's problem as spelled out by his former co-worker in response to the Chairman's request.

At HQ things were getting back to normal after the big move to Miami from Jerusalem.

"It's getting far too dangerous here," the Chairman had decreed. "You can't walk a block without getting accosted by some sect bum trying to wheedle a dinar or two for the current annual edition of a bible put out by some—probably unauthorized and not royalty-paying!—jerkoff sect.

"We'll move to that Florida place, where I understand 98% of the population are so old and/or handicapped that they can barely breathe, let alone hold out their hand for a handout. Much more civilized."

And so the move had been made, not without some teary demonstrations by a few weaker sex employees.

But on the other hand, almost all of the female employees handled it smoothly and spent their frothy-café breaks basking in the sun and being ogled by oldies who could barely remember what that damned tube between their legs was really for.

Except for, at the moment, Judee Black, the assistant department supervisor of the Internal Franchisee Supplies group.

A long title, but actually not much to ordinarily do; just make sure the monthly shipments of specially printed bibles and other 'holy' books were delivered on time to the correct sect, and that other miscellaneous supplies (crowns, dresses for senior prests in the older sects, naughty underwear for younger prests who still enjoyed cross dressing, and cheapo quill pens and pencils inscribed with uplifting messages ("Have you paid your monthly fees promptly?").

She didn't like to even think about the time her predecessor had mixed up shipments for a small mooslim branch in Eyeran with a box of supplies for a peaceable holy roller group in an eastern state of the Untied States.

The local h.r. bishopric had just about heart attacked into the void when he opened an attractive short treatise and began reading: "And our glorious leader has commanded us to cut the balls off every non-believer and infidel they find...".

But errors like that were rare. Almost as unusual was the request she was now looking at.

From some heavyweight with about five holies and reverends preceding his name, he requested that the euro Crapolics franchise 266-8B, of which he was the corresponding secretary and chief assistant to the sub-chief who in turn reported to the area assistant branch manager, be granted the exclusive GOD® euro franchise rights to market all holy-type candles, those with diameters and lengths less than 1 and 10 units respectively (so that the damn things would burn up quickly and have to be replenished) and that all non-licensed (by the Crapolics, naturally) vendors would be subject to immediate arrest, detention, even beheading, if local laws permitted.

She grinned.

Wow, those religious nuts were as bloodthirsty as the old-time pirates. But far more hypocritical than the boys with real swords had been. Anyway, how should she handle this idiotic request?

She thought about it, had a quick sip of famous pale-stein harmony tea—'guaranteed to relax your brain cells without reducing their power'—and decided to take the obvious step.

She grabbed one of those cheapo imprinted quill pens found everywhere in HQ; this one warned "HE will know if you cheat on your 10% assessment!", and crossed out her name, scrawled in her immediate superior's name, and added a short note.

"This is above my level of authority so I'm sending to you."

Her boss was a snob and that's all she had to do to get him to accept the problem. Matter resolved and solved.

Time for a little more of that great sun before the Chairman's daily pre-recorded 'Boost sales and your bonuses' news broadcast.

Chapter 16

"To desire immortality is to desire the eternal perpetuation of a great mistake."

A. Schopenhauer (1788-1860), writer and philosopher.

###

The Chairman was worried.

He had just finished reading a confidential report from one of his most trusted aides.

The investigation behind it had been authorized by the Chair and his secret group of seven senior advisers.

"Your information," he read, "as is usual" (the Chairman smiled, a little butter goes a long way) "was essentially totally accurate.

"One of our most senior Franchisees has been, and still is, actively hiding criminal acts of child molestation, assault, torture, intimidation, and at least in several cases, murder, both from their members and local police forces."

The Chairman frowned. This was even worse than they had feared.

I better notify my Senior Seven of a special meeting. The Chairman rang the bell which summoned his personal secretary.

"Are you sure it's this bad?" Sam Easterman waved his copy of the confidential report. He was the senior member of the Senior Seven, and inclined to caution. "Maybe this investigator got a little carried away?"

"Not a chance, Sam. I've used this man several times before on equally sensitive problems. I've found that if anything he's a little conservative.

"His report will be a very accurate picture of the real conditions. And, as you can see, it's bad."

Ellery Goode popped up from what appeared to be a deep hibernation.

"Bad? I think you're a little off base, Chairman. It's fucking terrible."

The Chairman disliked profanity, except when stealing a quick one with one of his always well-endowed secretaries; he found the timeworn four-letter words still had an aphrodisiac effect on the younger women; but he had to now agree with Ellery, who in spite of his perpetual polar bear trance actually had a sharp mind.

"What we have to do is decide, and fairly quickly, how to handle this major problem. Ellery, now that you've finished your hibernation, maybe you'd summarize for all of us what this report contains, and more importantly, what it means."

"Glad to, Chairman."

He paused to quickly speed scan the entire document, using his ever-present red quill to make a few marks, then cleared his throat.

"In five separate countries in Europa alone, the Crapolics—our largest single franchisee of course—are being sued in major courts, about half from individuals' lawsuits for everything from traumas brought on by various prests fondling and sexually abusing them when they were still children, to major criminal cases lodged by a variety of bodies: everything from municipal agencies to state, and now even a couple of federal prosecutors have started criminal actions.

"It looks like after a long period of basically 'Don't ask, don't tell', people have decided to take action against the perpetrators.

"And a large part of that long period was caused by the smart shuffling around of guilty prests from one church area to another before the local matter got too smelly.

"And this chief handler was really smart. For his entire working career in the Crapolics internal hierarchy he moved prests like pawns on a chessboard. As soon as one prest made too big a stink, this operator yanked him out and moved him across the country somewhere where his reputation didn't precede him.

"This report shows that some prests were moved in this fashion as many as twelve times over a period of 25 years. Quite an operator.

"And he knew where so many bodies were buried that even though he had never been active politically in the Crapolics, when it came time to replace a dead popey, he was feared enough that he nailed the job.

"And that even with a lot of strikes against him: he was from alemann, an area not usually beloved of the roman mandarins, and had been a member of that country's fascist forces while the then dictator was alive; after the dictator's death this guy 'didn't know anything' about the millions of our people who were murdered during that time.

"So, you can see that he's as sharp and slippery as they come, even though he now's starting to drool in public quite a bit.

"From our many previous meetings I know that our official policy has been to ignore political stuff as long as it doesn't get mixed up in our wonderful franchise concept."

Ellery paused; this was a sensitive area, and half the members agreed with it, half didn't, but the Chairman was in the former group, so he continued reading.

"The report contains no recommendations. I don't believe the Chairman requested any.

"But it does paint a pretty grim portrait of our largest franchisee, and if these lawsuits continue, let alone increase, we might be faced with declining royalty fees income from it."

He sat down. Any more editorial comment would get him into very warm waters.

The Chairman cleared his throat, took a drink from the container always on his desk, and looked at the Senior Seven members.

Their actions affected not only the GOD® franchise but the well being of the entire population of this society.

"The floor is open to suggestions. But please keep strictly to the topic, and keep them short."

Sam Easterman was the first on his feet.

"I retract what I said earlier. This is a terrible fucking report. How can we have overlooked these pricks all these years?"

It was a redundant question and everyone knew it.

"Regardless. We've got to do something concrete, and quickly, or we stand a good chance of damaging our basic franchise, the one that has kept our people solvent for a long, long time."

"No one is disagreeing, Sam," the Chairman agreed. "But let's stick to specifics. Does everyone here agree that some kind of action is needed?"

He looked around the room, and nodded. "Yeah, it's unanimous. Okay, specific ideas?"

Joel Wieder stood up.

"As chairman of the public affairs committee, I recommend that GOD® immediately start a major internet sneak campaign to press for total internal reform of this rotten group."

Eden Morriss stuck up his hand. "What's a sneak campaign?"

"Good question, Eden," Joel replied. "It's a carefully planned and orchestrated campaign, not identified in any way with GOD®, and apparently just a grass roots thing which is rapidly getting popular acceptance.

"We would do it by using friendly blogs, i.e., those published by people friendly to our cause but not identified with us.

"We could start by citing some actual cases, then ask questions like 'How many more victims will there be?' and 'Why can't these horrific abuses be stopped?'

"I assure you all that we've used these techniques very successfully in the past."

"Where?" Eden always aimed right at the point.

"Well, I'm limited by our state security rules, but I can say that our national budget is about half financed by another country. We accomplish that by portraying our country's security as very closely tied to theirs, so their politicos are actually convinced they have to kick in all this dinero."

He looked around at the members.

"One point is important, and essential to the success of any such campaign. It must be founded on basically accurate info. Despite what many dictators have believed about the power of the Big Lie, today with all the instant communication power available, to build a campaign strictly on BS would be a disaster."

"How much to get such a campaign going?" The chairman was always aware of budget constraints.

"Far less than any other even comparable effort. We can get it going for under a hundred grand, and in regular media that wouldn't buy more than a couple of back pages.

"It's not a terribly long process either. If I get our writers on it now, we could start seeing results within just a few weeks, even days."

"I'm still a little unclear on how this campaign would work, Joel. Without getting into all the guts can you just give us a rough sketch?"

"Sure. These kinds of campaigns have been used successfully by organizations from big business to political to even cockeyed individual things like mass sit-ins and nude parades.

"Basically, we use a simple letter approach. We address our friendly blog editors with a short inflammatory letter they can use to build interest and circulation—like any other medium blog owners make more money when their readership increases—and then also include a confidential note to the editor with enough hard stats to justify his taking the time to run our short letter.

"Then we follow up with timed letters using the same approach: a short letter apparently responding to the first letter, and starting the public wildfire, and again provide more hard facts for him to use or not as he prefers.

"By this time, just four or five days after the initial contact, others have responded to our first letter. It doesn't matter whether they agree or disagree with us, they're providing more fuel for the controversy fire. And that's what our blog editor wants: more readership, more controversy, more money from sponsored ads on his blog."

"Is that ethical?" Sam Easterman looked worried.

Joel laughed. "Sam, it may not be 100 percent ethical, but it 100 percent works."

The other members laughed and clapped.

The chairman rapped for silence.

"I think that questions of ethics regarding our largest franchisee are somewhat moot. Has anyone read our secret history recently?"

He didn't bother to make a count, he knew it would be zero.

"Anyway, back some time ago that franchisee thought it would get rid of some of the competition which was springing up, their popey and governing council felt they wanted the field to themselves.

"We weren't too concerned, as any result of their actions would just be to increase our royalty fees. But the techniques they used to get rid of the competition make questions of ethics concerning them laughable."

He paused to sip his drink.

"They simply murdered some of the new boys on the block. Others they hung, or beheaded along with entire families, or pushed into religious disgrace by falsely stating that the crap they pushed was heretical and directly from the devil's own lips.

"And of course their customers believed it, because from birth literally they had been brainwashed to do just that.

"In some parts of their franchise area they simply moved in gangs of rapists, thieves, and cutthroats, and paid them bounties for each dead or mutilated or raped, or all three, 'heretics'.

"No, I don't think any ethical considerations are necessary or warranted, Sam.

"But we do have to make a decision on Joel's proposal. Any questions on it?"

He waited. No one spoke.

"OK, then let's vote. All in favor of Joel's proposal..."

Before he could finish the sentence every member had raised his hand.

"Well, then, it appears unanimous. And I cast my vote with the rest of you."

Several members clapped their hands.

"The proposal is carried."

The Chairman couldn't think of anything else to say, so for once he didn't.

Chapter 17

"The religion of one age is the literary entertainment of the next."

Ralph Waldo Emerson, (1803-1882), writer.

###

"History is a load of crap. It's boring, boring, boring, and probably all lies anyway." Efran closed the big book and pushed it away.

Miriam smiled. She knew what he really wanted to do instead of studying 'The Official Abridged History of This World, Version 293-B'.

She had let Efran sample her blouse full of goodies last night, and from the telltale bulge in his tight jeans she could see he was thinking of that.

But her father had been as firm: "If that boy doesn't start getting better grades, Miriam, you can say goodbye to him, no matter how much dinero his father has. No daughter of mine is going to hang out with the village idiot."

But she really liked Efran, so she had decided to give him a hand—not the kind he would really like—and help him with his studies. He was particularly bad in history.

"It's not so difficult, Efran. Here's a trick I use to remember stuff in history. Just make up little stories about key events—remember how we used to do that in kiddey garden? —and that will trigger other stuff in the same time periods."

He tugged at his jeans, trying to get his swollen dick into a more comfortable position. If only she wasn't so damned pure; he knew some other girls would gladly help him to relieve the pressure. But he was going to have to work on Miriam slowly.

"Sure, that sounds good for you. But how can you make up stories about this crap?" He pointed to the very large volume.

She leaned over—accidentally on purpose giving him a renewed glimpse of the twin mounds he'd found so fascinating last night—and lugged up the book onto the coffee table.

"It's not hard, Efran." And smiled to herself; of course it was.

She leafed through the volume, stopping randomly. She read a few paragraphs.

"OK, here they're talking about the early founding of the Untied States.

"Way before the war with the Brits that actually started the country, a group of people known as Pilgrims had settled in some of the northeast coast areas. And back in elementary school I remember learning a little poem about that."

She rose to her feet, and adopted a theatrical pose, making sure her breasts were pressed tightly against her silk blouse.

"This poem was written by a man named Arthur Guiterman a long time ago." She cleared her throat.

"The pilgrims landed, worthy men,
And, saved from wreck on raging seas,
They fell upon their knees, and then,
Upon the aborigines."

Miriam smiled prettily, curtsied, and then blushed-
—almost as she had when Efran had first kissed her left nipple; by the time he had worked over to the right side the blush had been replaced by a general tightness in her lower body and a shortness of breath—and sat down.

"That was pretty funny, Miriam. Is it accurate?"

"As accurate as anything in history, I imagine. That's just about what they did, even though they were supposed to be very religious.

"You see, Efran, a simple little poem can bring back stuff about a time in the country's history when new immigrants simply wiped out the original inhabitants. Whether they did so out of fear, or stupidity, or just cruelty, who knows now? But it makes it easy to remember some history, doesn't it?"

Efran nodded slowly. "But that's only one example, Miriam."

Surprisingly the problem of an extremely obvious erection had somewhat dwindled, although the twin causes of it were still all too noticeable.

"You probably couldn't do that random selection thing again."

"Dare me?"

"I guess so." When she got into her female power character Efran was a little intimidated; she would probably insist on being on top.

She smiled a sort of victory smile and grabbed a bunch of pages. "Dare accepted."

She opened the book and spread it on the table. She read for a few moments, then looked up.

"This part is about stuff that happened in the mid and late 1900s. ASS, not BS.

"Now at that time, just like forever, there were a number of weirdo groups, all over the world. Among them you may have heard of hippies, the anti-everythings, the we-won't-goers, and a big bunch of others."

Efran nodded slowly. He remembered a couple of those names but nothing more.

"They were all drop-outs, you know, they didn't agree with the so-called establishment," Miriam said. "Some of our people, too, but not too many. Most were younger people from the sects that were franchisees, and where often weird rules were enforced.

"Anyway, one group got extremely obnoxious at all the airports—you remember, places where those early air machines landed and took off, long before our space continuum engineers fixed travel up—and short of shooting them on sight something had to be done. Even big business and political wheels from every country were being hassled every time they took one of those air machines.

"The problem was attacked by our Special Projects department, and they came up with a neat solution.

"Rather than let this group—known then as Hairy Krishnuts—bother everyone, they forced them to buy a sub-franchisee warrant solely for those air machine places.

"A special minor sub-franchisee tax was placed on all tickets sold for travel on the air machines.

"Part of this tax revenue was allocated to the Hairy group, and they were warned that any further harassment of passengers would immediately result in expulsion to the island of Erie Land where they would have to exist on potatoes.

"A simple solution," she said. "Problem solved. But just thinking and remembering about the Hairy group, and that will bring back memories of this world many years ago, the ancient travel means the people used, and lots more."

Miriam smiled. "Did I win the dare?"

She sat back on the sofa, straightened her hair, and took a deep breath, almost causing fabric dissolution of her fragile blouse material.

Efran's bulge problem was back in spades.

"Sure you did, Miriam. But that's enough history for now. Let's just sit here and relax for awhile."

Miriam smiled again. Relax? She wondered which side he'd try to start with today.

Chapter 18

"Life's but a walking shadow, a poor player
That struts and frets his hour upon the stage
And then is heard no more: it is a tale
Told by an idiot, full of sound and fury,
Signifying nothing."

William Shakespeare (1564-1616), playwright.

###

"We've got to stop this fucking crap." Erim was unhappy and it showed.

"What's the prob, bro?"

Sammie had been watching too many low-budget TV shows, and he had picked up an array of slang sayings from the equal rights channel. He didn't know what a bro was, but he figured it must be someone pretty intimidating.

Erim scowled at his assistant. "And also cut out that equal rights crap, it's as bad as the fucking crap I was referring to."

"And that is?"

Erim picked up a formidable looking scroll and pushed his thumb against it.

"This is what that is. This most recent monthly report on worldwide attacks on our protected GOD® trademark shows that the illegal and immoral pricks continue to test us. They seem to be coming out of the woodwork just about everywhere."

He flipped a few pages.

"Look here. In the period since just three reports ago—three fucking months! —there have been at least 20 reports of attacks on our trademark protection."

He paused to gather his breath. "Everywhere! Every fucking where!"

Sammie covered a smile with a cough. Listening to Erim was a tiring job, he used more exclamation points in one burst than Sammie did in a year.

Erim continued. "There's another bunch of idiots out there in the wild west, Idaho or somewhere, where a 'leader' claims to have had a personal visit from one of god's lieutenants. He doesn't specify which god he's chummy with, but our spies have captured a couple of his official reports to his followers, and he's slipping in the odd GOD®.

"That's a clear violation of our worldwide coverage, Sam, but the trouble is this jerk doesn't as yet have any tangible assets, so it's not worth our while to sue him. But that time will come."

Sammie expected another ! at the end of that sentence but it never came.

"And here. Look here!"

There it was, Sammie knew. That missing ! had just shown up. So he looked as directed.

"In that famous religious state of Illinois, which everyone knows has more criminals per capita than even Somalia, including probably 99.99 percent of the politicians, higher even than the national average of 99.98 percent, some fat former hippy says he knows the day, even the hour, when JC will make his reappearance, and in some of his verbal drooling he also has made free use of our protected GOD®.

"And also, like our Idaho buddy, he doesn't have the proverbial pot to piss in, so there's no easy or satisfactory way to at the moment shut him up."

From long experience Sammie said nothing, just nodded his head and looked grim.

"And it's not just in the Untied States where the pricks are on the move."

To lend authority to his remarks he now assumed the famous Nixon 'I am not guilty' pose.

Sammie thought he looked more like some third-rate television comic doing a bad impression of a drag queen but again his experience kept him silent.

"Overseas we have several groups in Frogville who have decided to start their own churches. Must be relatives of the late Ron Hubbard."

Sammie didn't have a clue as to who or what a Ron Hubbard was, but again silence kept him out of harm's way.

"And a Polish bunch, who say they are totally disillusioned with all existing religions, have decided to share their visions of the 'right' one with us, and use GOD® freely in their hand-printed crap.

"But it does appear a few of those handpicked have a few pesos, so I'm going to get our Polish lawyer to have a run at them. Probably won't even cover our expenses but we have to maintain our fences. Right?"

Luckily Sammie had been occasionally listening and his trained ear caught the significance of the question mark as opposed to the !, so he quickly nodded. "Absolutely, Erim, that's our job."

Satisfied that he had a rapt audience Erim carried on.

"Even further afield I have info here on a group in Morocco who has started the H. Bogart Institute of Eternity Studies.

"They claim it was actually founded in secret by the late actor who was in some movie set in that area, but probably shot on a sound stage in sunny Burbank Cal.

"And they too are very free with their use of GOD®. In just one booklet I counted 17 times they used it, none with the ® trademark symbol of course.

"So, I'm going to have our Gibraltar guy jump on the ferry and see if they have any sizeable assets. If so, he can get the legal wheels rolling, assuming that there even are legal wheels in Morocco."

Erim paused for breath, and Sammie seized the opportunity.

"I think you're doing great with our department, Erim. Just give me a minute here, I've got to take a tremendous leak."

And he walked very quickly out the office door before his boss could complain.

His tremendous leak, aka a quick smoke, took almost six minutes. He would have pushed it even more but he knew beyond seven and Erim was liable to come looking for him.

When he re-entered the office Erim was deep in conversation on the outside line.

He listened for a moment to make sure his boss hadn't ordered a hit on him, then he settled down into his usual half-hibernation state.

"Of course I want immediate action, Dennis! We can't have these jackals using our trademark and getting away with it. Sue the bastards!"

Not bad, thought Sammie. Only two out of a possible three !s.

Erim slammed the receiver down and looked at Sammie with a satisfied grin.

"There! That will teach those bandits in sunny Cal that they can't be free and easy with our trademark!

"It's that bunch up in northern Cal who have set up an 'official' headquarters for a major directive from God due shortly. And no ® mark to show our name ownership!

"I know some of those crooks have some money somewhere, so I ordered Dennis Diamond to get after them. He'll grind them back on to food stamps where they belong!"

Sammie had given up counting the !s.

He figured that his boss had exceeded the thousand mark this week alone. Enough! Fuck, now he was doing it. Maybe it was contagious.

Anyway, their department had a pretty good cost-revenue ratio. Last time he'd checked the figures, they took in, mostly from lawsuit settlements, almost six times as much as the shysters cost to launch them.

With a little whining from Erim, who was as good at that as dropping in the !s, they both stood to get healthy bonuses at year end.

Normally they could expect to split, in favor of Erim, the boss of course, an additional twenty percent of their net salary earnings.

Great!

Chapter 19

"Saint: a dead sinner revised and edited."

Ambrose Bierce, (1842-1914), writer and humorist, in 'The Devil's Dictionary'.

# # #

Sammie didn't feel all that good. He had, though. Earlier when he first got into the office that day. As usual, the weather in Miami had been warm, and clear, and the humidity hardly topped 98 percent. A fresh shirt would last at least six minutes before it turned into the equivalent of a used swim suit top.

But all that was before he had been handed, and signed for, an important-looking envelope from 'Legal Affairs, Headquarters'.

Anything from HQ was usually bad news.

Payroll checks, for example, came from the local office. News about bonuses, salary raises, and vacation days, all from local. From HQ? 'You're fired. Where are your overdue reports? Why are your estimates late?'

So this brown envelope was undoubtedly bad news. Should he open it now, or wait for Erim! to arrive?

The problem was resolved when Erim himself walked in. Immediately he saw the envelope in question.

"From HQ? Why haven't you opened it!"

Not a question mark as ordinary folks would use, but one of those damned ! marks he cluttered every conversation with.

"It just came, and because it was marked 'Confidential' I thought it perhaps would be best to wait for the department head. You," in case Erim didn't know who he was.

"Well, open the damned envelope! It won't open itself!"

A typical Erim! observation, Sammie thought, but he went ahead and ripped off the security seal Legal Affairs liked to use on everything they sent.

A single legal-sized sheet slid out. Sammie grabbed it before it hit the floor. He started to read it but Erim! grabbed it from him.

"Anything from Legal should be read first by the department head! That's me!"

Exactly what he had said to him a minute ago. What an idiot! And then he realized he was falling into Erim's habit of adding an ! to everything. Enough! Oh fuck, again. From now on just periods.

Erim! was engrossed in the document. After a few minutes he looked up, gazed for a few seconds at the ceiling, cleared his throat, checked out the ceiling tiles again, then finally spoke.

"You read it, Sammie! Then later we can get together and discuss any ideas you might have! Right now, I have to have a meeting with, ah, never mind! Just read the memo!"

Sammie knew all too well that Erim! had no meeting scheduled.

As always, he'd head to the next floor lavatory, and hide in one of the booths until he figured enough time had passed for Sammie to come up with some specific plans or proposals to resolve the Legal Affairs problem.

When would Personnel ever figure out that he, Sammie, was the actual head of his department?

Unfortunately, Erim! was still sleeping with the assistant personnel manager, and until she got tired of his exclamation point conversations Sammie was doomed to play second fiddle.

He took the page and retired to his own cubbyhole office. Office, he laughed to himself. More like an upended shoe box. And damned Erim! had at least three times as much space, and a much nicer desk and visitor chairs too.

He realized he had got through that internal conversation without using a single ! Way to go! Oh shit, would it never end?

He read the page. While couched in Legal Affairs doubletalk, the problem was basically simple. Not the resolution, however.

A bunch of fairly recent immigrants, apparently known in their local area as pipgrims—it was difficult to read, the clerk in L.A. was apparently on an economy kick and was using a machine ribbon whose expiry date was far, far in the past—had moved in and were literally squatting on what was once prime real estate development area. Of course, every square inch of land in the state, and even quite a bit of it currently underwater due, some said, to that mysterious global warming, but fairly close to shore, 'prime plots' too, as far as the real estate shark sellers were concerned, fell into that category.

The local sheriff had been summoned by concerned citizens, the same ones who would walk by an injured pedestrian because they didn't want to get involved, but who were like hawks diving on a prey when real estate values were possibly threatened.

The lawman was a good old boy from Alabama and usually at least listened awhile before he drew his 357 and fired, so he approached the squatters with a grin on his face and his cannon securely ensconced in his custom-built holster.

Several began talking immediately. In spite of their funny accents and quaint costumes—the men had high collars on everything, the females were completely protected against everything from mosquitoes to stalkers by acres of drab cloth wrapped several times around their entire bodies—the sheriff listened fairly attentively to their complaints.

In his report, highly condensed and summarized by the frugal typist, the facts were few.

The squatters, who had arrived in rather weather-beaten and poorly constructed open sailboats, were seeking asylum because they had suffered absolutely unbearable religious persecution from the atheists, agnostics, and even a few Crapolics, on the island they had come from, called, the sheriff had written, something close to inger or angland or even blighty. Their accents made anything possible.

Their problem appeared, the sheriff's highly condensed report said, to be one of geography.

Sammie paused.

He had never been good in that subject either, so an immediate wave of sympathy washed over him. He wondered if they also had problems with arithmetic. He never could quite grasp how those damned fractions worked. How could you add up one-quarter of one apple to two-thirds of another? Obviously the result would have to be applesauce.

He shook his head and continued reading.

The squatters, the sheriff reported, had aimed their boats at what they thought was a place they had heard highly recommended by some high school students, Fort Lauderdale, as a 'wonderful, open, understanding' place, especially, the students went on, for religious holidays like something they called Spring Breaking.

A new one to the squatters, but they were not so close-minded that they wouldn't at least consider a new religious day. And what they really needed was some place they could start afresh, set up things like they wanted in the way they wanted. If any of the locals didn't like it, they could just darn well learn the squatters' ways.

When pressed further by the sheriff, who by this time was edging his right hand closer to that packed holster, it appeared the squatters, or Pidgrims as they called themselves—that typist really needed to update her ribbon—had headed to shore when they espied a large group of religious people clothed and acting like themselves having a religious ceremony on the shore.

After a quick investigation by one of his deputies, it turned out that the group in question was the local rotary club getting some practice for a forthcoming new members' induction ceremony.

When the sheriff explained that the Pidgrims were squatting on a local real estate agent's prime seashore-view condo property, the problem arose. The real estate mogul wanted them off, and soon. The Pidgrims had no local money—they tried to pass some funny coins the size of small oranges, but no one would accept them—and their boats were incapable of further adventuring.

Legal Affairs wanted the problem solved.

The local God™ franchisee said the commotion would hurt his revenues from members, who were too busy watching the squatters to turn in their weekly tithes. He said the Pidgrims were casually using god this and god that without any acknowledgement of his area trademark rights.

L.A. was rightly concerned to protect all GOD® legal franchisees, even when their annual franchise fee contributions were pitiful compared to the big franchises.

Sammie sat back and thought. By this time Erim! must have saddle sores from sitting on the can was his first thought, and he grinned.

Then he forced his agile brain cells to focus. Until this problem was resolved to the satisfaction of L.A., he would be running a one-man department. Although he was largely useless, Erim! was handy to have around because he insisted on a quality brand of coffee for the office percolator.

Sammie had been to the dog races the day before, and as usual had bet only on dogs he saw have a huge dump before the race. A pro had once told him that was a good sign: the dog had less weight to carry and would run faster.

Someone had neglected to tell the dogs this, however, for every bet of Sammie's on a just-dumped dog did that also for his bet: dumped it.

But the dogs still stayed in his head. Why? What possible connection to this problem could they have?

And then the lightning flashed. Dogs. Greyhounds! He just had to use Erim's! favorite mark to honor his inspiration.

Twenty-three minutes later Erim! himself reappeared. Sammie thought if he was racing, he'd bet on him, he looked like he'd had a dump. Or maybe it was just the bathroom pallor.

"Well, any bright ideas, or do I have to solve things as usual?"

As usual? The last time Erim! had solved a problem was never.

"I do have an idea. Greyhounds."

Erim! looked at him, frowned, looked away, and looked back. "What do greyhounds have to do with the Legal Affairs problem?"

Even he couldn't work a ! into that last remark, Sammie realized.

"It's fairly simple, Erim. The squatters, or Pidgrims, or whatever they are, are bothering one of our franchisees. But the Pidgrims have no funds so unless that friendly sheriff throws the whole lot into the calaboose the problem remains."

Erim! frowned again. "And?"

Another victory for non-! sentences.

"Well, a greyhound can resolve both ends of this problem.

"Here's what we do, Erim. Right now, down in sunny Lauderdale the Spring Break festivities are in high gear. From a distance they could easily resemble some kind of religious celebration.

"So we swing for cheapo bus tickets on the Greyhound redeye special—I know they have dirt cheap group tickets on busses leaving after midnight—and tell the Pidgrims we're giving them a super gift, free transportation to a wonderful religious event down south.

"That immediately solves our franchisee's problem, makes the real estate guy happy, and unloads these yahoos on a bunch of other yahoos. They'll all fit in, at least at the start, and by the time they start killing each other our problem will have been resolved. I checked, and our nearest franchisee to Lauderdale is half a league away, so there should be no problem with it."

Sammie stood up, made a hand washing motion. "Everything taken care of, Erim!"

And this time the ! was definitely justified.

Chapter 20

"Because there is a law such as gravity, the universe can and will create itself from nothing. Spontaneous creation is the reason there is something rather than nothing, why the universe exists, why we exist. It is not necessary to invoke god to light the blue touch paper and set the universe going."

Stephen Hawking, 1942-2018, physicist.

###

"Do you mind if I tape this interview? It makes my notes more accurate, Mr. Cobb."

"No, in fact I'd prefer it. And please call me David."

"Thank you. And I'm Sheila." She leaned forward, just enough that her cleavage was peeping over the low top of her peasant blouse, and pressed the record button. It never hurt to make sure she had the interviewee's undivided attention.

"As you know, Mr...David, I'm here because Winner's Magazine wants to run a profile on you. You're on the right side of 40, you have started several successful businesses, and, incidentally," she gave him a big smile, "you are apparently filthy rich."

He smiled back. "I don't know that I'd describe my assets as filthy, but otherwise that's a fairly accurate thumbnail. Ask away."

"Okay. How many successful businesses have you started?"

"I've been involved in a number of start-ups over the years, but my own creations number just three. I started Mr. Wizzo Tinting, a vehicle and building window tinting company."

"That's the one that is now franchised just about everywhere?"

"Well, in a lot of places." He grinned.

"When it became common knowledge on how deadly the sun's rays actually were, the original business took off. I tried using company branch offices for awhile, but finding and training employees got totally time consuming, so I switched to a franchise system where local owner-operators could better handle these local problems."

"How many make up 'everywhere'?"

"Last count worldwide, 8,328. Pending, about 400. On these we're doing background checks and other stuff. By the end of the year I expect the total actually operating to be close to 9,000."

"In how many countries?"

"Over 135. Please don't ask me to name them all."

She smiled again. "I promise not to. I probably wouldn't be able to spell them all anyway."

She shifted a little in her chair, making sure the blouse top hadn't ridden up.

"Okay, business number two?"

"Once Wizzo got going, we, my family, had a home invasion," he said. "Three punks got in and terrorized my kids, ages 11 and 7, for almost an hour, before my wife got home, and realized from the dining room blinds being drawn that something inside was wrong.

"She very intelligently used her cell phone to call the police. Their special intruder-present squad responded, and acted in a completely professional manner. One of the thugs was shot, the other two surrendered immediately, and my kids were unharmed, aside from terrible dreams at night for several months.

"Right then I realized how unprepared our home was, so I started doing research. What I found was literally shocking."

He paused to drink some coffee, nodded at her cup to see if a refill was needed. She shook her head.

Cobb continued. "In spite of the increase almost everywhere in opportunity-crimes—those basically unplanned and simply resulting from what criminals see as a good opportunity—almost no one, according to police stats, was prepared for home troubles. So my second business was launched."

"That would be" she glanced down at her notebook, "Vida Life Alarms?"

"Right. And before you ask, the 'Vida' means life in Spanish, and is often even used in English, so I thought it appropriate in the hemisphere where over 98 percent of the people speak one of those two languages."

"Okay. And it basically took off too?"

"Well, like all 'overnight' success stories it actually took quite a bit longer than that. I could bore you with all the glitches that developed before we got a universally-capable alarm system."

"If I have it correct, Vida gives customers a small control box, about the size of a video movie package?"

He nodded.

She said, "And all the customer has to do is press the button and she's connected with a local office. The bilingual—English and Spanish of course—operator then speaks to her, asks what the problem is, and takes action accordingly, notifying the cops, firemen, or ambulance."

"Yes", David said. "But there are also extras Vida provides. If the customer can't talk—maybe she's fallen, for example--the operator then proceeds as above, and also contacts people the customer has previously specified, a neighbor, doctor, friend, or whomever.

"And since the early days all Vida operations now have a full line of accessories like motion detectors against intruders, automatic sensors that contact Vida if the customer falls, and other company-exclusive products that provide complete protection for any customer need."

"So whatever happens, whether it's someone trying to force a back door open, or an accident, Vida really can mean life?"

"Well put, Sheila. Are you interested in a Vida copywriting job?" He smiled again.

Not a bad idea, she thought. Probably pay a helluva lot better than the money she made freelancing profiles for magazines. She filed it in her 'consider later' file.

"Not right now, but later maybe. Okay, so eventually Vida is off and running. What happened next?"

"Much the same as with Wizzo. I soon found that I couldn't physically find, then train, managers for local Vida branches, so I turned to franchising again, it had worked so effectively to expand Wizzo."

"And the numbers, please." She held out her hand in imitation of always-smiling TV game show hosts.

"Here they are, Sheila." He pretended to pass her an envelope, which she realistically ripped open.

"Today we have 744 Vida franchisees in 65 countries. Pending, about 80." He leaned back in his leather chair.

"I'm really happy with Vida's growth, because from personal letters and feedback from Vida offices I know that our products and services have literally saved lives. Just yesterday I got a handwritten note from an 89-year old lady who said her automatic fall detector had gotten medical help to her in time to save her life. That's great stuff to read."

She saw that he was serious. "Of course it is."

She took a breath, big enough to put her nipples in clear view, small enough to keep her blouse from falling off completely. Time to move away from the hearts and flowers. "And business three?"

"That one is still in the formative stage, Sheila. During our most recent banking crisis, when the same people who had caused it were in political positions where they were going to 'solve the problem', I realized that many possible entrepreneurs—men and women who actually create something, who build companies that employ other people, unlike the politicians who are solely parasites and feed off others' successes—were being shut out before they even got started because they couldn't find start-up money.

"Banks, Wall Street financiers, all these crooks had easy and repeated access to taxpayer money, but the small guys were excluded. I thought it might be a good idea, and a good business, to act as a go-between, taking in funds from people who wanted higher than rip-off rates from their 'friendly' local bank, and offering loans at favorable rates to deserving entrepreneurs. I started small, just a few internet pages, and a little publicity. I found the need was great. More than I had even optimistically forecast."

"So Entre-Middle", she glanced at her notebook to make sure she had the right name, "was open for business. That's a great name, David. Did you come up with it?"

"No, credit for that goes to my son. He's only 14 but he's really interested in words and names, and when I told him I was looking for a name he said he'd work on it. A week later he gave it to me, I paid his very reasonable creation fee, and liked it and started using it immediately."

"At the moment this one is still wholly owned by you, right?"

"Well, by a company set up for that purpose. But it is still owner of the whole shebang. This time, though, I'm thinking of something a little different. While it might fit into a franchise mold, I am thinking of getting it listed on some exchange and offering stock to lenders and borrowers who use it. That way they'd have a direct interest in a company which was also serving their financial needs."

"When you have an IPO please make sure I get a notice." She smiled. "And I will make clear to Winner readers that IPO stands for initial public offering, although I imagine most already know that."

She finished her coffee, then shook her head when he raised eyebrows to silently ask if she wanted a refill.

She picked up her notebook, and had to bend over fully to do so, accidentally again exposing a little more of those creamy goodies barely held by her blouse.

"The editor gave me a list of topics he wanted covered. Let's see, after business successes he wanted some info on religion. Okay with you, David?"

"Sure, although I don't have a religion. In fact, I'm anti-religion. I think all the religions have done more to screw people than all the dictators put together. They have brainwashed kids long before they're old enough to know what's going on, they've kept entire countries in economic poverty by their demands for outrageous tithes, by using people's money for grandiose buildings and monuments used only by the big shots of that religion, by their insistence on keeping the people ignorant and uneducated, by..." He broke off and laughed.

"You haven't even asked a specific question, and I've answered with a monologue. Sorry about that, Sheila, it's just that religion is one of my hotspots."

"I can see that. No problem, David. Let's start with your childhood."

"My parents were both Jewish. Not especially devout, but synagogue-going on a more or less regular basis. I was too, until I got into my mid-teens, and started reading a lot, especially on our world, our universe, even our universes.

"Almost immediately for me religion became just another con, a giant confidence trick perpetrated over the centuries by a whole rogue's gallery of tricksters, everything from a group of fraudsters who ended up with the richest business in the world, to former freelance writers—like yourself," he grinned— "who got tired of working for nickels and decided to start a church.

"Whatever the denomination, whatever the 'god', the desire was to trick gullible people into believing, believing that the trickster had the answers to puzzles which have already been solved by science, but which too many people refuse to understand.

"It's obvious that a large percentage of the world's population needs a crutch to lean on. That's not bad in itself, but when the crutch is fabricated by a crook, the end results are bad: ignorance, poverty, unfilled dreams." He cleared his throat and grinned at Sheila. "Almost like a sermon, isn't it?"

She smiled in return. "Did your childhood religion, or your later non-religion, cause problems?"

"Until I was eight or so I never even thought about religion. In the city we then lived there was a large minority population: different languages, customs, religions, including some Jews, so I never felt ostracized. In public school religion was tolerated but not emphasized. As I grew into my early teens, I became aware of prejudices—we all do, no matter who we are—and I got a fairly normal amount of anti-Jewish insults.

"They didn't especially bother me, because I've always been a little on the introvert side and didn't get involved in a lot of high school social activities.

"As my reading expanded, and I came to view religion as the con I mentioned briefly before" -- he smiled at Sheila—"any anti Semitic insults just rolled off me, I didn't view myself as any kind of religious person, Jewish or otherwise.

"Of course, I didn't wear a 'I'm not a religious Jew' sign, so the insults continued, and even increased after my first business became successful. I am a Jew by birth, but that's all. Like Einstein once wrote, the Jews to him were no better or worse than anyone else, they were just people.

"That's my view, so the insults continued to hurt a little, simply because they were aimed at me as a person. But I got to the point where I realized they had all the significance of a puff of smoke."

He paused, looked at Sheila, and then smiled again.

"Would it be accurate to say that your childhood, your teenage years, were blighted by the insults aimed at your religion, or even later your no-religion?"

"Absolutely not, Sheila. Every kid gets insults. You're skinny. You're fat. Your old man's a drunk. Your mom's not pretty. And on and on. They all hurt, but as we get older, and hopefully a little more understanding, we realize that, like the rhyme many of us learned, 'sticks and stones can break my bones, but words will only amuse me.'

"I don't view growing up as a Jew any more debilitating than growing up as a dirt-poor kid, or a kid from a broken home, or a kid who has no friends. That's life. It hurts all of us sometimes. But we get beyond that. So please do not even imply that my youth was blighted by my parents' religion. It wasn't." He frowned slightly to show that he was perfectly serious.

"You have my word, David. No moaning about a tough life."

She glanced around the room, noting the real leather chairs and sofa, the apparently real paintings by people even she recognized, the thick Persian carpets, the bookcases crammed with real books, books which looked like they had had a lot of use, not the shelves of books used by lawyers and sometimes doctors to impress.

"Regardless of your younger years, it does appear that more recent times have been rewarding," she said. "Before I came to this interview, I checked your credit rating online, David. I got severe eyestrain from all those zeros before the decimal, not after like mine. I did a fast count. Looked like eight or nine of the little nothings before the decimal. And then a four or five in front of them."

"Numbers are just that, Sheila. A way of keeping score. They don't mean much by themselves."

He got to his feet. "And now, how about some lunch. There's a company dining room on the top floor, and I thought you might enjoy it up there on the rotating roof, you get a new slant on the city in just 30 minutes or so."

"That sounds great, David. I'm starved. Let's go." In her haste to arise her peasant blouse slipped a little, and one brownish nipple was on view for a second. She smiled. And he did too.

Chapter 21

"Luther was guilty of two great crimes: he struck the pope in his crown, and the monks and priests in their bellies."

G. D. Erasmus (1465-1536).

###

"We've had some great presidents, Norm."

"More like interesting presidents, Sol. Take Kennedy, of example. No one can accuse him of being great, but he sure was interesting." He finished his bourbon and signaled to bartender Steve for a refill.

"Look at his old man. Just 15 years after WW2 ended, and with still a fair amount of hostility to Hitler and his thousand-year Reich, this rich kid gets elected—or his father buys the job, probably more accurate—by a man who was one of Adolph's biggest fans."

"In fact," Norm continued, "as the US ambassador to Britain, Kennedy Senior kept counseling against even getting into the war, long after Hitler's atrocities became common knowledge."

"The very fact, Sol, that he got to be an ambassador. He had made the family fortune running booze from Canada during prohibition. And he was a firm Crapolic, as was JFK. At least in spirit," he grinned to show he'd made a pun, "but certainly not in body. How many presidents give out private keys to the White House to Hollywood sex queens?"

Sol nodded to show he was actually listening. His pal Norm tended to run off at the mouth.

"And talk about interesting. Look at Clinton. Didn't have too much on the ball, but he sure had balls"—another smile to indicate another pun— "and could sweet talk young gullible interns into giving him blow jobs under the Oval Office desk. Not what you'd call great, Sol, but truly interesting."

"True, Norm, but our assignment today is to do a quick and dirty review of what some of our most profitable franchisees are doing to stimulate business, and see if their ideas can be modified for franchisees that are doing crappy business."

Norm sighed. Sol was okay but a little too conscientious at times. Like now.

"So who do we look at first?"

Sol opened his full-sized notebook, reached into some interior pocket and pulled out a pen, then cleared his throat.

"The Crapolics are doing some good stuff. One plan they're pushing right now is a bonus program for their field sales managers. They award points for each step achieved. The points can be redeemed for prizes at their head office retail store, where they flog overpriced candles to their members.

"Some of the prizes are the usual trashy junk made especially for them in slave labor camps in China and North Vietnam, but a few are actually pretty good deals. Like a simulated leather case to hold their authorized books. It looks like real leather..."

"Okay, Sol. I get the idea. What's the prize setup?"

"It's pretty simple, Norm. The field sales managers can keep all the points, or let their sales people share them. In any case, they award 10 points for each kid fully Crapolic-brainwashed by age 6. They give 15 points for those BWed" --he noticed Norm's look of puzzlement— "brainwashed, Norm, and 25 points for those done by age 4. And for those who have been completely BWed by age 3 or even under, they give 50 points."

"Does the plan work?"

Sol hesitated.

"Well, to be perfectly honest, maybe not as well as it should. The problem is that so many of the field sales people, especially the prestos who have first crack at the kids, have already got most of their customers' kids BWed even earlier. But it does seem to be stimulating revenues a little in areas where the prestos have been occupied with, ah, more physical matters."

"You mean abusing the kids?"

"I guess you could call it that. But that term never shows up in official Crapolic sales materials so it's difficult to quantify it."

Norm snorted. "Of course the term doesn't show up, buddy. In many areas where the Crapolic bosses haven't got the local law enforcement fixed it's still a criminal offense.

"In places like New York City, where the badges and guns get passed down from Irish Crapolic pop to son for generations, there's no problem. Those 'officers' either ignore reported cases or manage to 'shoot while resisting arrest' those who won't shut up."

Sol shifted uneasily in his chair. "That kind of stuff is not for us, Norm. We're not in the History or Crimes sections, so let's stick to sales promo ideas we can perhaps share with other franchisees."

Norm and Sol had had these arguments many times before. The result was always the same. Sol was able to convince his friend that no good, and certainly no year-end bonuses, would follow if they strayed from their appointed duties. Several acquaintances in the Crimes section had even lodged internal complaints against their sometimes too-descriptive reports.

Norm sighed. "What's next?"

Sol smiled. They were back on safe ground.

"In most of our eastern franchisees they are showing great gross revenues and dandy nets because they have been able to keep their costs really low. By utilizing tied-in sweatshops to build their religious toys they've been able to keep product costs below 10 percent of retail. That's a wonderful record, and maybe we could get some of our western franchisees to emulate their successes."

Norm looked dubious. "How could we do that?"

"For example, if we could get a couple of the more established areas, especially where they have had a history of 'organizing' labor, to adopt more of a sweatshop attitude. You know, like the Eyeties. Our profitable franchisee Benito was able to tie in with the Crapolics and create a joint profit-sharing deal that boosted revenues for both."

"And don't forget Adolph. He really proved, especially in the heavily Crapolic areas, that a joint profit arrangement with them paid big dividends, and with their active support also helped to chloroform the rest of the people so they stood by when he moved all those people into the camps."

"Yes, those time slots were wonderful for our western franchisee revenues. It's just too bad that we were never able to sign up Joe. He was always too much of a loner. He told our reps several times that he liked our franchise idea but he was convinced he could do better on his own."

Norm frowned. "Yeah, and unfortunately the little prick was right. Then after he croaked, for awhile it looked like we'd succeed better with one or more of his successors, but then the country was taken over by hard core criminals who weren't interested in paying us any franchise fees."

Sol shifted around on his chair. "But we do have a pretty good chance in Chinee. Looks like the newer guys can see the merits of a God™ franchise.

"And as our reps have pointed out to them, it's not just the revenue, but it gives them a chance to BW all their people just like the Crapolics have done. And with all those people to control that's an important consideration."

"Sometimes it takes a while for these so-called leaders to really see the franchise light," Norm added.

"Remember how our sales reps had such a tough job with Mahatma, Sol? He had built his image on poverty and all its associated ills. But eventually he came to realize that poverty was bad for business. With everyone broke there was no revenue for his organization, no money for anything.

"So, he slowly came around to realizing that it was better to have followers with some assets and incomes, so that he could carve off a healthy slice. Not in public like the Crapolics, of course, but the backdoor approach where he signed up some rich guys who wanted his brand of salvation, and were content to be silent sponsors."

Sol squirmed with excitement.

"Yes, that's right. If I remember the facts correctly it took our reps a long time to sign him up, but once he did, he was a good franchisee, and our revenues from that big area doubled, maybe even tripled, year over year for about 9 years."

"Sometimes we can even slide into a good franchise. Our 'Winning Case Histories' series had a good story from Aleman. Long before Adolph, of course, but similar in a way.

Norm nodded. "Did you ever read about that guy Luther? He had been operating as a sub-franchisee for the local Crapolics but he got pissed off because his territory included the Black Forest, and as he found not many customers lived there.

"He lodged a complaint with the Crapolics but they just threw it out, said he was a trouble maker and was lucky to have any franchise area at all.

"That really pissed him off. He sat down and wrote a proposal, based very loosely on the then current Crapolic dogma—that was their version 78 or 79, I think—but modified in several key areas to make it different enough to qualify as a unique franchisee request."

Sol nodded quickly. "Yes, and our Head Office okayed it and awarded him a brand new franchisee, even though it was physical territory that the Crapolics had milked for a long time."

He laughed. "The Crapolics bitched and complained to us, but Luther's proposal was unique enough that Head Office stood by their decision, and he was off and running.

"We learned that time that having two conflicting franchises in the same geographical area is not necessarily a bad thing.

"In fact, our revenues from both franchises increased steadily, because each one was determined to undermine the other. They both began trying to BW customers' kids the moment they were brought home from the hospital.

"Sometimes," he laughed again, "sales agents from the two different franchises would be outside one house at the same time. What a wonderful time for our revenues!"

"Our legal guys had to step in finally," Norm said. "It was getting bad for overall franchisee revenues, and not good for our public image.

"So they got both franchise operators to agree to a new recruiting rule: the first franchisee to immerse a new child into a pan of water and have the parents swear a sort of loyalty oath, had the exclusive rights to that kid and any revenue he was responsible for, coming at the start certainly from his parents."

"Wonderful times for revenues." Sol gazed into some distant vista where competing franchisees could be signed up in otherwise exclusive territories. "How I would love to be involved in something like that."

"You never can tell, amigo. The way the Untied States are separating, I expect we'll have chances soon to have two, maybe even three, competing master franchisees in the same areas.

"Take that western section, Sol. Quite conceivable we could have franchises for Luther's group, for the Crapolics, although like the frog language worldwide they appear to be disappearing from that scene, a franchisee of that seventh or eighth day bunch, the multi-wives group, and quite possibly a group from one—or even more—of the eastern mobs which appear to be getting fairly popular now with all the attention on world-ending propaganda."

"Oh, Norm, how wonderful you make it sound. We would be kept busy just implementing new promo ideas, adapting them as necessary between the differing—and competitive! —groups."

He rubbed his hands together.

"We would probably need to expand our staff both here and in the field, and for pros like us, with solid experience behind us, we'd be in line for moves up to full management slots. More prestige, both internally where some of the more active types think we're just desk jockeys, and externally, where we'd have to be active in the field. Wonderful possibilities, Norm."

"Well, don't come in your pants just yet, Sol. Probably a while to get to that point, but I honestly can see it happening within a few years.

"And when I'm named overall department manager, old buddy, I'll make sure to find a spot for you."

"You have no reason to think you'd be made the manager, Norman. I am just as qualified, and have just as much experience, as you do."

Sol sniffed. "But I know you're just joking. You are, aren't you? Norm, aren't you?"

In the New Business Department, Andrew was finishing dictating a memo to his secretary Lorraine. She was just 18, and on her first job, and had been easily convinced by her boss that it was best for him to give and for her to take dictation when she was balanced cheekily on his right knee.

"That way you will hear every word I say correctly and you won't have to redo work because you didn't hear me clearly."

Lorraine, although trained as a secretary, had the classic figure of a sweater model. As she shifted on his knee to maintain her balance, Andy got a full and continuing look at her firm breasts, and even occasionally when he shifted weights from one leg to the other, one or both of the beauties would rub against his chest. And all this because he was such a caring boss.

"Finish the memo like this: Remember that back in the '60s, Kokie wanted a merger with us, Russell. Their ad people thought it would be great if they could use this slogan worldwide, without having to modify it for local consumption: 'No matter what god you believe in, worship with a Kokie in every pew!' Wasn't that a dandy?"

He shifted his legs again, and was rewarded with a firm thrust of Lorraine's right boob.

He looked over at his second in command. "Have you read about that, Oliver?"

Oliver slid the racing form back into his top drawer. He was sure he had the longshot who would definitely finish first in the fifth.

"Read about what, boss?"

Andrew shook his head disgustedly—and also managed to get both boobs in lovely motion—and looked at his secretary's face for a change, seeking consolation for the third-rate employees he had under him.

"Try to forget your fucking races for a minute, Oly." He knew his assistant hated the nickname.

"You'll never beat them anyway. They're all fixed, everybody knows that. You'd do better just throwing a dart at a list of numbers. Well, if not better, no worse than what you do now. And that's terrible.

He frowned to show this was a serious matter.

"I asked you if you had read in the company history about Kokie way back in the '60s sometime, when they wanted to hook up with us to promote a Kokie in every pew, no matter what god a person believed in."

Oliver quickly tried to banish the vision of that longshot crossing the line first, and himself shouting for glee and holding aloft his ticket worth... "Uh, no, boss."

Andrew shrugged, just enough to force Lorraine to quickly move her left leg to maintain her balance—oh what sweet dreams that caress conjured up—and reached backwards to get a pencil—another balancing move needed! —then threw it at Oliver.

"Ouch! What'd you do that for?"

"Just to make sure you weren't dead. Anyway, I want you to read that stuff up and write me a short, say two pages, report on the Kokie ad promotion. That way you'll be improving your knowledge of important company advertising history."

"And wasting a lot of my valuable time," Oliver muttered. "Sure, boss." Right after I get my longshot bet down.

"Okay, now let's get this show on the road." Andrew loved show biz talk. Reluctantly he slid Lorraine off his lap— she probably wouldn't notice the fairly impressive boner she had left behind, and if she did it would just be one more step ahead in the Lorraine Seduction Drama he had mentally constructed.

He was sure she was a virgin, and thus he had to move carefully, but smoothly, to ensure her first trip to sexual heaven was ecstatic.

Unfortunately, Lorraine was one of those girls who had matured early. She had been screwing since 14, and viewed her boss's seduction attempts at somewhere lower than rank amateur. But a soft and good paying job was worth a little play acting.

"Head Office wants us to develop an ongoing special deal geared to the miracles which so many franchises use in their internal promotions."

Andrew grabbed a huge marker pen he loved to use—obviously making up for a small dick, Lorraine felt— and flipped to a new page on the stand-up easel board near his desk.

"These miracles apparently are a significant source of revenue to several of our biggest franchises.

"The Crapolics, for instance, try to have a new miracle discovered at least every ten or so years.

"They've found the best recipe for one is to choose two or three totally illiterate kids in some backwoods spot, and thru fairly innocuous but thorough coaching laid on by the local prest beforehand, get these morons to agree on some 'miracle' they witnessed, preferably one that is vague to start with—a vision of an angel, or a cactus plant talking to them—and obviously one that cannot be repeated. Or verified, that's very important.

He started marking on the easel. The figures didn't have much resemblance to any known alphabet.

"Sometimes a more advanced local franchisee employee will supplement his oral conditioning of the chosen kids with a little of the local 'magic powder" to make everything even more cloudy and thus more believable to people who already have suspended all their critical faculties to believe in our franchisee's spiel."

Andrew made a couple of large slashes with his marker pen on the now sullied sheet.

"So our job is to develop a franchisee deal which, with minor modifications to permit peddling it to a variety of 'god' franchisees, will yield a nice ongoing revenue stream for our company."

Both Lorraine and Oliver looked at the easel slashes. Lorraine thought it was Andrew's Freudian wish for a large handy vagina. Oly felt it represented the only thing of his longshot winner that the following horses would see.

"Is that clear?"

Both subordinates nodded enthusiastically.

"Right." He smiled contentedly. Being an effective and inspirational leader wasn't all that difficult.

"So let's get our plan started." He peeled off the top sheet, and scrawled a giant 1 on the next sheet.

"Oliver, you get the honor of being first. What's the leadoff point in our miracle promo?"

After several years under Andrew's tutelage Oliver knew his role perfectly.

"Point one, boss: We need a promo plan which can be ongoing."

"Perfect, Oly." He jotted down some graphics which someday would stump a team of expert archeologists.

"Lorraine, my dear," --he felt the avuncular approach would help to get her natural female guard down— "would you like to give us point two?"

Like Oliver, Lorraine was already an experienced hand in keeping Andrew happy.

"Sure, chief. Second on the list should be that our plan has to be easy to package and sell to our franchisees."

Andrew resisted the urge to massage his growing penis. His people were doing splendidly.

"Right on, my dear." That would help to reinforce his image as one who kept up on relatively-recent jive talk. "And now we have two important parts of our plan. I will add number three, now that we are getting into dangerous territory." And territory that you two flunkies might have problems navigating, he thought.

"For three, I think" he paused to stroke his weak chin, having read this indicated that he was actually thinking, "that we need something specific, something eye-catching. How about a complete miracle-promo package that has everything any franchisee needs to implement it almost immediately?"

Both assistants seized the bait.

"Great point", Lorraine quickly said, again thinking of the Freudian connection.

"Exactly what was needed." Oliver really needed that longshot to win the race. His bookie was starting to make leg-breaking motions every time he saw him.

"Wonderful, we all agree."

He carefully placed the marker pen in a vertical position on his desk, next to the pen and pencil set he had won a few years ago in a company 'best money saving idea of the month' contest.

Lorraine and Oliver both relaxed. They knew that at least for today the pressure was off.

"I think we have made an important start on this miracle promo plan," Andrew said. "And I am a firm believer in letting our subconscious help in our creative efforts."

Lorraine grinned to herself. Good luck, she thought; you really need it.

"So I propose we put this plan on standby for a day or so, while our brains work on it. For next time, I want to move on to at least point six, and points four thru six should deal with specifics of the plan. In general, of course. Once completed each franchisee plan will be modified to fit its unique 'god' and 'miracles' parameters.

"For now, I want us to give a little time to a somewhat minor problem that the New Business V-P laid on me" --he threw a quick look at Lorraine, maybe she'd get his seduction plan by osmosis— "when we were having coffee together the other morning."

It never hurt to remind his troops that he did fraternize with upper management, even if it only actually happened rarely.

"The V-P (he felt titles were more impressive than names) mentioned that some franchisees seemed less adept at increasing income from supplemental sources. That in turn means that our company gross royalty revenues take a hit, even though it's minor overall."

"As an example," Andrew continued, "he said that the Crapolics had this down to a science. Everything in their buildings was a money earner.

"Right inside the entrance door, he said, there were candles. Each customer was expected to light a candle— you'd think the buildings would be awfully smoky—and he had to in effect buy the candle by putting money into a special box. Then if the customer was remembering someone or something special another candle would be needed. Another purchase. Those Crapolics are wonders!

"And that was just one example, the V-P said there were lots more, but they illustrated his point. While the Crapolic franchisee was able to squeeze sometimes literally the last coin from their customers—as we know, the Crapolics make most of their money from customers who are the poorest in the world, and yet they pay for those incredible edifices for the Crapolic prests, many of whom are pedophiles—but I'm getting off the track."

Are you ever, both listeners shouted silently.

"On the other hand, some franchisees are terrible at boosting their, and our company's, supplementary incomes. As a for example, the V-P mentioned the Buptists. They apparently not only are against everything, but they can't get customers to buy fuck all."

He looked quickly at Lorraine to see if the crudity had stimulated her. She yawned. Oh well, maybe she's just covering up her insatiable appetite.

"So he wondered if we here in this New Business section couldn't come up with some scheme that the poor sales franchisees could incorporate to boost revenues."

He looked at Lorraine, then Oliver, then Lorraine again. She did have tremendous boobs.

"Any ideas?"

"It's a little off the point, boss," Lorraine knew Andrew liked the title, "but I have been doing some thinking, and there's something that really has me puzzled."

Andrew smiled like a hungry lion to a baby zebra.

"If you have a question that's bothering you, my dear, it's never off the subject. I'm here to help you in any way I can." And I can certainly think of at least three ways to do that." So open up, he laughed to himself, and I'll answer your problem.

"Thanks, boss. I know that our company succeeds by selling franchises to other companies and organizations, and they in turn peddle our crap, er, valuable materials, to their customers. Am I right so far?"

"Perfectly, my dear." He was getting too avuncular, he'd better get back to some jive talk so she didn't write him off as a has-been. "And your specific problem, babe?"

Babe? Was he back in his slick talk mode? That was even worse than his friendly uncle approach. "Well, Andrew, my problem is that I can't understand where our franchisees find all their customers. Are there really that many ignorant people out there?"

"An excellent question, sweetie. And one I puzzled over also when I first joined GOD®. After thinking about it long and hard", and it really was getting there again, "I figured out the main reasons for our, and our franchisees', success."

He smiled at his subordinates to show that even he, head of this department, had once upon a time had problems. No more, of course.

"Here's what I finally concluded.

"First, most people are such failures in this life that they have to believe in some future life where all their dreams, wet and dry", that was a clever shot, he thought, "would be magically fulfilled. So, they are the first and best customers for our franchisees.

"The second reason is that a majority, a large majority, in fact, of the rest of the world's people are like sheep. Even more accurately, dear Lorraine, they are like lemmings.

"You know, those stupid creatures who follow a leader over a cliff in a gigantic suicide leap. These people don't even like to think, they just want to follow someone who appears to know what he's doing. Ask any politician; these kinds of people are his prime audience." He looked around as if searching for a politician to verify his conclusions.

"And the third reason, my faithful associates? Simply that the vast bulk of the remaining world population is brainwashed almost immediately after birth.

"Look at our most profitable franchisee, the Crapolics again: they get their brainwashing, including using cold water to scare the living shit out of tiny babies, into high gear as soon as the kid is brought home from the hospital.

"By the time that kid is four or five he—or she," he smiled at Lorraine to show he wasn't biased, "has been subjected to enough hours of indoctrination that it's a wonder he can even go to the bathroom without getting some prest's approval. Even people who would ordinarily be reasonably intelligent can't withstand the mental assaults these franchisees bring to bear.

"It's a proven technique, brainwashing, and it has been used in a variety of situations: war, spying, and, and other stuff." His knowledge of things in general was somewhat limited. "And believe me, I've seen some of what these successful franchisees do, and it's amazing. They can turn a normal person into a non–thinking robot.

"Great for their business. And even better for us." He always liked to end one of his explanatory expositions on an upbeat note.

"And always remember, folks, how the underlying framework of our most profitable franchises were started. All three of the biggies were originally started by illiterates. None of them could even write, and at least two couldn't read. They all had failed at previous jobs. Their only skills were the ability to stimulate a small cadre of followers who in turn were basically ignorant and stupid enough to take care of their leader.

"What's more, my loyal associates, is that for a long time after these leaders bit the dust and proved themselves totally mortal, nothing happened. Then, finally, some really clever people got hold of their earlier ideas, re-packaged them—in one case even completely writing a text which they fobbed off as being 'created' 400 years earlier—and began promoting them to the idiots I told you about earlier."

Oliver was feeling so good about his racing prospects that he was inclined to add his contribution to Andrew's monologue.

"So, chief, can we say that these early forerunners of our best customers today were just basically anticipating Ron Hubbard's 20th Century decision to make a fortune with his new religion—Scientology—rather than stick with piss-poor pennies a word as a pulp fiction writer?"

Andrew was shocked into silence. Neither of his subordinates had ever before contributed a salient bit to his orations. And worse, although he wasn't positive, he sort of felt that Oliver had successfully summed up the situation.

"Not a bad comparison, Oly. Glad you're doing some real work here, besides keeping your bookie busy."

Time to get this situation ended before idiot Oly actually started to add further relevant comments.

He looked at Lorraine. Then he actually looked up at her eyes. "Did I answer your question, pretty girl?"

She was going to puke if he kept up. Better close out this teacher-student farce before he started to froth at both ends.

"Perfectly, Andrew. Just perfect. And now I guess I should get thinking about finishing off your points four through six on that miracle plan for franchisees."

She dropped her pencil, bent over slowly from her waist to retrieve it, displaying her tight round ass—might as well leave him with something, no matter how small it might be—to remember her, added her memo book, and headed out to her desk.

Like a penniless orphan wistfully looking at a cake-filled display case, he watched her taut behind wiggle away. Some day, he promised himself.

Oliver promised himself that his longshot sure thing would pay in big double digits. It has to, he realized, he couldn't walk well on a broken leg. He too left the hallowed inner sanctum and flopped down at his own desk.

Two days later Andrew again summoned his creative crew.

"Okay, everyone"—both Lorraine and Oliver were present— "let's carry on with that miracle package for our franchisees. Anyone got some ideas to get things started?"

Lorraine was wearing a sweater today. He could actually sketch each breast, including the nipple. Should he just adjourn the meeting and fall on her? Probably not, he thought, although the idea had merit. To the bold went the booty, or something like that.

Oliver was reasonably optimistic. His sure thing longshot had somehow managed to end up seventh, in a field of seven, but his bookie had had a good day otherwise, and he had granted Oliver a three day stay of execution, or leg breaking more likely, and in three days he knew he could pick a couple of sure thing longshots.

The silence from Andrew's crew was deafening. Time for the boss to show command skills.

"To get our collective creative juices stimulated" he didn't even glance at Lorraine, he was proud of himself, "I did a little research in the company library, and found an interesting story about how miracles can be used to really goose business." Had she smiled when she thought about that goosing?

"So without further ado," what the hell did that mean? "here's a story how one of our most profitable franchises used a simple miracle to turn a dying area around.

"Back in the Great Depression time, times were tough for a lot of towns and cities everywhere. But a Crapolic prest, for some unknown reason, got interested in a small town in Belgium; maybe he had really scored there. Anyway, he started to look around for a good miracle prospect.

"There turned out to be a whole lot; few people got any real education other than the usual crap provided by the prests themselves. But finally he selected a young— read really impressionable—girl of 11 years."

He checked his crew to make sure they were still awake. He had had bad experiences in the past when he had spoken for more than a couple of minutes. Once Oliver had actually fallen asleep and off his chair, and Lorraine had been totally preoccupied filing her oh-so-long nails. But today both seemed awake and reasonably attentive.

"The girl's name was Mariette Beco. She was one of seven kids in a poor family. After a little helpful coaching, Mariette discovered that someone identified by the friendly prest as 'virgin Mary' had appeared to her eight, count them, eight! times.

"Of course she had always been alone and in secluded locations, but that's pretty well par for the miracles course.

"Regardless, her whole town of Banneaux profited from her miracle. Or more accurately, I guess, her eight miracles. Today, according to official Crapolic figures, over a million loyal customers daily offer up little memorized speeches to the 'virgin of the poor'."

"Is there a separate virgin for the rich?" Lorraine asked. She was always interested in making sure the group she aspired to was well represented.

Andrew smiled. At least she was paying attention. Oliver seemed very busy with marking notes on what looked like a sheet of newspaper.

"I don't know about that. Nothing was mentioned in the library. But I do know that the town of Banneaux certainly profited from those miracles.

"It has become sort of a second Lourdes, one of the Crapolics really successful promotions, and there are a lot of Crapolic buildings, churches, places where men sit around doing not very much, and other stuff as well.

"It's amazing what a few, well, eight, miracle sightings can do," contributed Oliver. He had finished his handicapping, and he almost certainly had at least two longshot winners spotted later at Santa Anita. Things were looking good.

"Very true, Oly. Now let's move on to some other forms of miracles, which we might be able to modify and then package for our less profitable franchises.

"Here's another dandy I uncovered in the company library: transubstantiation. Does anyone have any idea of what it is, or does?"

Lorraine smiled.

Andrew knew it meant she knew. How the hell did that dumb broad come up with these exotic answers? It was more than enough that in that sweater she looked better than any nightclub pole climber.

She said, "That tongue twister refers to the Crapolic teaching that the bread and wine of their communion service become, in substance, but not appearance, the body and blood of their hero Jesus." She smiled again.

"Sounds like one helluva way to cut costs," Oliver said. "No need to dig up body parts, just run in a cheap supply of water and dago red."

"Okay. That's correct, Lorraine, and good work. Now how can we modify and package that simple brainwashing concept for other franchises?"

"Maybe it has possibilities for ones like the Buptists, the ones who don't really like anything at all," Lorraine said. "You know, we could offer it as a cool way to get new customers: Come in for some neat singing and get a free buzz-on at the same time."

Andrew stroked his non-existent chin.

"Maybe. Let's put it in our 'Possibles' file. Now, moving on, what about other miracle-type promos, and let's even include a couple which have misfired, just so we know both the ups and the downs of miracles."

He would sure like to put some ups and downs into play with Lorraine but she was busy writing something in her notebook.

She finally looked up. "On the down side, remember that guy named Jim Jones, back in the 20th?"

Both Andrew and Oliver shook their heads. "Not exactly a distinctive name", said Oliver.

"No, I guess not, but anyway, he was a sort of successful prest-type promoter who assembled a small but dedicated group of believers."

"One of very many," Andrew said. "A great number of people are attracted to the prest career. It appears ideal: no real work, no qualifications needed, sometimes lots of available broads for the picking" he slanted his eyes at

Lorraine in what he felt was a sensually meaningful fashion "and always lots of customers just waiting to be gathered in."

Lorraine ignored the interruption.

"After huddling around together, mostly in the western part of the Untied States, Jones decided that he needed a new stage for his activities. He announced that he and all his flock would decamp the wicked U.S. and head for the cleaner, greener, and less regulated, shores of some southern countries."

"I've always wanted to taste the delights of warm southern beaches." Andrew imagined Lorraine, clad in the briefest of bikinis, walking with him on a sandy shore. But she punctured that balloon as she kept talking.

"Now the story splits into two versions," Lorraine said.

"The first, and probably the most popular, is that Jones and his bunch of loonies made landfall down south. He had privately decided that his prest run on this world had approached its zenith, and to expand even further he needed the opportunities of space. Or eternity. Or both. The hard record is pretty clouded here.

"But what is known that after summoning all to a giant clambake, he served them all a healthy shot of what turned out to be poison. Adios, this world, Hello eternity. And that was the final chapter in Senor Jones' conquest of this world."

"Did he manage to duplicate his recruiting success in the next?" Oliver seemed genuinely interested.

"What was the other version, Lorraine?" Andrew loved to hear her talk about otherworld experiences; he just knew she'd be fantastic in his thisworld experiences.

"It's slightly more complicated, and certainly less accepted", she said.

"The theory is that Jones had a sub-franchise from one of the bigger religious operations. Not one of ours," she added hurriedly. "Jones refused to pay higher fees as his flock increased, and he split the U.S. in an attempt to eliminate the fees completely. But the bigger group had other ideas. Like the mafia, they didn't believe in letting former members just say I quit and walk away.

"So, at that big barbecue Jones had organized on those sandy shores, what he thought was a mild aphrodisiac, something to stimulate his female followers even more, turned out to be a one-time-use-only treatment which effectively proved to other backsliders that quitting the group was not a good idea."

"Wow. That's quite an ending, Lo. Do you think it is accurate?"

"No one knows, Oly. All those who might have answers are either dearly departed or have lips so tightly sealed you'd need a federal injunction to even get them to smirk."

Andrew had to regain control of this group, his group.

"A good example of a bad ending, Lo." He might get some mileage from using Oly's nickname for her. "But let's move on to other miracles, or at least good examples of smart promotion ideas."

"I did some serious research myself in preparation for this meeting," Andrew said, implying that neither of the others had. "A success story? How about Luz del Mundo, or Light of the World for those of us who aren't fluent in espanol? Any info?"

The silence was deafening. Andrew nodded as if to confirm his worst suspicions.

"Okay, I'll give that info.

"It was started in Mexico—just imagine taking on the Crapolics in their very best customer country—in 1926. It now has almost two million paying members. To collect the customers' fees it has close to 4,000 temples worldwide, with about one-quarter in the founding country."

"Ranks right up there with our old friend Scientology, doesn't it?" Oliver said.

"Yes, but like most—all? —such groups not all was sunshine and roses. In the late 1990s a son of the founder was charged by both young girls and boys for 'molesting them' at official retreats in the early '80s."

"So what happened?"

"I didn't pursue the research, Oly. I wanted more examples. But why don't you do that, and report back to us on what happened."

Oliver knew he should have kept his mouth shut. Next time he would.

"Moving on, group, there are a number of fairly recent success stories. Nearly all of them had very limited lives, although one or two have managed to hang on even to the present.

"An example of that is Christian Science, started by a broad named Mary Baker Eddy. Anyone with three first names is automatically suspect," Andrew grinned to show his human side to his subordinates.

"Any connection with the Scientology bunch?" Lorraine asked.

"Not that I'm aware of. But with the incredible increases in our real knowledge of this, and probably other, universes, it is becoming popular to invoke the word 'science' in some form, to make the religious crap more believable, I guess."

Andrew checked his list.

"One who was far more fleeting was a Father Divine. He preached mainly to the real downtrodden and for awhile had a growing group. But he came and went as did many others who didn't have the lasting promotion skills to keep their messages fresh and income-producing."

Lorraine stretched and he almost lost his place.

Regaining a measure of his composure, he continued.

"There were also a number of fringe groups, often in southern U.S. areas. Some aimed their efforts at 'upper class' members. Included here were the Episcos, the Presbys, the Methods, and of course the Buptists. They all carved out small marketing niches and aimed their promo pitches directly at that small population slice.

"They're still around but none of them will ever get beyond a small customer audience, even though each group is convinced it has the answers to every question.

"And most of them are even more puritanical than the original puritans, who were among the worst of all religious groups in their liking for offing the heads of all dissenters."

He looked closely at Oliver. Were his eyes actually shut? As if by osmosis the person in question cleared his throat, opened his eyes—if they had actually been shut—and smiled at his boss.

Well, he'd catch him next time.

"One thing all these groups had in common," Andrew said, "was their total desire for their own popey. They all realized that much of the continuing success of the opposition Crapolics was their popey, someone who really was tuned into direct contact with whoever their god was.

"But they also shared a common problem: they couldn't afford our very reasonable, but to some of them extremely high, franchise fees for their very own popey."

Lorraine was moving around. It was the subject of money. It fascinated her.

"Were our fees actually quite high? Or were they reasonable, as you said?"

He focused his attention on her eyes. He'd show her he was more than just a tit man. "Well, like most questions, Lorraine, it depends on your point of view.

"From the GOD® side, we had to get a fair return on our products.

"As has been discussed in almost every one of our general meetings over the last couple of millenniums (or was it millennia, he hated those weird Latin words), franchising out a popey is a tricky deal.

"On the one side, we know it will definitely increase the gross revenues—and our resulting fees—of any franchisee who can offer some form of popey to its customers. That one feature alone, combined of course with the automatic weekly washing of all 'sins' through their confession gimmick, has probably been responsible for the Crapolics keeping more than one billion customers.

"But there's a big downside to us. Like a hooker alone in a room of horny sailors, there's a very definite value to exclusivity."

Andrew noticed that Lorraine didn't even flinch over his hooker example. A good sign.

"If we started letting any franchisee, even the 'here today and in jail tomorrow' fast buck ones who are usually prepared to spend big money on quick return promos, start offering popeys, their value to us would decrease just as quickly as that lone hooker's would if half a dozen of her colleagues joined the party. Even the value of pussy to a needful sailor depends on the available supply."

This time Lorraine actually nodded! Fuck, was she getting turned on? But then she immediately picked up a pencil and started jotting figures on it. No, it was just her basic and absolute interest in money, not his colorful hooker analogies.

"So we have to carefully control the quantity of popeys we franchise, Lorraine. And as we all know, to date that has been just one. If the Crapolics hadn't been such smart marketers we undoubtedly would have offered more.

"But so far the closest has been a modified version to the Anglicoulders in Angleterra. And they've only got a relatively few million customers so they're no competition for the Rome rascals.

"Looking at it from our other franchisees' viewpoints, Lorraine", he was sure that Oliver had dozed off again, but he didn't care, it let him concentrate on luscious Lorraine's various goodies, including those two in her blouse that had definitely sprouted erect nips since he started talking dirty, "each one would love to be able to add a popey to their attractions. Most of them don't even think, or care, that a flood of popeys would rapidly diminish their promotion values. They just want fast action, fast returns, big bucks, and fuck the competition."

Andrew was now really getting into this dirty talking. But he watched Lorraine carefully to make sure she wasn't getting ready to throw something heavy at him. But no, she was still screwing around with her pad and pencil.

"In short, Lorraine, in spite of their messages of everlasting joy to be enjoyed somewhere above—I wonder, do Chinese franchisees refer to heaven below? —nearly all of them want their returns to be here and now."

That spiel had sounded good to him. Too bad he hadn't recorded it. He could have used it on any new subordinate—female of course—he hired to replace Oliver.

"So, to wrap things up"—a neat idea for her—"Lorraine, the popey question remains somewhat unanswered. It would mean immediate big returns for us, but probably rapidly dissipating returns, and short-term boosts for franchisees, against which they'd have to weigh our undoubtedly stiff fees."

Stiff fees. A snappy adjective to throw in.

"Have I explained the problem of popeys to your complete satisfaction, Lorraine?" And that's what I'd give you.

She looked up, surprised that he had stopped talking.

If he'd just keep going another five minutes, I'd have my monthly budget all figured out. Each month I go through this hassle. I really should make up a firm budget and stick to it.

Well, I guess I could get that new guy in my apartment building to do it for me, I heard he was an accountant somewhere, and I'm sure he has the hots for me.

Chapter 22

"If you wish the sympathy of the broad masses, you must tell the crudest and most stupid things."

Adolph Hitler in 'Mein Kampf'.

###

"Nathan, can you come in here for a few?"

Oscar Snellings was the chief honcho of Laurencomin Research Associates, Inc, and didn't really have to beg his field flunkies, but he felt it added a democratic aspect to what was actually his despotic managerial style.

Nathan was glad to oblige. Usually he encountered Snellings only when some aspect of a field research study had gone sideways.

"Sit down, my boy. Make yourself comfortable."

That was a good trick in itself. The furniture in his office—except for his own plush leather swivel chair—was designed specifically to move occupants out as quickly as possible, hopefully before the thick metal ridges on the backs tore into the skin. One of LRA's early clients had been a fast food chain, and from them Snellings had learned and remembered that short occupancy times meant higher returns. In his case, Snellings settled for keeping his employees on the move. He associated movement with results.

"Here's what we are faced with, Nathan. I've been working on this prospective client for quite a while."

Nathan knew that meant Snellings had phoned him three times over a period of a couple of weeks.

"I think we stand a good chance of bagging him. He's starting what he hopes will be a chain of dance schools for young girls, those in the 6 to 12 or so age brackets. But he doesn't want to wait years for his promotion programs to build up to the point where the chain will be profitable. Then I remembered that survey report you'd done on religion some time ago, and in it you referred to something about how some groups actually did brainwashing on kids of their customers. Remember?"

"Sure, boss, that was in my report on a branch of the Crapolics, way back early last year."

"Was it effective?"

"You wouldn't believe it, boss. They actually had a chart—for internal management use only, of course— showing how effective the BW—that's how they referred to brainwashing, they didn't like to use the actual term much—was, based on how old the kid was when the BW started."

Nathan paused for breath. He was actually surprised that Snellings had let him run on that long. The boss felt that anything more than one sentence from a flunky was time wasted. Obviously this was a potentially lucrative client.

"Do you want any more detail, boss?"

"Of course I do, idi...Nathan. What else do you remember?"

Nathan stroked his goatee. He'd been trying to grow it for almost three months, but now he felt he was making real progress. He could actually feel a tuft of hair where before it had been as smooth as a baby's ass. He thought the goatee made him look older, more mature.

"Today, Nathan?"

He blushed. He wished he could stop that. "Absolutely, boss. I was just trying to marshal my thoughts.

"Seems to me, boss, that their basic BW chart started at age 0, or right after the kid was born, and continued up by one-year periods to five years, when the kid was thrown into contact with other kids, in kiddy garden or even grade one."

"Great, Nathan. And do you recall any of the data results they showed?"

"I think the next column listed percentages of BW achieved at each age group, boss. Offhand I don't remember the exact numbers, but I think it ranged from almost 100 percent at age 0 to something like 65 or 70 percent at the five-year mark."

"Great fucking balls of eternal fire!" Snellings grabbed his flunky by the shoulders and hugged him violently.

"That's our answer, Nathan. If we can just show our dancing impresario how to translate that kind of results into dance school sign-ups, he'll make a fucking fortune. And so will we."

Snellings mentally rubbed his palms together, vicariously feeling the torrents of money that would pass between them if he could put this BW idea into practical terms.

"Here's what we have to do, Nathan. We have to first keep the source of this BW info absolutely secret. If the Crapolics get wind of our using their techniques, they'll be on us, like a horny bishop on an orphan boy, for a cut of the profits. Is that very clear, Nathan?"

"Absolutely, boss." He zippered his lips to reinforce his secret-keeping ability.

"Second." Snellings was a fan of lists. "We need to develop some workable plan on how our dancing maestro can set up and implement our BW technique. In spite of his desire for speed we'll probably have to scale the plan in over several years."

Snellings grabbed a pad and marker pen from his desk.

"Third." He scrawled a giant 3 on the pad. "We have to give him a simple workable way to set up our plan. He's probably not a relative of Einstein so we'll have to keep it easy to understand, easy to use. Right?"

Nathan nodded. He was good at translating exotic ideas into simple workable programs.

"Maybe, boss, we could show him how to implement the plan over a couple of years. He could start by advertising his exclusive dance academy, or whatever they're called, to new parents. Make it sound like if they don't register their new kids the kids will have a blighted childhood, scorned by all their dancing friends."

Snellings was smiling. This was why he paid Nathan the big bucks. Well, reasonable bucks. No point in spoiling the kid. When Nathan got going, creative marketing ideas spurted.

"Once we, or he, get the kids enrolled, he can start our BW program. Not called anything like that, of course.

"If he can get one-year old kids signed up, by the time they're in the second year of dancing heaven they will be well on the way to partial BW. And by the third year, he'll have to have limits on new enrollments."

Snellings was ecstatic. This was going to be a gold mine.

"Above all, Nathan, we have to keep our proprietary interest in the BW techniques absolutely secret. Unfortunately, we can't slap a trademark on the whole process; that would just get the Crapolics bitching for a cut.

"But if we play our cards right, and tight, on this one, Nathan, my boy, we can use that BW stuff on almost all our present—and future—clients."

Nathan understood the significance of 'his' BW idea. He was creative, but he also had strong financial acumen. Like a hooker whose monetary price can decline greatly as time passes, he knew that now was the time to get Snellings by the short and curlies.

"It will be a truly great profit generator, boss. And just as we have to keep the BW techniques out of the public eye, we have to keep a tight internal lid on it.

"You know as well as I do that any of half a dozen of our current employees wouldn't hesitate to copy, or even steal outright, our", he leaned heavily on the word our, "proprietary secret. And right now is when we—you and me—have to come to some agreement on this valuable creative idea."

Snellings testicles tightened. That prick. Trying to put pressure on me, after all I've done for him.

But then Snellings realized that Nathan actually was in a position to pressure him. What he had to do now was strike a deal that cost him as little as possible.

How could he do that, and still keep Nathan on his team, a team that could, possibly, become an extremely profitable team if those BW techniques worked the kind of marketing magic he expected.

Snellings smiled. When it came to his ability to slash another's share to the very bone, he had no equals. And compared to his shmuck employee—trying for months to grow a fucking goatee!—it was no contest.

"Okay, Nathan, assuming that this BW thing, which of course is not original, not even with the Crapolics who merely stole it from earlier users, is something we can use in my" he said the word my in bold caps, "firm, which I started as you well know from scratch myself many years ago, and is something we can keep buttoned up internally, and of course externally, you'll recall that it first came to light in a research study which I set up, and paid for." Snellings was losing his train of thought, and he felt he'd better close things down for a moment. "So, what do you think would be fair?" He actually hated that last word.

Nathan was young, and in high finance totally inexperienced. But the heritage of hundreds of generations of negotiators was his, and he wasn't about to let his slippery boss bamboozle him. He stroked his goatee to give him a few moments respite, and then charged ahead.

"Oscar", (he thought it important to make the change from boss to first name seeing they were actually discussing a type of partnership), "Oscar, it's important to set up something fair to both of us, and also something which can remain for a long time. I feel that if we concentrate solely on the BW technique, and on our present and any future clients we can employ it with, our negotiation will prove simpler. Is that agreeable?"

What the fuck was he talking about? "I'm not too sure what you mean, Nathan. Please explain more fully."

Here it was. Time for the 100-mile an hour pitch. His big chance to get onto the gravy train. Think of the broads he'd be able to wine and dine. And screw, with or even without that fucking goatee.

"First thing, Oscar, is to get as much legal protection as possible. Give me a day or so and I'll design a program encompassing our BW formula as an integral part. Then we can get trademarks and service marks on every aspect of it; it will be unique the way I lay it out."

Snellings listened with a mixture of pride and fear. Pride in how quickly his flunky had grasped the essentials. Fear because he was deathly afraid that the little prick was manoeuvring himself into a large—shit, maybe even fair—share of the golden bonanza.

Nathan gathered his breath.

"Then we can get Jack Diamond, our slippery legal counsel, to try and get the entire process, or at least the key elements, patented. That will limit the time we have a monopoly, but long before the patent expires, we should be able to come up with insignificant, but legally acceptable, moves to extend its life, just as the sleazy drug companies do."

The fear in Snellings' gut was getting larger by the minute. This damned clerk of his was starting to sound like he actually knew what he was doing.

Snellings knew that education of employees was always a dangerous sign, just as the religious zealots and scammers had always known.

"Now, with that framework in place," Nathan continued, "we need a legal entity to own it. I suggest a corp. And to keep ownership of our secret BW weapon as tight as possible, a simple 50-50 share ownership would probably be best."

Nathan tugged at his few goatee hairs to show he was temporarily finished.

Snellings felt the floor giving way. That's what came from trying to treat fucking parasite employees as human beings. Give them an inch and they took a foot, or meter, or whatever goddamned measurement system they were using today.

But he hadn't piled up the wealth he had by letting his emotions dictate business decisions. In spite of that fucking goatee he realized that Nathan was pretty sharp. Very sharp. In fact, really fucking sharp.

"Well, I am not sure right now that a simple 50-50 share split would be best for us, and the BW idea."

Snellings saw that Nathan had immediately squinted his eyes, a very bad sign. "But that doesn't mean we can't reach a satisfactory arrangement, my boy." A little grease never hurt, he thought.

"Let's do this. Each of us, in absolute confidence of course, will think about this program and how it should be marketed after we have all possible legal protections." If he could get Nathan-the-prick using his proven marketing skills before any agreement, Snellings would have more leverage, his flunky less.

"I don't think we should spend time now on marketing plans, Oscar. That will follow naturally once we have the corp, and the legal stuff, set up. I have no worries about coming up with some red hot marketing ideas. But first things first."

Fucking cocksucker. I wish I had the ability to think up marketing ideas the way he does and I'd chuck his ass out of here.

But Snellings' good business sense intervened. He knew that without Nathan he would have a very difficult time developing the BW program.

"Maybe you're right, Nathan. Okay, let's each take a day or two to think this whole thing through. Each will put his ideas on everything from the basic corporation to the patent stuff on our shared computers, but password protected.

"And let's make sure we use at least 12 digits in those passwords, to protect against our"—fuck, he hadn't intended to use that pronoun—"sleazy employees."

Sharp-eared Nathan noted the 'our'.

I've got this buffoon by the balls already, he gloated.

He could see his new marketing empire stretching ahead for a very long time.

And a very profitable time, too, he mentally added.

Chapter 23

Question: What seems more plausible to you, that we've existed in past lives, or that there is a god?
Answer: Neither seems plausible to me. I have a grim, scientific assessment of it. I just feel, what you see is what you get.

Woody Allen, actor and film director, interviewed at age 74.

###

The city council was winding up its regular semi-monthly administrative committee meeting.

Everyone was tired, bored, and thirsty. Dealing with the peoples' business, particularly when there were no lucrative new bridge or highway repaving contracts, with suitable fringe benefits for benefactors, to award, or even discuss, was a pain in the ass.

Councilwoman Edith Chalmerson, as thirsty as they came, unfolded from her comfortable position with her red head cradled in her arm, and got to her feet.

"If there's no further business, I move that we adjourn…"

Before she finished the sentence, acting Mayor Taylor Wimsby, ever on the lookout to be heard last on any subject so a sleepy and lazy reporter might quote him first, interrupted.

He knew he wouldn't make mayor on brains, so he had to use everything possible to get noticed by the power brokers, only one of whom appeared tonight to even be awake.

So he cleared his throat more noisily than usual, and was rewarded as the senior power broker actually opened one eye to see what the disturbance was. That's a start, he figured. Now if I can only get him to keep at least one open.

"There is one additional piece of business. I couldn't find a regular spot on our packed agenda"—was the senior PB watching? Yes, he was, "so I made the executive decision to keep it until after we had completed our normal business."

What a pretentious twat he was, Chalmerson thought, a thought mentally voted on and passed unanimously by every other thirsty council member.

Wimsby, who affected a phony English accent that sounded like he was giving the punch line on some cornball joke, cleared his throat again. Never hurt to make sure.

"We have received a formal complaint from the exec director of the area airports." He liked to abbreviate titles, he felt it gave him an 'insider' image. Mostly it made his laughable accent even more impossible to understand.

"It seems that the airports have been plagued with some sort of religious group. While the airport people are all in flavor of religious freedom—as of course we are too—they now feel the problems caused by this group are actually impeding the smooth and safe flow of airport passengers. In consequence of that decision, they have asked us to make a binding ruling on how this group, and others like them, can have access to public places like airports where safety and speed are critical issues."

Wimsby paused, took a handkerchief from his sleeve, and dabbed it against his drooping fleshy lips.

I expect he also uses that rag to jerk off in, thought councilwoman Edith Chalmerson who was becoming increasing thirsty and thus even more critical of her colleague's mannerisms.

"What's this group's name, Wimsby?" She had to do something to speed him up, otherwise her dehydrated body would just return to dust.

"Ah, let me see." Wimsby ruffled a few pages, although the name was on his topmost page. "Oh, yes," he lisped, "here it is. They are the Hairy Krishnuts.

"Not a major player in the religion field, perhaps, but apparently they do have quite a few followers, or believers, or whatever they call their, ah, followers."

Jeesus Keerist, Chalmerson thought. Each word he utters plunges him further into a cesspool of distorted language.

"And what problems are the hairy ones causing," asked Donnie Kilbrain, a councilman who had been catching up on his sleep until Wimsby started repeatedly verbally puking.

"According to the official complaint, which I have here in my current business file should anyone wish to see it", Wimsby continued, "the Hairy Krishnuts are causing passenger traffic congestion.

"This group evidently relies on soliciting the public directly to receive the bulk of their contributions, and unfortunately much—maybe even most—of the traveling public are not in sympathy with the group's goals, or even their manner of buttonholing passengers in a hurry to get to where they are going and continuing to pester them for a donation even after the passenger has declined to do that."

"In short, Wimsby, the hairy guys are panhandling." Would she ever get a drink?

"Perhaps a little strong worded, councilwoman Chalmerson, but in essence somewhat correct." Wimsby straightened his ascot-striped tie which had become a little loose during his frequent throat clearings.

"So what is our solution to this earth-shaking dilemma, oh great leader?"

Was that sarcasm from the councilwoman? No, it couldn't be. I guess she was just giving me my actual inferred title.

"I jotted down several possible solutions, Edith." He had once read that the way to treat equals, even superiors, was to call them by their first names. So that's what he would do with the sometimes problem-causing councilwoman.

"Great," she said. "Let's hear them, Taylee."

Wimsby flinched at the nickname he hated, but carried on; he cleared his throat, tightened his tie, and started reading from his top notebook page.

"First, we could simply pass a bylaw, completely outlawing, and prohibiting, any kind of public solicitations at places like airports, those places which are critical to smooth movement of large numbers of passengers."

Several councilors started to move around in their chairs so Wimsby rushed ahead to forestall them.

"Of course, that bylaw would probably be appealed in some court, possibly as an infringement on peoples' rights, or even religious freedom grounds."

Wayne Goodly, an opponent of anything involving any group having the right to hit up passersby for money, immediately jumped to his feet.

"Bullshit. No one, anywhere, anytime, has the right to bother me by sticking out a grubby hand and begging. I say we should just authorize an automatic fine, say of a grand or two, to make these jerks pay attention."

Several councilors nodded vigorously and Wimsby saw his meeting command slipping away.

"That's an interesting observation, Wayne, but I doubt if we have the resources to back up such a draconian solution."

Each day Wimsby diligently forced himself to learn a new word but he rarely got to use the esoteric words he adopted. He felt a glow of pleasure at finally being able to work in that dandy draconian.

Goodly mumbled what sounded suspiciously like a sexually-oriented expletive but collapsed into his chair anyway.

Wimsby had to get his meeting command back in order.

"That was my first suggestion, even though it's of doubtful use. Second, we could pass a bylaw authorizing various groups to solicit donations in public places like airports, but attaching several tough restrictions. For example, we could specify that solicitors could not approach within five feet of people, that they could not touch them in any way. And we could make the license fee for such permissions quite high, say $500 for each location."

He saw Goodly nod his head. He was on the right track.

"To control it, we could have some of our parking meter maids wear a special enforcement badge. It seems to me that too many of these m.ms seem to spend too much of their time sitting in coffee shops. If any member of the group did not have a valid sticker, he or she would be subject to the specified fine.

"Refusal to accept a violation ticket, or to pay the fine within a specified time, would be a misdemeanor, and more than say four or five such failures would result in the total group losing its license."

"And then what?" Councilwoman Chalmerson was rapidly approaching terminal dehydration.

Wimsby shuffled his feet awkwardly, a sure sign he didn't have an answer ready.

"To be honest, Edith, I haven't completely resolved that issue. I have considered it at length, but because of its complexity I felt this was an issue we all should reflect on, and consider all the options."

Shit, what a fucking jerk. Chalmerson was getting close to throwing her very solid desk paperweight. She could feel her skin becoming crisper by the minute as all her body fluids evaporated.

"Good idea" she said. "Let's all ponder the crap out of this subject and discuss it in excruciating detail at next meeting. Agreed? Then I move for immediate adjournment. All in favor?"

Even though most of the members had their eyes closed, reflex actions shot up their hands.

No doubts, it was a landslide for adjournment.

Chalmerson hoped she could make the nearest bar before collapsing.

Chapter 24

A man said to the universe: "Sir, I exist!"
"However," replied the universe, "That fact has not
created in me any sense of obligation."

Stephen Crane (1871-1900), writer.

"Just how accurate is this?" Bill Corey asked.

"My source has a secret tape recording of much of the final session." Although a few years younger than Corey, Jim Johnson's face conveyed sincerity.

"How the hell did he get that by those hawks?"

"It wasn't easy, but he's been in the organization a long time, and is pretty well respected—and trusted—by the powers."

"I mean, Jim, if this turns out to be someone's idea of a practical joke, you and I, and probably your informant, are not going to have to worry about pension plans anymore. Those guys wouldn't think twice about offing all of us. Fuck, they've been doing that for a couple of millennia."

Johnson drained his glass, and waved it aloft to catch the bartender's eye.

"I know that, Bill. I know just how ruthless these people are. And I have no desire to check out their promised heaven before old age takes me off."

The bartender, obviously working on a percentage basis, quickly exchanged Johnson's empty for a full glass. He looked at Corey who shook his head.

"But I have heard part of the tape. There's no way it could have been fabricated. It's simply too authentic. You can even hear some of them belching and clearing their throats. The kind of stuff that someone faking it wouldn't even think of. No, this tape is the real thing."

Corey sipped at his bourbon. He wanted to keep his head clear. What his friend and fellow reporter had told him was dynamite, and very possibly deadly to anyone associated with it.

"Can I hear it?"

Johnson put down his glass which had been halfway to his mouth.

"I don't know, Bill. It was a hell of a job for him to agree to me hearing any of the actual tape. He's awfully nervous, of course with good cause. He told me, quite seriously, that if his name leaked out, he would be dead before sunset."

Corey fiddled with the mechanical pencil he always had close. He pushed the end to lengthen the lead.

"You know, Jim, I was on the police beat for a bunch of years, and I got to see a lot of crime stuff. Mob professional killings, idiot amateurs who decided to correct a bunch of imaginary wrongs in one bloodbath, perverts who went crazy. A lot of blood and guts. But even with that gory background, I know this group of yours makes the mob look like a kindergarten for bad guys."

Corey hesitated, then continued.

"Do we really have the balls for this, Jim?"

Johnson chewed his lip. That was exactly what he had asked himself a dozen times since his informant had first contacted him. He was young, eager, and willing to take risks to advance his career. But reasonable risks.

These risks were of a different order. This group had the resources, money, and willingness to do anything to keep their extremely profitable business, reputed to be the largest in the entire world, safe and functioning as it had for a very long time.

He knew that Jim Johnson wasn't even a fly in their eyes. They'd swat him without even blinking.

"I'm not really sure, Bill. Believe me, I know the clout these pricks have, both legal and otherwise. Shit, half the fucking judges bow down before them once a week. If it even ever came to a legal trial our gooses would be cooked before noon.

"And on the dark side, they probably have more people willing to maim or kill than even the Untied States do."

He drank, then looked at Corey.

"So, no, Bill, I'm not at all sure we have the balls for this. But it's obviously a reporter's wet dream come true. You and I both know the chance of another scoop story like this coming along in our lifetimes is almost zero."

"Assuming those lifetimes last beyond today," Corey said, frowning to show he was serious.

He finished his glass and waved at the bartender, who had a new drink poured before he lowered his arm. "Christ, this bartender must be a mind reader."

The drink was delivered before Corey spoke again.

"Okay, let's look at the facts, whatever the fuck they are.

"You've heard part of the tape, Jim. What's it all about?"

Johnson cleared his throat, looked around to make sure a spy hadn't crept up on them—the bar was deserted except for a rummy crying in his beer at the far end of the counter, and the mind-reading bartender seemed to be engrossed in a TV ballgame.

"Of course I only heard part, Bill. And the whole plot was obviously not spelled out in that one-minute excerpt. But my informant did rough out what the tape contained, so I'll try to summarize his comments."

Corey was on the verge of throwing a glass at his colleague in order to speed him up, and then thought better of it. After all, Johnson had voluntarily included him in this scoop of the century, as he thought of it. Scoop? He hadn't even heard that term since he was a kid and he used to watch Superman cartoons, and Clark Kent was always on the trail of some scintillating scoop.

Johnson primed himself with another healthy drink.

"It appears the group is facing declining revenues in some of their normally very profitable regions," Johnson said. "The problem is twofold. First, competition is moving in. And second, existing customers are leaving."

Corey had his pencil out but it hadn't moved.

Johnson drank again before continuing.

"Now, the problem of competition is apparently not new. There have always been new guys out there peddling a new message. Some even got to be pretty successful. But when it's happened before, to any significant amount, like in the earlier centuries, this group simply took steps to eliminate the competitors.

"They'd get them on false charges, have judges in their pocket who literally said 'Off with their heads', or something like that, and the competition was snuffed.

"If phony charges didn't work, they simply roused the local peasants to believe the competition were witches or vampires or something else scary, and the local idiots wiped them out for the group."

Corey shifted in his chair. He still hadn't used his pencil on the little notepad he carried. Now he looked at Johnson.

"That stuff is ancient history, Jim, and certainly not new. When do we get to the interesting part?"

"Okay", Johnson said. "Well, now days it's getting difficult, sometimes impossible, to use either of those approaches. Even though maybe half of all judges belong to the group, they can't simply act like they did in the old days.

"And direct action by the group, although no moral or even physical dilemma, can only take care of a few competitors. Wholesale wipe-outs a la Hitler or Stalin are pretty difficult to arrange."

"Again, Jim, common knowledge." Corey was starting to fear that his friend had played up a simple page four item into page one above-the-fold importance.

"Sure, Bill. But now we start getting into the juicy parts."

"About fucking time."

"Along with the two competition problems I mentioned earlier, the group is facing declining market share. Even where they have locks on the locals, like in parts of Mexico and US states like Massachusetts and New Mexico, the peasants are starting to get educated.

"As they do, the group's grip on them weakens, and eventually, my informant said, after about the second or third generation of educated people, the group loses its stranglehold almost completely."

"Poor them," Corey said. Would Johnson ever get to the meat of his pitch?

Johnson grinned. He knew that Corey was squirming in his seat, waiting for the kicker. Well, he'd give it to him.

"Until now, for a couple of millennia, the group has survived on its own. With education only a recent development, and the ability to literally annihilate competitors, the group has provided a great living for all its managers. Consider a normal company, Bill. In this situation, giving constraints on further growth, and even present markets threatened, what choices does a CEO have?"

Corey was silent.

"Seeing that my star pupil doesn't have a ready answer, I'll give him a clue. Diversification."

Corey gagged on the drink he was taking. "Diversificashun?" His unswallowed drink dribbled down his chin. "Diversification?"

He jumped to his feet and wiped his face with a napkin. He cleared his throat, finished the drink, and carefully set the glass down.

"Would you like to explain that?"

"Sure", Johnson said, "if you're finished puking your drink."

Corey looked at him but said nothing. Johnson felt he'd better continue.

"My informant said most of the special meeting was devoted to that. To diversifying."

"That's it? Nothing more?"

"Oh yeah, lots more. The meeting members agreed apparently on the need for D"—he was tired repeating the multi-syllable word—"and once that was established, they considered all the ways to accomplish it."

Corey picked up his pencil again, dropped during the choking episode. "Are you telling me that this group, probably the largest profit-making bunch anywhere, are actually considering diversifying?"

"Si, senor, that's exactly what I'm telling you. Is that news or what?"

"If we can verify that, it is absolutely news, old pal. We will get page one, maybe even a banner on top." Corey could already see the plaudits, the praise, the fucking envy, from every other reporter in the city. City? The whole fucking country. Maybe even the world!

Similar thoughts had raced across Johnson's mental screen as his informant had summed up the meeting's agenda. But in the time since he had realized that info from an informant, who wouldn't admit to word one, was not exactly the same as seeing his copy immortalized on any paper's page one.

"Slow down, cowboy," he said. "While I have my informant's info, he won't corroborate any of it. If he did, he wife becomes a widow before the sun sets in Dodge.

"We have to figure out some way to get his confidential info verified before we can print any of this."

Corey was jotting scrawls in his notebook. No one else in the civilized world would be able to decipher them, and even he frequently had problems.

"What else did he say? Did he give any corroborating details?"

"I don't know if they are corroborating," Johnson said, "but I did get quite a bunch of other stuff, some of which we should be able to use to get the overall scheme verified."

"Start talking. And no more pauses until the end, amigo, or your wife may start wearing widows' weeds, whatever the hell they are."

"I'm not married. Anyway, I made some rough notes when he was talking to me."

Johnson reached into his sports jacket inside pocket, pulled out a dog-eared notebook a little larger than Corey's, and thumbed through it, finally settling on a page which looked like a menu in a Chinese restaurant written in Chinese.

"Here we go," he said. "First on my list, the method or methods to be used in D. Most important, the members agreed, was the simple one of buying control in the major competitors."

"Hold on. Most of those aren't even public companies. They maybe are private firms, but how the hell could they buy control of that?"

"Obviously they couldn't 'buy' control, amigo. But my informant said that 'buy' was simply a euphemism for 'take'. As in, we want in, give us what we want."

"In short, what they've been doing since time began," Corey said.

"Yeah, pretty much. But whereas before they simply eliminated the comps, now they are going to take them over internally and keep them going. In not too long a time, my informant implied, their goal was to control more than 51%, whether that's an actual figure or simply a goal, of all major religious groups."

Corey took a long drink. "How soon does this plan get underway?"

"According to my spy, it's probably underway now. This taped meeting was several weeks ago, and this group doesn't like to sit on new objectives very long. From what he said, and implied, this meeting was ended—that's not on my sample clip—on a 'get going' basis."

"Any idea of the time frame involved to complete the action?"

Johnson checked around for eavesdroppers.

"No, I got the impression it would be ongoing, taking as long as necessary. These guys have been doing their fun and games for a long time, and I don't imagine they're in any particular rush."

"If we're going ahead on this, Jim, we have to agree first on two things." Corey shut his notebook.

"First, we're on a story which could get us both killed. Quickly. And second, we have to keep it absolutely to ourselves. Any digging we do has to appear to be on something completely separate, something these pricks won't find in the least threatening. And third, I just expanded the list, we have to get together on this as infrequently as possible.

"Whatever research we do must be on independent subjects, and normally we don't spend a lot of time together, so we have to keep those appearances as normal as possible. Agreed?"

Johnson nodded his head.

"Absolutely on all three, Bill. Believe me, I know how rough these guys play.

"Remember I covered that story a couple of years ago in Mexico. In one state this group owned the political party that was in control. A couple of enthusiastic but amateurish reformers tried their luck in getting elected. They didn't achieve that. Their bodies were found in a land fill dump. That message left a definite impression on my young mind."

"Good. And keep it uppermost," Corey said. "Okay, let's set up a rough plan of action." He pulled out his notebook. "Any preferences for what you dig into?"

"Well, given my past work and admittedly limited experience in the area, how be I try to do some research in the overall all-embracing aspect of the group, how they have their tentacles in so many different parts of peoples' lives?"

"How would you cover your research?" Corey looked doubtful.

"I could say I'm doing some background on a piece on how religion is so important in so many different ways.

"If I make it look like I'm actually fishing for a fat fee from the group for what will apparently be a glowing testimonial to them, I may be able to dig some dirt."

"Sounds okay to me," Corey said. "And with my background in finance and all the dirty tricks the pros in that field use to screw the public, I can let it be known that I'm working on a series of stories about how such finance tactics are finding their way into a variety of fields. Like, ah," he scratched his head, "like even education, maybe, and possibly even a little into our old friend religion."

Johnson frowned, drank a little, frowned again.

"I guess you could make that angle believable. But probably best to make sure religion is at the end of whatever list you make up. Let's not make it too easy for these cocksuckers to get a line on what we're actually doing."

"Sure. Now what about some kind of timetable on this? We can't just drift around out there in the big world. Let's put a specific date on our next 'drinking session'. Not too soon, obviously, but sometime before the next century."

Johnson, his junior partner status mentally ever present, said "So what do you suggest?"

Corey flipped his notebook to the center where he had pasted a calendar of the year.

"We should be able to get at least a start on our digging in a couple of weeks—remember it has to be done slowly—so let's meet here in two weeks, about the same time in the afternoon as today. At that time few other reporters have ended their shifts so there shouldn't be anyone we know floating around."

"The occasion?"

"If anyone asks, we have just found we both have an interest in horse racing, and we met in common cause to pick a few longshot winners. And to ease the pain of the inevitable losers with a little liquid solace."

"Good. And in the meantime, whenever we meet we're just fellow scribblers, right?"

"You have it, my boy," Corey said. "Carry on, like the limey movies said, and good luck.

"We're both going to need lots of that."

The bartender lifted one eyelid in silent query. Corey nodded, stuck two fingers up to indicate drinks for both men, and slid into the booth.

With the same speedy service the bartender placed the drinks on the table and vanished back to the bar.

"If I ever own a bar that guy is going to be my number one bartender," Jim Johnson said. "Even if he steals more than usual he's really good."

"Based on what I've accomplished," Corey said, "it sure doesn't seem like two weeks has passed. "How about you?"

Johnson drained half his rye and water and wiped his lips. His mother had been an unrelenting teacher of manners.

"Afraid I have to agree with you, Bill. Doesn't seem like I accomplished much of anything."

Corey stretched and made a full visual sweep of booths around them.

"We have the place to ourselves, excluding Simon the souse there at the bar, so let's get what we do have on the table."

"Fine, I'll start." Johnson pulled his battered notebook from his inside sports jacket pocket.

"To commence, mister chairman, my assignment, you'll recall, was background on a piece on how religion is so important in so many different ways."

Corey was tempted to reach over and punch his junior colleague in the mouth but he held his irritation in check.

Johnson noticed Corey's ire so he decided to stop horsing around.

"First I did some library checking on world stats on the various religions.

"Our group, as might be expected with their inherent dark-seeking criminal tendencies, doesn't take the top spot in any category. Close to the top in a couple but never right in numero uno. I feel that's deliberate, a strategy followed by under-reporting actual member numbers simply to avoid the spotlight of being top dogs.

"And nothing, in any of the respectable references I checked, showed even a hint of desires to expand through diversification. The official stats, of course, come from each religious group, so ours would have no trouble in cooking them to whatever extent they wanted.

"And the stats, assuming they have any real credibility, do confirm my informant's info that this group is in trouble. Even in regions like Latin America, where traditionally they've had a total lock, because there babies are brainwashed right after birth, and grow up not realizing they've been had, the numbers are bad for them. As more kids get better educations, membership falls off.

"When you look at membership broken down by ages, the younger segments, say under 30, drop off almost dramatically. In one country, for example, the under 30s show just 38% membership, whereas the over 50s are about 93%. That's a tremendous drop in membership, and confirms what little I heard on that tape."

"Anything else?" Corey was already thumbing through his notebook, trying to read scrawls that a professional code breaker would give up on.

"Just one thing."

Johnson shifted in his chair, looking at the ceiling, then at the very unattractive walls. Finally he moved his glance around to Corey.

"Maybe a small thing, Bill. I'm not even sure if it actually is a thing. But it's got me a little spooked."

Corey again resisted the urge to punch Johnson. Just as he had almost given in to it, Johnson resumed talking.

"Here's the problem, Bill. The last couple of days in the libraries, and I was in four different ones in total, I got the impression, or feeling, that someone was there watching me. Different people each time, all men, but a couple of big guys, one medium, one shrimp. No ethnic matches either. One black, one tan, two more or less white."

"So what makes you think they were eyeballing you?"

"That's just it, Bill. Nothing overt, nothing obvious. But a couple of times when I looked up quickly, I got the impression the watcher had been watching me, and turned away a second earlier as my head movement tipped him off."

Corey scratched his left ear lobe. It seemed to itch far more than the right one. Maybe showed latent left-wing tendencies?

"That's pretty skinny, Jim. How many other people were in the various libraries when this happened?"

Johnson grimaced. He knew his suspicions were sounding more and more like an old maid's belief that every male was trying to get into her bloomers.

"It varied. A couple of times there were several others, maybe four or five, fairly close by. Once my watcher was solo, once he had a dozen or so other people around. That was in the public library."

Corey interrupted. "So there was no routine to it. I mean it wasn't always one guy alone, or a watcher with a bunch of others as camouflage?"

"And never the same guy, Bill. And to me that sounds more suspicious than the same guy. In that case it could be just some nut, maybe somebody who thought I looked hot. Or thought I was in some secret service, or something.

"Whatever, if this is our group doing all this library research, it means two things. Both bad."

Corey finished his drink but didn't even lift a finger to summon the super bartender.

"And they are?" He hated to admit it, but Johnson's report actually seemed to make a weird kind of sense.

"First, that our group is aware of something. Our specific research, or just something possibly unpleasant is being undertaken, and they want to keep any eye on it."

Corey nodded. Unfortunately, that point seemed reasonable.

Johnson cleared his throat. He looked at the bar again and lowered his voice.

A little dramatic, Corey thought.

"And second. It probably follows, if the first assumption is correct, that they also know who we are."

Corey grinned. "Well, maybe they have you spotted, Jim, but as I haven't been hanging around any libraries recently, they don't have me in the picture frame. So if you're on their wanted list, you're hanging out there all alone."

He thought the joshing would help to relieve his colleague's anxiety.

Johnson managed a very weak smile.

"Nice to know you're so firmly part of this team, Bill. But I'm afraid you're a little too optimistic."

"Why? Did I leave a trail of bread crumbs or something that they were able to follow?" He felt it possible that Johnson was actually crossing over into paranoid territory.

"No, I think it was simpler than that, Bill." He tried to get rid of that damn frog in his throat.

"Take away the 1940s raincoat, shave him a little, and that rummy slumped over at the end of the bar looks quite a bit like the watcher I spotted in the law library."

Corey froze. One talent his partner had was a very good ability to remember faces and bodies. Corey knew it had served him well in his years as a cub reporter. He had an overwhelming urge to turn around and stare at the man Johnson had identified. But he fought it down.

"How sure are you?"

"90 percent. Even more, 98. I've been watching his mannerisms, the way he reaches into his pockets, the way he rests his left hand on the bar like he was holding something in it. And several more. No doubts, Bill. That's my watcher from the law library."

"Is there any chance our bar scumbag is during the day a respected lawyer who often bones up in the law library?" Even to himself the question sounded puerile.

"Allowing for the fact that all lawyers are by definition scumbags, I'm afraid your question is sort of, well, puerile."

Now where the fuck did he get that word? Corey thought he had an unofficial trademark on its usage.

"The facts are simple, Bill. The same guy who spent several hours last Thursday watching me read law books is now spending time in one of our sleaziest bars, doing what? Obviously watching me, and now you too."

Corey shifted in his chair but refused to look at the bar, even though he was desperately in need of a large drink. He leaned a little forward, hopefully not far enough to get the watcher's attention. Damn. Now he was verifying that the scumbag was a watcher.

"Listen, Jim. If you're right, and with your known talents for ID-ing people I have to assume that you are, it means we are into a shitty situation.

"When we started this story, or at least the research for it, we both knew and agreed that this group had at least some members who would have made Adolph and Joe look like beginners in the maim and kill Olympic events."

Was he being too dramatic? No.

"It also seems like we've skipped a couple of moves on this game board, and we're now well beyond the 'quit, collect $200, and go home and forget everything'. Agreed?"

Johnson nodded, keeping his glance at Corey but slanted slightly to take in the bar sleazebag.

"It's a new game, Jim. And now we have to decide. Do we proceed, up against as it now appears at least a reasonably well funded operation by the opposition in keeping tabs on us, or do we try and extricate and walk away from this now obviously major story?"

Johnson felt a weakness in his knees and a fairly strong urge to piss. But his character as a dedicated reporter pushed through his fear.

"In spite of the increasing stacked odds against us, Bill, I say we go ahead." His voice had cracked a little there at the end but Corey didn't comment.

"You are aware that if this group can marshal so quickly at least four different men to spend time following you, now us, we have to also assume they won't hesitate to play a lot rougher if they perceive a need? In short, pal, this activity could get very unpleasant for us very quickly."

Johnson tried to mentally pro and con the reasons for staying on the story. Pro was the instant fame, and maybe even some big bucks, which would rock the journalism world if the story panned out. Con? Bodily injury, maybe even of a fatal type. He knew this group viewed human life as a very disposable product.

"Even with the now apparent downside, Bill, I still say" he tried to find some fucking saliva, "yes."

"Okay. Reluctantly I agree. But now we have to work out a definite plan for our future meetings.

"We obviously can't meet here, where they now have a lock on it. It should be someplace where there are other people around, yet not so many that we, more likely you, won't be able to spot any watcher. A location where we would have a professional reason for being together, besides a place where two intrepid conspirators are trying to throw at least a little sand into this group's continuing takeover of the religious world. Or at least a little light on its malfeasances."

Corey yawned and sneaked a glance at the bar. The sleazebag watcher, cum sleazebag lawyer or whatever, was still on duty. That looked like the same drink in the same glass he's nursed from when Johnson had first made him.

"It should be somewhere fairly close to the paper, Bill. That makes it easier to be part of that world, at least to a casual watcher. And somewhere where there's in and out traffic, but not too much, so I can try to spot any new watcher."

Corey nodded. "But still private enough so we can talk without whispering or being easily overhead. If their watcher has to be obvious then he's blown his usefulness.

"How about the Scoop coffee shop just across the street from the paper?"

"Wishful thinking, Bill?"

Corey grinned. "Maybe. But how does it sound?"

"Pretty good. I think we're both in and out of there often enough that it shouldn't raise suspicions. We'll just have to be careful that we don't enter or leave together."

"And not any oftener than absolutely necessary, Jim. The more I think of these watchers, already hot on the trail, the more nervous I get."

Johnson nodded. "Right. And I guess we should shut down this meeting as quickly as possible. Until now it could look just like a couple of colleagues having a drink together. Let's get it wrapped up in a few minutes."

"All we need is a quick breakdown of who's doing what research. Seeing that you have the informant— incidentally, is he going to be a continuing source or has he shot his load?"

"He'll be on tap, I think, but only as an emergency contact. Even that will take some doing.

"He gave me a box number at one of those mail drop services, but that would take at least a few days to send him a very disguised note—he told me how to word it to make it look like a solicitation from some obscure veteran's org— and for him to phone me from a public phone. And even then he just gives me the word 'quicksand', and I have to phone him back from another public phone to a number he gave me. It's really cloak and dagger stuff, but after seeing all these watchers already I now believe the precautions are absolutely necessary."

Corey finished his drink but didn't nod for a refill.

"Then let's get research assigned. You do all the background stuff, seeing you already have it started.

"As soon as you give me a few names of the outfits being targeted, I'll start basic research on them, and try to build up a couple of good contacts, people who may be in positions to know if a takeover move is being made."

"But of course you won't approach it from that angle?"

Corey looked at Johnson as a junior college instructor would look at some pinhead student who had asked a particularly stupid question.

"No, teacher, I won't. I'll use all my reportorial guile to sneak up on the real subject. Probably disguise it as a survey feature we're considering on the changing faces of today's religious groups. Something like that, anyway."

"Sounds reasonable, Bill. How about our next meeting?"

"How soon can you quietly get me those names?"

"I have all my research on this, ah, let's call it a research project? in a separate notebook I keep in the trunk of my car."

He saw that Corey was about to interrupt. "Yes, partner, don't worry. I have it in my own shorthand code. Even the top cryptographer wouldn't have a chance in deciphering it.

"As for the names, I can dig them out tonight and leave them in your work in-box tomorrow some time.

"I'll ID them as 'possible leads for your possible religion feature'. That should be sufficiently innocuous even if they have an employee as a watcher."

"I think you can eliminate the 'even if', Jim. From what we've already seen, I wouldn't be surprised to find they had watchers in a great many places."

"I agree. So our next meeting?"

"It'll take me a few days to get things organized. Let's make it Thursday, say mid-morning, how about 10.30 or so?

"But make sure we don't leave the paper at the same time. I'll go first.

"You can see my cubicle from yours, so watch and see if anyone seems to care, and then carefully drift over there five or so minutes later."

Johnson nodded and got to his feet. He pulled out his wallet and threw a few bills on the table.

"That should cover my share, Bill. See you around."

He left without looking back or over at the bar. Corey was impressed, his temporary partner was already acting like Bogart in Casablanca. He hoped he could make as graceful a spy exit.

Chapter 25

"To be positive: to be mistaken at the top of one's voice."

Ambrose Bierce (1842-1914), in the 'Devil's Dictionary'.

###

Johnson hurried over to the table, almost knocking a fullback-sized waitress over. He grabbed a chair and sank into it.

"Jesus Christ, Jim, I thought we agreed to make these meetings look accidental," Corey whispered the words. "Not that you didn't almost cause a fucking accident."

Johnson grabbed Corey's coffee cup and drained it in one swallow. "It doesn't matter anymore, Bill."

He reached into his jacket pocket and pulled out a crumpled sheet of newsprint. Stacks of it were always scattered around the newsroom for reporters to use as cheap doodling paper.

"Look at this." He almost threw the sheet across the table.

Corey grabbed it, looked around worriedly, and then smoothed out the sheet. Scrawled on it in large printed letters was a simple message:

'You and Corey had better stop. If you don't—X.'

"When did you get this? Where?"

Johnson looked around, caught the linebacker's eye, and held the empty cup aloft. "Two more, Mildred."

He turned back to Corey.

"It was on my desk when I returned after taking a quick piss. I had watched you leave. Nobody seemed to give a fuck. So to kill the five minutes we agreed on I went to the can. I was in there a couple of fucking minutes. When I went back to get my sports coat it was on my desk, crumpled all to shit like you saw it."

Corey knew Johnson was on the edge, he rarely cursed as richly as he had been.

"And I know fucking well what the cocksucking X stands for, Bill. They're threatening us with death."

Mildred brought the two cups. "I hope you had a good feel, you pervert." She smiled. "Next time just ask and I'll let you have a real feel."

Corey nodded to Johnson. He couldn't disagree with what X stood for.

"You know what this means, Jim. There's somebody in the reporter pool who's on their side. Somebody who saw you head for the can and acted very damned quickly."

Johnson gulped his coffee, almost choking. He wiped his chin with his hand, then grabbed a napkin.

"Of course that's what it means, Bill. The pricks are everywhere. And they know everything we're doing."

"It looks that way." Corey paused.

He had to get Johnson settled down before he blurted out everything to the coffee shop audience. Probably including one of their watchers, if Jim was right.

"I know this is bad news, Jim, but keep your voice down. It won't help if everyone in town knows what story we're working on."

Johnson seemed to relax a little, although his tensed shoulders still showed the stress he was feeling.

"Yeah, okay, Bill. But that note really scared me. I had thought they might be in a lot of places but I never expected their fucking spies right in the god damned newsroom."

Corey looked at the note again.

"With that large printing it would be impossible to match this to anyone's writing. And if we asked all the guys in the newsroom to give us handwriting samples, they'd laugh us out of the building."

He rubbed the cheap paper with his thumb.

"Did you get a look at who was actually in the newsroom??

Johnson shook his head.

"I was too shaken once I read it, I just wanted to get out of there. And you know what it's like anyway; those fucking cubicles—and there's got to be over 30 of them--can hide all but someone standing up."

Corey nodded. He was still nervous about Johnson talking too loudly.

"Let's look at where we stand on this, Jim. Have you come up with anything since our last meeting?"

Johnson drained his cup and waved it overhead to get a refill.

"I had another quick meet with my informant. He's getting as spooked as we are right now after that fucking note. He feels that they may be on to him, or at the least suspicious of what's he's doing. He did tell me that the big cheese, the guy at the very top, has apparently given his okay to this whole diversification idea.

"He said that one of the group leaders at the most recent assembly had read out some figures. The group is apparently losing members at an alarming rate, something like down 18 percent overall in just the last year.

"And the declines are coming everywhere, even in the once-solid countries like Italy and Spain, and even big losses in Mexico and several other South American spots.

Seems that education, and information generally, especially coming from the internet and all that mobile phone texting, is causing departures far faster that anyone anticipated.

"So the big D had been okayed and is being implemented in several areas as we speak. Negotiations are in progress in a couple of European hotspots, and more are scheduled for the New World areas. These guys are really moving on this."

He paused while new coffee was added to his cup. Corey shook his head when the waitress looked at him.

"Even in England, where the official group has what looks like a lock on members, an emissary of this group has started talking to one of their wheels. Seems they are feeling the pinch as well as our group—'our group', fuck; they're trying to kill us—and they want to get new bodies paying dues as quickly as possible.

"My informant said that at one such meeting it was suggested that they all work on shutting down the internet, because most of them held it responsible for much of the information that former members were relying on to pull the plugs. This proposal was actually debated, he said, and only defeated when all agreed it was too big to take on.

"Imagine, Bill! This group actually considered shitcanning the internet."

Johnson laughed and Corey felt a little relieved. His partner in this weird story seemed to be settling down.

"That's great stuff, Jim. Anything more?"

"Christ, isn't that enough for now. And the note," he added, looking at it near Corey's coffee cup.

"Sure it is, partner. And with this new info, I'll be able to start digging deeper into the groups in the areas you listed.

"So far, I've got basic research files on the main group, its internal structure—it makes the U.N. look like a kid's game in comparison—and even some of its key figures.

"One of the head honchos, for instance, was a valued member of Adolph's group even though pretty young, and following that he spent an interesting career as a fixer of those prest, or whatever the fuck they're called, perverts who should just have been castrated. Or shot. Even better both."

"You said one of the head honchos", Johnson said. "I thought the group had one guy in charge of everything, sort of like a king but far more powerful."

"A very popular and prevalent misconception, Jim. Despite that image which the group promotes for public consumption, its members are far easier to herd along if they think the top guy has a direct line to heaven. All he really has is a sometimes-direct line to one of the real wheels on their board of directors."

"Are you sure, Bill? That's really news in itself."

"Of course it is amigo, and just the tip of the proverbial iceberg. This group has more fucking turns and bends than a horny snake. But remember, it's been around for a long, long time, and it's had to adapt to a lot of different times and political and economic changes."

Corey straightened his shoulders. Johnson knew this meant a real revelation was forthcoming.

"And news so hot that my lips are burning even as I speak. I've had rumors, some from what I have found to be pretty accurate sources, that our group, big and powerful and worldwide as it is, is just a part of something even more powerful. That it's just like a branch store or whatever."

Johnson's face went even whiter.

"Jesus fucking Christ, Bill. Are you serious? Where did you pick up that scoop? Fuck, if it's even remotely true, that could explain why already we're on this group's 'do not resuscitate' list."

"You betcha, partner. I think we are on the biggest story of this century, maybe this millennium.

"And I also think we'd better do two things. First, move our asses even faster before they get blown away. And second, we'd better start using evasion tactics just like if we were at war.

"Which, actually, we are, Jim. We're taking on a group so big, with so much money and so many members and top contacts, that it makes any single country's powers look like a BB gun shooting against a mortar.

"I think we should get this meeting wrapped up pronto. There're a couple of guys in here who easily could be spies or at least snitches for the group. It's far too open. Any good shooter could take both of us out from any of half a dozen positions across the street."

Johnson wiped his sweaty forehead.

"Thanks, Bill, that really makes me feel good. I agree, I think our future meets have to be somewhere secret, and safe. After that note proved that there's at least one snitch right in the newsroom, I think we have to keep our relationship there strictly to good mornings."

"Agreed, Jim. And by next meet I should have something more on this possible connection of our group with something or someone bigger. If I can verify even the loosest rumor it will mean we're on the road to multiple Pulitzers."

"I'll try to milk my informant for any corroboration he can give to your rumors, Bill. If we get two completely different sources giving even a hint of that connection, or whatever the fuck it is, then I agree that the Pulitzers will be coming in wheelbarrows."

A new waitress stopped by their table. "Anything more, gents, or should I just bring you pillows and blankets?"

"Actually, sweetheart, that's not a bad idea." Corey grinned. "But for now just the check. Next time, I promise, we'll even order something besides coffee. Maybe a piece of pie or something exotic like that."

"Sounds like you guys are real big spenders. I'll look forward to your next visit."

She smiled and scrawled out a check and gave it to Corey.

"Let's get together this Friday, Bill. After work, say around six. Most of the guys will be deep in the sauce at the Newsmen's Club by then, so we should each be able to shake off any tails, at least those from the newsroom. It'll be light enough then to make that easier."

"Good idea, Jim. Where?"

"It can't be at either of our places. Too easy to spot, and maybe even to bug. Let's face it, this group can do just about anything.

"How does this sound, Bill? I have an aunt living in the Stanton Hotel. You know, that residential place on Boundary, near the big mall. It's one of those spots for older people. Each apartment is separate but there's good security and a button alarm brings help if a tenant falls or just needs help."

"What about your aunt? Any problems with her?"

"None. She's always on the move, and she said she'll be out on Friday. I have all her duplicate keys.

"Because of visits to my aunt I'm known there to the main door security people. If I leave your name you'll be able to get in. It's not foolproof but most casual followers would be kept out. What do you think?"

"Great. If you, or me, has a last-minute change, just scrawl the new time and date on newsprint, crumple it, and drop it on the floor in my cubicle. After I read it I'll flush it in the can. From now on we have to start being really careful, Jim."

"I totally agree. Those Pulitzers may be looming on the horizon but it would be nice to have them presented in person, not posthumously."

"I'll get the check when I leave. You go first, Jim, and keep your eyes open."

"I will. See you Friday, Bill."

Chapter 26

"Nothing is so firmly believed as what is least known."

Michel de Montaigne (1533-1592), philosopher.

###

"Any problem at the door?"

"No. The doorman just asked my name, then smiled and opened the door for me. Said Mr. Johnson had asked him to do that."

"Good. Here." He held out a water glass half full of a clear liquid. "Thought you might like this before we get underway."

"Vodka? Great. First all day." Corey swallowed half then set the glass down carefully on a coaster Johnson had provided. "Yeah, we don't want to mess up your aunt's place. Where is she?"

"She and a girl friend—girl, she's in her seventies—decided to get out of town for a few days, and they went to Vegas for a wild weekend. She does stuff like that pretty often. I hope I can do as good when I'm her age." His face darkened. "I hope I get to her age."

"Likewise. Okay, let's get started. I'd like to finish before dark, just so I can keep an eyeball on possible followers a little easier. I left my car a half dozen blocks away. I figure the walk there might make it more difficult for a spy. If there's a back door to this place I'll also slip out there."

"There is, Bill. Good thinking. I'll do the same, although my car is just a block away. Got anything new?"

Corey smiled and straightened. Johnson knew something good was forthcoming.

"One of my top sources, he was responsible for that break I had on the defense minister's kickback scheme, came up with, well, I can only say, astounding info."

"Strong words. And to back them up?"

Reaching for his scuffed-looking briefcase—Corey often claimed his father had carried it through the entire Vietnam War, and it looked like it—he almost fell off the anemic looking rocker he had chosen. "Christ! How does she stay in this thing?" He got up and switched to a straight-backed wooden chair.

He fumbled inside the case, then pulled out a dog-eared piece of legal sized paper.

"My contact mailed this to me, at my apartment. No return address, nothing on the sheet to indicate where it came from. And everything is printed, so not even any handwriting. But he said he was sending it so I know it's from him."

Corey extended the paper and Johnson took it. He looked down at it and read for a minute.

He looked up and frowned. "What are all these figures, Bill? It doesn't mean anything to me."

Corey smiled. "Good. It's not supposed to. But it wouldn't hold out long against even a poor cryptographer, Jim.

"It's just a simple number for letter substitution code. Each number represents the letter but one space to the right of its actual place in the alphabet. For example, the number 5 means the letter D, 7 indicates F. Got it?"

Johnson thought for a moment. "Sure. So there won't be any number higher than 26, no, 27. Right?"

"Exactly, amigo. It's simple but works to deter casual viewers. They'd be able to figure it out pretty soon but if they don't actually have the paper that long it works."

Johnson nodded. "Okay, I follow. And I assume that you have already worked out the real words?"

"Yes. It's actually a two-part letter. The first part deals with payoffs to other denomination big wheels, the people who can grease their group's takeover by our group."

"That sounds great, Bill. So now we have some hard data on how our group is suborning other religious groups, and getting control of them surreptitiously."

Corey frowned. "That's right, Jim, but remember this info is not attributable. My contact sure as shit won't back it up publicly. It's just like a cloud. Now we can see it, and know that your informant's info has been verified, but that's it.

"We can't print anything. We need far more concrete stuff, tapes of people discussing payoffs, photos of money changing hands, something like that."

Johnson bounced from his chair. "I know that, Bill, I'm an experienced reporter, remember? But this is the first corroboration we've had of what my informant gave me. I believed him but it was only one source. Now, with this material, we have that vital second source. Great! I feel good, Bill."

He looked at his partner. "Why aren't you smiling like I am? Are you so jaded that good news fails to even bring a grin to that ugly puss?"

"Well, Jim, it's not because I'm jaded and totally cynical. I guess it's because I've also read the second part of this thing."

Johnson quickly sat down into his chair.

"How about sharing that news with me, Bill."

Corey got to his feet and walked to the balcony side of the room. He parted the curtains a few inches and looked out, down at the street five floors below. It seemed empty. He turned and walked back to near where his partner was sitting.

"The second part covers a one-time assignment to any 'observers' reading it. According to my informant, when we spoke before he sent this to me, he said that observers was our group's code word for 'doers'."

"And what are doers?"

Corey cleared his throat, then did it again.

"They're assassins."

Johnson sat very still, then he lunged to his feet and grabbed the sheet. He read it again then looked up.

"Does it say what their assignments are?"

Corey nodded and took back the sheet. "Here, in this last bunch of coded numbers. This section right here."

He pointed to the bottom third of the sheet. He took a red ballpoint pen from his inside pocket and circled a series of numbers, then corrected the circle to include a few more numbers.

He passed the sheet to Johnson.

"Can you quickly estimate the names buried there?"

Johnson retook the sheet and sat down. He took Corey's red pen and started to enter letters above the numbers Corey had circled. Once or twice he slashed out a letter and replaced it.

It took him less than two minutes to finish. Silently he handed the pen back to Corey, then remembered he was holding the paper and returned that as well. Then he sat down slowly. He looked up at Corey.

"Those numbers translate to two names, Bill." He hesitated a moment. "Our names."

Neither man moved or spoke. Johnson's aunt had a very old miniature grandfather's clock on the kitchen wall and now its swings and resultant wheezes and groans could be heard clearly.

"Our names are on a hit list that our group apparently sends out wholesale to its current list of doers.

"Motherfucker, Bill. I can't believe this fucking group has done this. It sounds like a cheap late-night TV crapper. In this day and age two reporters get marked for murder because of a story they're working on? Is that really possible?"

Corey folded the marked-up paper and put it in his jacket's inside pocket.

"It's really possible, Bill. We now have a price on our heads."

Chapter 27

***"Every man must do two things alone; he must do his
own believing and his own dying."***

Martin Luther, (1483-1546).

###

"From now on, Jim, we have to really take precautions. This is no longer a make-believe thing, these assholes really are prepared to pay to have us killed.

"First, we have to prepare a record of what each has done on this story, and then combine the two parts into one. When that's done, and we should do that now, tonight, before we leave here.

"Each of us should then leave copies with at least two reliable friends, even lawyers, who will make them public if we are eliminated. We can make copies back at the paper."

"What good will that do to help us stay alive?"

Corey shrugged. "I don't know. Maybe if we make it known to one or two loudmouths at the paper about what we're working on, and hope it gets back to someone with authority to cancel this killing order, it might work to at least get a temporary reprieve.

"After that we have to do one of two things."

Johnson watched him but remained silent.

"We can work like hell and hope to get the story completed, and published, before one of those doers gets us. Once it's out even this group will probably think twice before re-issuing a kill order, the publicity would be great and possibly too much even for them."

"And the other option, Bill?"

"Walk away from the story, and again make sure the blabbers at the paper know that. We can just say our sources dried up, there's no story left."

"So we quit?"

Corey nodded. "If we can get the story before a doer finds us, we're probably safe. What odds do you give we can do that quickly?

"My source has probably shot his load with this sheet he sent me," Johnson said. "I doubt if we'll get more good stuff from him. What do you think about your informant?"

"Over time, Jim, he might give us enough to print it. But how much time that would take I have no idea. I do know that if I went to him now, and said we had to get enough to publish, because his group had a murder on sight offer on us, he'd evaporate like piss on a hot stove.

"Our choice is clear, Jim. We proceed with unknown sources and hope we can dodge the doers, or just throw in the towel. What do you vote for?"

Chapter 28

"When one guy sees an invisible man, he's a nut case; ten people see him, it's a cult; ten million people see him, it's a respected religion."

Richard Jeni, entertainer and actor (1957-2007).

###

There was complete silence in the room. Even the grandfather's clock in the kitchen seemed noiseless.

Each man was motionless, his eyes looking at something beyond the room, maybe in the skies outside, maybe deep inside his brain's mazes.

Finally Bill Corey spoke.

"I vote..." His voice broke and he cleared his throat. He looked at Johnson and managed a slight grin.

"A little stage fright I guess. Anyway, I vote to charge ahead. To be honest, Jim, I have a feeling that we've already passed the quit-option line. With this kill order out to who knows how many crazed killers, a retraction now might not even reach all those yahoos in time."

Johnson's glance slid around the room, then finally settled on his partner.

"I guess that's the situation, Bill. It's scary, hell, I'm frightened to death. But pulling the plug now would probably be like you said, too late. All we'd accomplish would be to prove we were quitters, and probably dead quitters at that."

He looked at the notes scattered on the dining room table.

"It seems very doubtful, but maybe if we put on all the pressure we can muster, call in every favor owed to either of us, and beg the news ed for all the help he can assign us, it's just barely possible that we can cobble up enough hard info to get something in print.

"I agree that that's our only hope; get a story out in the public and hope that the fear of more publicity will convince this group to leave us the fuck alone."

Corey nodded slowly. He didn't look happy.

"Neither one of us is really enthused about carrying on, but that seems to be the only possible workable solution to this giant fucking mess," he said.

He walked to the front window, hesitated, then moved quickly to the side, out of view perhaps of a shooter with a rifle.

"Shit, I'm already paranoid, Jim. But I guess from now on, till we get something in the paper, or..." He didn't want to finish that sentence so he didn't.

"Realistically, Jim, how soon could you apply that max pressure to your contact, and what do you estimate your chances are of getting some solid info from him?"

"As to timing, almost immediately. I can contact him first thing manana. But when I say contact him that means to leave a message with his dropbox. We agreed on a coffee shop we both use, and when I want to contact him I leave a note in the can, on top of an unused medicine cabinet. No names of course.

"Usually he has coffee both in the morning and afternoon, and so far he's been pretty prompt in getting back to me.

"As to what success I'll have when I actually talk to him, who knows? I'll play up how far along our story is, and if he co-operates again I'll guarantee him that his part will never come to life.

"On the threat side, all I can do is try to scare him shitless. I'll say that if he doesn't come up with hard info almost immediately, I'll have to quote him in the article. He'll know that's an even faster death sentence than ours.

"I just don't know how he'll react. Up till now he has seemed genuinely interested in exposing some of the group's more egregious crimes, but when I put him to the wall he'll either crumble and work with us, or just say fuck you and hope their freelance killers do a quick job on us."

Johnson had a very glum expression on his usually smiling face and Corey knew he wasn't very optimistic about his contact's performance when directly threatened.

"And what odds do you give on your contact, Bill?"

About 100 to 1, Corey thought, but hesitated to put that figure into the already gloomy conversation.

"Just like you, Jim, it's tough to put numbers on it. Maybe less than even money, and realistically not likely better than one in 10. But I know that even longshots can come in sometimes, and I will absolutely give it my best shot. As I know you will. We both know the downside if we can't get these contacts to open up."

Both men stopped talking. Each was thinking of the very real possibility that this group, that they had joked and laughed about in the past, was now showing its real claws, the same claws it had used over a couple of millennia to shut up other, much bigger, much stronger, opposition.

Finally Corey cleared his throat again.

"Okay, Jim, let's get on with it. Here are my notes. I think you can read most of my scrawls. How be you mesh my stuff with yours? We're not doing finished copy here, all we want is a written resume of what we've learned so far, right up to where we found out about the death contracts.

"As you're combining, I'll look over your shoulder and try to rewrite the rough stuff into something at least readable.

"When we've got a tight piece that covers all we know, then we should head back to the paper and make several copies for each."

Johnson nodded, but then shook his head.

"Not to the paper, Bill. That's too obvious, and we already know there's some fucking spy there keeping tabs on us. We can just stop into the first printing or copy store we see. After we've made copies we can split and go home and decide who's going to get a copy. Those copies should be emailed or snail mailed first thing tomorrow."

Corey nodded.

"Good thinking, Jim. Let's do it that way. Who are you going to send copies to?

Johnson paused. "Hadn't really thought about it. Hmm, guess my lawyer for one. He's not too bright, but I'll attach a note explaining what it's all about. I think he cares enough about the law that he'd take some action if needed."

He scratched his chin.

"Other copies? I have a cousin who's a federal prosecutor back east. He'd do something. I'll snail mail him a copy. And maybe one to the editor of 'Sneaky', that crap magazine that just loves conspiracies. I once did a couple of freelance pieces for him, way back in the olden days, and he seemed to like them, even asked for more, so I think he'd do something in print."

"Good choices, Jim. I'm going to send copies to my lawyer. I still owe him some on my divorce, but he's a pretty decent guy and I don't think a few bucks would deter him from doing something.

"And I think my doctor will get one. Every time I visit, about once a decade, he gets onto the subject of the free press, and how important it is to everyone. I'm pretty sure he'd take some concrete action, ignoring any possible risk to himself. He's that kind of man.

"And I may think of one or two other people who would probably stand up for justice if the need arose."

"The more the merrier, Bill. This is one time we want to have several people on our side, unconnected, and even geographically separated.

"Our group has incredible contacts. And most likely hit men, almost everywhere, but even it might not be able to shut down several reputable voices before the damage was done.

"That's our only hope now. That the fear of possible really bad publicity may convince these rotten people to hold up, to cancel the kill orders already out on us."

Corey nodded. "Right. Okay, let's get this write-up done, Jim. And following your scenario, after the copy shop we'll split and go home, so let's make a firm time and place now for our meet tomorrow. How's your schedule?"

"Fuck my schedule, Bill. Right now dentist appointments seem to be pretty unimportant. Let's get together early, say eightish, at Tommy's Cafe. It's a little off our usual watering-hole path but that's probably a good idea."

"That joint on east Waterton? Okay, I'll wear my flea-proof jacket. Meet you there close to eight."

Chapter 29

A recent University of British Columbia study found that analytic thinking can decrease religious belief, even in devout believers. The study, which was published in the April 27/12 issue of Science, finds that thinking analytically increases disbelief among believers and skeptics alike, shedding important new light on the psychology of religious belief.

###

Corey checked his watch again. It still showed 7.58, just as it had a few seconds ago.

There were just three other early patrons of Tommy's Cafe hospitality. Two looked like maintenance workers associated with the city truck illegally parked right outside, and the third was apparently a man of leisure, if his threadbare jacket and no socks were accurate indications.

Corey cursed under his breath. Who gave a shit what these guys did? Where the fuck was Johnson?

His watch had jumped to 7.59. Time marches on, he thought, remembering watching old-time WW2 newsreels with that slogan from the rerun movie channel.

He finished his coffee, spilling the last few drops on the counter. He grabbed the napkin dispenser. It was empty, so he wiped his sleeve and made the spillage disappear.

Where was Johnson? Was it possible he had slept in on this fucking morning?

No, he didn't think that was possible.

Maybe he was being unfair. It was only now—his watch clicked over, finally! --8.00, so he wasn't really late. Yet.

He signaled to the waitress who was talking with one of the maintenance guys, and held up his cup. She nodded, and grabbed the pot, and hurried over to his table. Guess she was trying to impress him that she could handle four customers without breaking down.

8.01. Now Johnson was late! How could he be late when they had so much really important stuff to do?

He drained his cup, shit, he'd have to be taking leaks all morning, he rarely drank that much coffee so early in the day. Where was he?

8.06. Now he was getting really worried. Johnson was a rare reporter who usually was early for his appointments, unlike most of the breed who felt time commitments were for others.

The waitress, now down to just two customers, the maintenance guys had finally moved on, smiled and pointed to his cup. He shook his head; any more coffee and it would squirt out of his ears.

Corey cast around for something to look at, anything to take his mind off the time. He glanced at the man of leisure who was still sitting in the same position at the counter. Suddenly he shifted, as if aware of Corey's stare. He shuffled his feet and wrapped his jacket more tightly around himself.

Corey looked away, then quickly back. Hadn't he seen that gesture somewhere recently? The guy's left shoulder was lower than his right, and when he shrugged, as he had just done, he seemed tilted off center.

He rubbed his eyes, tried to think back. Today? No. Yesterday? Possibly. Trim the time down a little. Last evening?

He and Jim had walked from Johnson's aunt's apartment and headed west on Grandview until they found an open copy shop. They entered and Corey had finished his copies first, so he had ducked back out for some fresh air, the shop reeked of some kind of solvent.

He had looked inside at Johnson pushing his copies into an envelope, then glanced casually across the street to where a bum had been lounging against the front display window of a closed beauty shop. When the bum noticed him looking he had shrugged and turned to look into the shop, as though women's beauty products were of great interest.

That's it! As the bum turned his left shoulder looked off kilter, just as the guy's at the counter did.

He opened his eyes to look again at the counter. Where the bum had been was now empty space. Out of the corner of his eye he noticed the outside door swinging closed. The prick had skipped.

He checked his watch. 8.11. If he left now, to tail or confront the bum, he might miss Johnson.

No, he'd better stay. They already knew that the group had people watching them. He just hoped the bum didn't have a sawed-off shotgun tucked away in that flea-bitten jacket.

Would the group be stupid enough to have a killer shoot them in broad daylight? Yes. In a public place, if you could call this greasy spoon a public place? Yes again.

Those pricks would do anything to keep their secrets. After all, it was the biggest business in the entire world, and obviously worth taking a few chances to keep its money-making goliath grinding out the bucks.

He caught the waitress's eye and nodded at his cup.

He'd give Johnson a few more minutes, say until 8.20.

If he hadn't showed up by then he'd leave, to get his copies mailed and delivered, and catch up with his partner later in the morning.

The paper always had a routine meeting at 10 a.m. each work day. The news editor, or his assistant if he was traveling or otherwise busy, would quickly go over the local news with the reporters, and make any new assignments necessary.

Older reporters like Corey and Johnson thought of the meeting as a sort of recess, a time to relax and gossip with other reporters before the day's real work began.

But most reporters showed up unless they were on an actual assignment elsewhere, and Corey was sure Jim would be there this morning as they hadn't arranged any other meeting place after Tommy's Cafe.

8.17. Just a couple of minutes more.

Chapter 30

"When a well-packaged web of lies has been sold gradually to the masses over generations, the truth will seem utterly preposterous and its speaker a raving lunatic."

'Dresden James' [Donald James Wheal], writer, 1931-2008].

#

10 a.m.

"Okay, guys, settle down. The boss is away but he left instructions on what he wanted done today."

Assistant news editor Stan Kolby was a former night scene reporter who had tired of the constant drinking and schmoozing with so-called entertainers and 'celebrities' who made up most of that beat, so when the job became vacant with Diamond's promotion to news ed he had applied for it and won. He was well regarded by the current reporters and considered a knowledgeable editor.

He looked around at the group scattered on chairs and standing outside the news ed's office. Kolby's office consisted of a desk, two chairs, and an old-fashioned iron coat rack. Hardly enough room for three, let alone the dozen-odd staffers now assembled.

He looked at the bunch. "Where's Kendall?"

"The boss sent him out on that drowning near the Habas Lighthouse." The speaker was Henry Gimble, an old timer who functioned as an unofficial assistant assistant news editor when he wasn't occupied with his gardening beat.

"Okay." Kolby looked around again. "And Johnson?"

No one answered, and finally Corey finally spoke up.

"He asked me to tell you he had a hot tip on some stock market funny stuff. Said he'd check in with you ASAP." It was the best Corey could do.

Kolby knew Johnson was a good reporter and usually diligent about staff meetings.

"Okay. Let's get on with the new assignments."

Kolby pulled a dog eared and grubby notebook from his back pocket and flipped through it until he found today's notes.

"Starting off, Bilchuk, you are covering the teachers' strike action. Diamond wants a half dozen paras on what action the school board is going to take."

Kolby carried on with the day's assignments, and the reporters peeled off to get underway as he checked off their names.

Corey listened with one ear. Mostly his brain was churning like yesterday's warmed-over stew. Where was Johnson? Why hadn't he made contact?

After leaving the greasy spoon earlier that morning—8.20 had come and gone with just a couple of arriving customers, none of them Johnson or the mysterious bum—Corey had delivered a copy to his still-owed lawyer, Ben Stanhope, giving him a sealed envelope and telling him simply that he could open it if anything 'deadly' happened to Corey.

The lawyer had laughed, asking that if that happened who would pay his outstanding divorce bill, and tucked it away in his office safe.

Corey had then gone to a sub post office branch where he mailed the rest of his copies, five in all. He had thought it best to have too many rather than too few. Who knew how far the group's tentacles reached? No, he corrected himself. He knew only too well how far those slimy grabbers reached: almost everywhere.

There had been a lineup at the post office, and by the time he finished it was close to 10, so he had headed to the paper for the news meeting. He had hoped there might be a note or a phone call slip in his mail box at the paper from Johnson, but there was nothing.

Now all the other reporters had been given assignments and left. Usually his name would have called in the rough alphabetic order Kolby used but today it hadn't.

Kolby closed his notebook and wrapped a thick rubber band around it to keep the pages from falling out.

"What's going on, Bill? Kolby put one foot up on a wooden chair.

"What do you mean?"

"Johnson rarely misses these meetings, Bill, unless he's really on something hot. That bit about stock market funny stuff is so much crap. He would have turned that over to Stephenson the markets reporter, or at least cleared it with me or Diamond. And you look like you're expecting someone to stick a shiv in you."

Corey considered about telling Kolby what was really going on. But was it possible he was somehow controlled by the group? Of course, anybody could be. And what could he do anyway, even if he believed what to most people would sound like some crazy conspiracy theory.

Nothing really, so Corey decided to keep mum.

"Nothing much, Stan. I think Jim is on some possible story but that's all I know. And I just fell into a tub of vodka last night. As long as I never take a drink again, I'll pull through."

Kolby smiled. "I've been there, done that. Okay, Bill, if you see Johnson tell him to call me or Diamond, just so someone knows where he is."

Yeah, that's what I'd like to know. Corey nodded and headed out to interview a flunky in the highways department who claimed to have discovered an amazing new highway coating material that would last forever and wouldn't require any maintenance. Another Edison. They came along every month or so, but still had to be checked out. Maybe they did have a new light bulb.

On the way out he stopped at his desk and tore a sheet off his scratch pad.

Jim, missed you this morn. Let's meet at the Gables Bar around 1. Bill.

He stuck the note under a paperweight of a nude bikini-clad beauty on Johnson's desk. He'd also leave a message at the switchboard in case he phoned in for messages.

Now, in spite of the background worry that seemed a part of him now, he left the building and picked up his dented and dirty Oldsmobile in the company lot. A shame they stopped making these beauties, he thought. His had over 300 thou on the clock and still ran pretty good. He hated cars and owned one simply because he had to for the job.

Onwards to the invention story of the century, he thought.

Chapter 31

"It is error only, and not truth, that shrinks from inquiry."

Thomas Paine, writer (1737-1809).

# # #

He looked at his watch. 12.46. He had better make his way to the Gables, where he had told Johnson in his note that he would meet him.

The world's highway maintenance problems were now solved. For ever. If the twerp bureaucrat was to be believed, and he personally didn't believe a word of what that asshole had spewed out.

He had asked the correct questions, nodded occasionally to show he was awake and paying some kind of attention, and finally closed out the interview by telling the bureaucrap (in his mind he always changed the final letter from t to p) that he would check out the details with the paper's science editor.

"If he thinks it's a story, I'll get back to you."

The man had smiled, already counting the millions he could cream from his own department if his invention panned out. Corey left hurriedly.

He slammed the Olds into a parking slot behind the hotel, boxed in on one side by a pickup truck and on the other by what looked like a brand-new car of some exotic manufacture. He slammed his door open and saw with pleasure that it had nicked the newbie, which had deliberately been parked so it took up more than one slot.

The bar wasn't crowded, just a few regulars who enjoyed matching wits with the barmaid. Marie was a well-endowed brunette of early thirties, and she loved slinging insults and double entendres with her customers.

Today she was wearing a tight pink sweater which contrasted well with her hair. It also emphasized the full breasts which rolled pleasantly below it every time she reached behind her to grab a glass. The regulars knew that, and as frequently as possible asked Marie for a "fresh glass, please, Marie, this one is a little soiled".

He quickly checked each face. No Johnson. He checked his watch. 1.03. Jim wouldn't have left because he was a few minutes late.

Where in the fuck was he? Corey was starting to think that something had happened to him, something involved with their group, and that meant something bad.

He sat down at an empty table and mouthed "a beer" to Marie, who had a cold dripping bottle and a napkin in front of him almost before he closed his mouth.

"What took you so long", he grinned at Marie, who in turn took a false swipe at him with her bar cloth.

Usually he would engage in a short sparring insult contest with her but now he had no heart for it, and she seemed to understand that. She smiled and walked back to behind the bar, where her appreciative audience had her bending backwards in no time.

Had the group grabbed Johnson? Or even worse, taken him for the proverbial ride often featured in second rate crime novels?

In the background Marie had turned a radio to a classic music station, which she loved, and he half listened to one of Tchaikovsky's immortal compositions. The bar phone rang a few times before Marie grabbed it.

Should he go back to the paper and talk it over with Kolby? He seemed pretty straight, but then weren't most of the bastards in the group?

"No sleeping at the table, Bill. You have to rent a room for that. And maybe even a companion, if you're not really that sleepy."

He focused his eyes, he must have dropped off for a few seconds. He looked up and Marie was at the phone, holding the receiver towards him.

He jumped to his feet, spilling the bottle.

"Sorry, sweetheart, it's not one of your floozies. Just a guy. Although maybe your tastes have changed?" Marie was smiling and he took the phone from her and nodded thanks.

"Bill?"

He recognized his voice immediately.

"Where the fuck have you been? I figured maybe you'd fallen into those pricks' clutches."

"I damn near did. Listen, I don't think this phone is safe so I have to make it short." Johnson sounded out of breath. "Let's meet right where you are, say in one hour. It will take me that long to shake off my watchers."

Corey wanted desperately to learn more but realized Johnson was badly frightened.

"Sure, okay, here anytime after 2 this afternoon. Okay?"

"That's good. See you then. I hope." And Johnson was gone, the phone slammed down abruptly.

What did he mean, I hope? Was he actually in imminent danger? Where was he? Why was it going to take an hour to get to the Gables?

He handed the receiver back to Marie, threw her a kiss, which she acknowledged receiving by returning a big juicy one to him, and went back to his table. He was about to order another beer, to replace the spilled one, when he saw that the table had been wiped clean and there was a fresh beer on a new napkin. Christ, if all women were only as considerate.

He checked his watch again. 1.12. Almost an hour to wait. He'd have to watch the booze, he didn't want to be half buzzed when Johnson got there.

If he did.

Chapter 32

"One of the cleverer and more mature of my undergraduate contemporaries, who was deeply religious, went camping in the Scottish isles. In the middle of the night he and his girlfriend were woken in their tent by the voice of the devil — Satan himself; there could be no possible doubt: the voice was in every sense diabolical. My friend would never forget this horrifying experience, and it was one of the factors that later drove him to be ordained. My youthful self was impressed by his story, and I later recounted it to a gathering of zoologists relaxing in the Rose and Crown Inn, Oxford. Two of them happened to be experienced ornithologists, and they roared with laughter. "Manx shearwater!" they shouted in delighted chorus. One of them added that the diabolical shrieks and cackles of this species have earned it, in various parts of the world and in various languages, the local nickname 'Devil Bird'."

Richard Dawkins, b.1941, evolutionary biologist and author. He was the University of Oxford's Professor for Public Understanding of Science from 1995 until 2008.

###

For what seemed like the fiftieth time he checked his watch. 2.10. Johnson was overdue. Again.

He carefully nursed his third beer. He would have liked to switch to straight whisky or even vodka, but he knew he had to be clear headed when, or even if, Johnson showed up.

This whole story was getting out of hand. As a reporter he fully understood that sometimes stories involved hardship, even physical risks, but until he and Johnson had started on this story, he had never felt his very life was in danger.

Where was his line in the sand? At what point would he feel justified in calling it quits? Was it a macho thing, something he had to do to prove he was really a man?

Bullshit. He had grown out of that nonsense years ago. He remembered the time a very attractive college coed had tried to get him to do something to prove to her he was a man. He had trouble even remembering the dare she had given him. Something about drinking a lot, then driving fast on a normally deserted at late night country road.

He had gone as far as doing the drinking, and staggering out to his car. The prize, getting into her pants, seemed worthwhile. But as he was clumsily sticking the key into the slot he had suddenly realized. There was no pussy, anywhere, anytime, worth the risks he had been about to take. Risks to himself, to any other innocent drivers on the road.

He had laughed, pulled out the key. "Find yourself some other slave, sweetie", he had said, and stumbled into the back seat where he had luckily passed out for several hours. When he awoke he realized that he had made a crossing of sorts. He had understood that no other person's teasing or dares should or would override his own sense of responsibility.

He laughed aloud. Here he was afraid for his friend's life, even his own, and he's rhapsodizing about his coming of age moment years ago. He must be losing it.

"I thought you were asleep."

He shook his head and looked up. Pulling out a chair and sitting down was Jim Johnson, his almost given-up partner on this fucking story.

"Yeah, I was getting ready to dream about living a normal life again. And where have you been, and what have you been doing?"

Johnson swivelled, caught Marie's eye, and held up two fingers. She nodded and reached into the beer cooler.

"Let me get a drink first."

Marie placed the two bottles on the table, smiled at them, and left. She seemed to have an inherent sense of when people wanted to be alone.

Johnson took a long drink from the bottle, swiped his lips, and took another hit.

Corey watched him carefully. Nothing obvious about his physical appearance, but he seemed stressed, nervous. Maybe even frightened.

He sat up straighter in his chair. "Bill, you are not going to believe me. I can hardly believe it myself."

He cleared his throat.

"Four men, their heads covered by plastic cartoon masks that kids play with, grabbed me when I was leaving my apartment this morning. They gave me a choice. A lot of money, a real big lot, or death."

Chapter 33

"Convictions are more dangerous enemies of truth than lies."

Friedrich Wilhelm Nietzsche, philosopher (1844-1900).

###

Corey looked at Johnson. His mouth felt dry. "What do you mean?" Even to him the words sounded trite, stupid.

Johnson looked around, then back at Corey. "Just what I said, Bill. Those creeps in Halloween masks gave me just two options." He took another drink.

Corey watched him closely. Was this some sort of gag, some elaborate pulling of his leg?

"They said," Johnson cleared his throat again, "said that I had those choices. The easy one, they said, was to take a shitload of cash, quick, and all tax free. Or a shitload of death, just as quick."

He sort of grinned at his partner, the same look a feral dog gets just before he sinks his teeth into your leg.

Corey cleared his throat. Must be contagious, he thought.

"So exactly what happened?"

Johnson leaned forward, almost touching Corey's legs with his. He pushed his bottle aside so he wouldn't knock it off the table.

"Like I said, when I opened my apartment door to head out to meet you, this mob of masked yahoos pushed me back into the apartment. All had those stupid masks on, you know, Superman or Spiderman or whoever the fuck they are, and when I started to shove back, one of them pulled out a gun. Looked like an automatic to me, but I'm no expert."

Johnson adjusted his legs so he wasn't on top of Corey's. He leaned even closer.

"What looked like the leader, he was wearing a Lone Ranger mask, then grabbed my arm and shoved me over to the sofa and pushed me back down onto it. He stood over me like he was going to smack me or something, but he just started to talk."

Johnson leaned back in his chair, groped for his bottle, and drained it. He held it aloft and Marie saw it and nodded.

"Will you get to the fucking point?" Corey was getting increasingly nervous."

Johnson started to speak, then hesitated as Marie brought his refill. She looked at Corey and he shook his head. She turned back to the bar and Johnson started again.

"As I remember it, and remember I was a little fucking scared out of my wits at that point, he said that he and the others represented a 'concerned party' that had become concerned because of our 'misguided' attempts to create a story out of nonsense.

"He said that ordinarily this concerned party would just laugh off our feeble attempts to turn fiction into fact—those were his exact words, so it sounds like he might be in the writing field somewhere—but because at the present time that party had a number of 'problems' elsewhere, they decided it would be best to get this little problem resolved quickly. And permanently. He emphasized permanently."

Johnson was sweating, and he used his left hand to wipe his forehead clean.

Corey was also feeling very uneasy. "So what specifically were his options?"

"He said we each could get a hundred grand by this weekend, in cash. In agreement to stop this 'silliness' immediately, and permanently."

Johnson wiped his freshly wet forehead again.

"Or by this same weekend, he said we could have the other option. Death."

Chapter 34

"Moral certainty is always a sign of cultural inferiority. The more uncivilized the man, the surer he is that he knows precisely what is right and what is wrong. All human progress, even in morals, has been the work of men who have doubted the current moral values, not of men who have whooped them up and tried to enforce them. The truly civilized man is always skeptical and tolerant, in this field as in all others. His culture is based on 'I am not too sure.'"

H.L. Mencken, writer, editor, and critic (1880-1956).

###

Both men shifted in their seats. Corey pulled a napkin from the dispenser and tried to casually mop his forehead. Johnson did the same but had to get a second napkin to complete the task.

"What do we do?"

Johnson asked the question but did not look too hopeful about getting an answer.

Corey cooperated by sitting as silent as Abe Lincoln on one of his many statues.

Finally Corey cleared his throat—it was contagious! —and said "Well."

He stopped there for several minutes, trying to marshal his thoughts. The problem was he didn't really have any thoughts to marshal.

After what seemed like several hours Johnson leapt into the conversational gap.

"Pretty simply, Bill. Two choices."

Corey looked at him as he would at a religious tract vendor soliciting a donation.

"Brilliant, partner." He sat up straighter in his chair and slid it closer to the table and Johnson's chair as well.

"Okay, we get rich very quickly or apparently we don't have to worry about whether our pension plan will still be around when we retire."

He looked closely at Johnson.

"How serious were these guys?"

Johnson didn't hesitate.

"I got the impression that if the Lone Ranger had received instructions via a mental beam from his boss, he would gladly have pulled the trigger right then." He paused.

"I don't think he was kidding, Bill."

Corey nodded.

"Are we going to take the big bucks? I vote no." He looked at Johnson.

"Although I know I should have my head examined, I have to agree, Bill. If we can get scared off a great story by a bunch of cowards wearing masks, we're definitely in the wrong business. Fuck, we're reporters, not wimps working in the civil service."

A hidden thought popped up. "Jim, did you get your copies mailed or delivered?"

Johnson looked sheepish.

"Not yet. I intended to do that this morning but my masked friends interrupted. I'll do it later. How about you??

"I dropped off a sealed copy with my lawyer. You remember friendly old Ben Stanhope, the reporters' friend in need? I still owe him bucks but he didn't press it. I mailed a couple, and I'll get the rest out probably this afternoon or" he looked at his watch, "more likely tonight."

Johnson nodded. "So what's our next move?"

"We have to plan things pretty carefully from now on, Jim. We're definitely in rough waters. How be we get out of here pretty fast? You should make an appearance at the paper, I tried to cover for you, but it sounded weak even to me. I'll make a couple of phone calls I have to make on stories I'm supposedly working on, it'll take me an hour or so. Then let's get together somewhere quiet and private and work out our next moves."

"Sounds good. My place, say in two hours?"

"No, it's obviously well known by our masked idiots. Make it at my place at, let's see, how about 5.30?"

"Fine. I'll hit the paper then head over. Your extra key is still in that phony plant in front of your pad?"

"Yeah, Jim, at the back, stuck between the fake soil and the back of the pot."

"Good, Bill. See you there about five and a half."

Chapter 35
Several years earlier

More than half a billion years ago a spineless creature on the ocean floor went through two successive doublings in the amount of its DNA. This simple "mistake" eventually triggered the evolution of humans and many other animals, says a new study from the College of Life Sciences at the University of Dundee, Scotland.

(Reported in the 7.25.12 issue of Discovery News.)

Alan Goldmann hammered his gavel on the heavy oak desk. Nobody seemed to hear it. So he did it again. And again. Finally he thrust aside the gavel and shouted, "Shut up!"

That got through to the noisy group and slowly the talking and rustling of papers and other sounds died down. The 10 men looked at him expectantly.

"Okay, already. Do you people have to sound like a freshman class of acne-riddled kids learning for the first time that broads have tits?"

He shuffled the small stack of papers on the desk.

"We have some big decisions to make today, and even though Ben Stone and Steven Haltfalter are off sick we have plenty to make up the necessary two-thirds of the full board required for major votes. Now I hope we can keep the sparring and posturing down to a minimum so we can get all our new business cleared before sundown."

He looked at each member for a few seconds, then slid his glance to the next.

Each man showed an air of innocence that you would expect from a 10-year-old who had just successfully fingered his eight-year-old brother for a misdemeanor that he had committed. But he knew that each was just waiting to start the bickering, the objectioning, the wrangling for which board meetings of GOD® had become infamous.

Fuck it, he thought. He'd push through today's agenda or die trying. This was his first meeting as chairman where major decisions were needed and he was determined that Alan Goldmann would not fail.

"Fine. Let's get started. I have here"—he pulled a thick stack of bound pages from his pile— "a report from Adam Worthy." The named member smiled and waved to his fellow members. Shit, they're all movie stars, though Goldmann. "It covers the current situation of our main franchisees, especially those headquartered in Eye-tie areas and now in several Latin America cities."

"You mean the Crapolics, right?" Wain Gooder was a believer in naming names, in getting quickly to the matter at hand.

"Yes, Wain, the report covers mainly our Crapolic franchisees. But it also has details on several other franchisees that are also causing problems."

Arthur Westinham was a senior member of the board, and a senior as well, both of which positions he filled to overflowing with well meant but meaningless and useless objections and clarifications. Now he partly stood, as when seated his 5-foot zero frame was almost invisible.

"Mr. Chairman, I think we should all be very clear on what those problems are, before we start analyzing possible solutions to them."

Motherfucker, would he ever just shut up? Goldmann nodded and cleared this throat.

"Thank you for that, Arthur. I was just about to do that before you, before the interruption.

"The problems, gentlemen, are the same problems which this board has discussed several times before. Let me just quickly enumerate them.

"First, and probably most important, is the declining membership of all our religious franchisees. But that decline is especially noticeable in the Crapolic franchise, which in just the last decade has slumped over 27 percent. And that decade is not unusual. If you look at a graph of total Crapolic membership over the last 50 years—half a century—the decline has been consistent and increasing.

"And while we at GOD® do not care a rat's ass about that decline per se, we sure as hell do care about the resultant decline in our franchisee fees, which as you all know were perhaps foolishly tied in to a franchisee's total membership, instead of what we have been doing recently, just levying a large flat annual fee, and let the franchisee worry about declines.

"And because we are men of honor, we have to respect that original franchise agreement. But under it our annual franchise fee revenue has dropped almost one-third just in the last few years. The trend, unfortunately, continues down. As more people who once believed the religious pap now see that science has disproved almost every one of its 'principles', fewer new members are joining or remaining in these religious groups."

Goldmann paused to take a drink from the decanter on the desk. An unwritten rule held that the chairman, and only the chairman, was entitled to have a decanter filled with wine. The board members, unfortunately, were restricted to water. This was the result of too many board meetings which had to be postponed, even cancelled, due to shouting and/or swinging matches between men who viewed arguing as normal as breathing. Some would even say more normal.

Several members held up their hands—a new rule implemented for the same reason as the water rule—but Goldmann ignored them. He knew the dangers of letting anyone start talking before he was completely finished.

"Second. Not only are we losing franchisee revenue from lower memberships, but most of the franchisees are now complaining that the worth of their GOD™ franchises are declining. They repeat much of what I have just said under the previous reason, and add to it that we are not properly marketing the franchise name. They say we should increase our franchise marketing budget from the current 3 percent of gross income to a much higher figure.

"Several have even suggested that 10 or 15 percent would be more appropriate in this time of reduced religious beliefs."

Several members struggled in their seats, trying to get around the 'no standing' rule, imposed for the same reason as the previous two rules. Muttered 'those pricks' and 'fuck all those cocksuckers' were heard but couldn't be tied to any specific member.

"Yes, I agree with all those sentiments," Goldmann grinned. "Here's something for comparison."

He reached to the bottom of his stack of papers and pulled out a single sheet.

"This sheet, which I will have copied and made available after this meeting, shows our group's total annual revenues. That is 100 percent."

He pointed to a circle completely filled in. "And the red part is the income from GOD®. You can clearly see that it is by far the biggest income element in our total revenue. That has made it the most significant part of revenue. Until now." He paused to let that fact make an impression.

"Next figure shows total GOD® revenue. That's this circle here. You can see that the filled in part, which was once 100 percent, is now partly empty. In fact, the filled in part is now at only 48 percent."

Several members gasped.

"Yes, it's that bad. Our GOD® revenue is less than half of what it once was."

Every member's hand shot up. Again Goldmann ignored them. This is what absolute power means, he thought, and it's wonderful.

"These next three small graphs show our analysts' predictions for the next 10, 20, and 50 years. You can see that they get emptier and emptier. Even by 20 years out they look almost empty. A sad change from when our forefathers started this wonderful franchising venture. It has supported our people through some difficult times, when we were basically all alone and surrounded literally by enemies. Without this franchise income we quite possibly would have perished."

He paused to let that sink in. No one raised his hand, or even muttered loudly. Each member was thinking of how close to catastrophe they had been. Again.

"It is now essential that we create some new sources of income, and pretty damned soon."

Arthur Westinham again was waving his hand. Goldmann looked at him, smiled, and continued talking.

"Fortunately, some years ago our beloved late Jacob Brenner, who served as board chairman for a record 36 years, could see this problem looming on the horizon. He set up a special and very secret committee of some of our best scientific and business members, and charged them with finding and developing solutions to the problem.

"That same secret committee, now composed of nearly all replacements for the original group, has continued to work on this matter, and today, I am proud to announce, they can see a solution in sight."

He waited while the members stared unbelievingly at him, and then started en masse to smile and grin.

Goldmann held up his hands like a boxing match winner.

"And they did it, even without Albert Einstein's help." The group erupted into laughter.

"I can't divulge everything yet, fellows," Goldmann thought it important to meld a little down-home familiarity with his dictatorial manners, "but rest assured in due time you will all be privy to exactly what they have come up with. It really opens up this whole problem area and proposes a solution that will amaze you. Yes, amaze," as he saw a couple of more cynical members slant their eyes at him.

"It will once and for all resolve both the problems I expounded on before. It clears up both declining memberships, and the resultant lower fee income, and the demand of some franchisees for much larger marketing budgets, from us, of course, not from them."

Several members ignored the rule and pushed back their chairs to stand and applaud. Then the rest joined in. As the waves of appreciation washed over him, Goldmann decided that a temporary violation of a rule was justified.

After allowing the rule violation for several minutes, Goldmann restored order.

"Based on the most recent report I've had from this secret committee, just yesterday in fact, it seems like the final touches will soon be applied to their conclusions, and they expect to be able to appear as a full group before us. That should happen within a year or two. It takes time, of course, for all eventualities to be considered, and tried out and kept or discarded. Their orders are to present to us a foolproof solution."

He hesitated, letting the tension build.

"You could say," he grinned broadly, "that they are developing our own 'final solution'.

Again every single board member jumped to his feet and began clapping excitedly.

Goldmann let the enthusiasm play out, finally holding up his hands to signal a time out.

"Now let's get the rest of this board meeting completed. We have a bunch of regular business to hear and vote on."

Chapter 36
The present

"You only live once, but if you do it right, once is enough."

Mae West, actress (1893-1980).

###

The three fire department trucks skidded to a stop inches before the ladder truck. A police department bomb disposal truck was parked halfway up on the sidewalk. Two uniformed cops were unrolling 'Police line-Do not cross' tapes in front of the building. Another two were repeating the process further out, partitioning off the entire block.

A city ambulance screeched to a halt, its siren winding down as the back doors opened and two uniformed medics jumped down, reaching back for stretchers. Two more ambulances kept their sirens screaming until uniform cops forced motorists caught in the chaos on the street to move immediately.

An unmarked black car pulled up totally on the sidewalk, three plain clothed men got out, showed passes to the uniforms guarding the entrance, and moved inside. From apartment buildings on both sides of the street occupants leaned out of windows, or stood on balconies if they had them, to watch the activity.

At the corner of the two streets a crowd had built up. Three uniforms were trying to keep control, and pushed back forcefully against too-eager viewers.

A pall of smoke covered the whole block, and a dusting of soot-like material lay on all exposed surfaces.

A young woman held out her press pass and showed it to one of the uniformed cops.

He looked at it quickly. "No good, beautiful."

"What do you mean no good. It's perfectly valid, just renewed it a week ago."

He smiled at her. "Still no good. Orders are that no one, not even the pretty ones, get through today. It's a totally closed site."

"What's the big deal, handsome?"

She objected to any nouns used about her which indicated the user was looking at her as a sex object rather than a reporter. Of course she often used that sex object image to gain access to places her male colleagues were shut out of.

"Quien sabe, as they say in Russia," he laughed. He had the dark good looks of a Latino, and she figured he was joking her. "Just following orders, miss." He smiled again.

She relented and also smiled. "Well, what's going on here?"

He smiled rafishly. "If I knew, babe, I'd be glad to fill you in."

She blushed at the double entendre and immediately felt foolish for that.

"Well, muscles, who does know?"

He looked around, and spotted a couple of men in suits.

He pointed his nightstick at them. "Try those guys, they look like dicks. They should know something."

She looked where he was indicating. One of them she knew, Lt. Ben Gonzales.

She waved her press pass and shouted. "Lt. Gonzales. A few words please?"

In spite of all the background noise from the various trucks and the rapidly expanding peanut gallery he heard his name and looked over. He nodded at her, said a few words to his companion, and sauntered over.

"Hi, Patricia. A little late to get a scoop, I'm afraid." He motioned to the TV remote broadcast trucks now forcing their way forward against the slowly giving-way mob.

"Screw the scoop, Ben. I just want to learn what's going on here. Our news desk just got a tip that there had been a major explosion."

"That part's right, Pat. A helluva bang. Took out almost half of this apartment building. It's a smaller place, just eight units, but still a major blast."

She had her notepad out and was jotting what looked like kindergarten scribbles.

"Any idea of cause?"

"The fire captain thinks it may have been a gas stove. That's unusual, though, to cause an explosion this big. So he qualified his initial finding by adding that some kind of accelerant might have been added, although if so the chances of finding any hard remaining evidence would be zero, there's just too much damage."

"Any fatalities or injuries?"

He grimaced. "Plenty of both. The two units below the explosion site were leveled. One was occupied, an older male and female. Both disfigured beyond immediate identification. Other apartment was empty at the time."

He turned as his name was called, and he nodded at the uniform calling him. "Two minutes."

He turned back to the reporter.

"The explosion site was rented by one of your people. A reporter, name of" he pulled out his notebook and flipped a few pages, "Bill Corey. Know him?"

"Yes, of course, he's one of the best. Was he home?"

"Unfortunately, yes. And had a fellow scribbler there with him too." He checked his notes again. "James Johnson."

"Son of a bitch. Jim Johnson. He worked with Bill on a number of good stories, he was a junior reporter but coming along."

She looked up from her notes. Her eyes had reddened. "Were they both, ah..."

The detective put one arm on her shoulder. He cleared his throat. "Sorry, Pat. Yes, they were both blown to smithereens. ID has been made by their wallet docs that survived the blast."

Chapter 37

"Do not ever say that the desire to 'do good' by force is a good motive. Neither power-lust nor stupidity are good motives."

Ayn Rand [1905-82] novelist and philosopher.

###

The paper ran both obituaries in boxed sections on page three, above the fold.

Deaths of the two reporters were listed as the result of an unfortunate gas stove accident when both reporters were together in Corey's apartment discussing current assignments.

There was no mention of any accelerant.

Laudatory comments from editors and fellow reporters who had worked with Corey and Johnson were included after factual data.

On the regular obit page there was a small item about the death of local lawyer Benjamin (Ben) Stanhope, who had perished in his office fire.

Cause of death was attributed to a smoldering cigarette which had turned the office drapes into an inferno, and which then fed on the wood paneling until almost beyond control.

A little unusual in that the cigarette ashtray was at least three meters from the nearest drapes.

The entire office contents had gone up in flames.

EPILOGUE
In the near future

Everything in this world is made of star dust. We come from dust thrown off by stars or planets or moons in this universe. We return to star dust which helps to form some other star or planet or moon in this or some other universe.
Many leading physicists now believe that this universe is one of perhaps a score of universes. Perhaps hundreds or even millions.

###

The room was jammed with people and attaché cases and carry-on suitcases. It looked more like some airport waiting room than the board room of GOD®.

"Everyone, listen up. Sit down somewhere and be quiet." The chairman looked sternly at the crowd.

"This is a regular board meeting, and I have only loosened the rules so that immediate family members could be observers. Observers, not talkers, not shouters.

"So for the last time, sit down!"

The crowds slowly found places to sit, many on the cases they had brought with them.

"All board members have already received copies of the Secret Committee's final report, so I won't go into detail on that."

Immediately the crowd began talking, to each other, to no one.

The chairman held up his hand. He knew better that to believe he could actually control this crowd for more than a few minutes.

"But I will summarize that confidential report for the family members that board members have authorized to be here."

And far too many, he thought. He had told them only immediate family members. Some had authorized distant cousins, in-laws, family hangers-on. What a bunch!

He pulled out from his inside pocket the notes he had scribbled earlier. As he unfolded the sheet the crowd settled down.

"As most of you now know, we have decided to vacate this planet. Our franchisees, which for a very long time were our main income producers, have become unruly and obstreperous, and generally a pain in the you know where.

"Here on earth, which was once a green and watery paradise, conditions have deteriorated greatly. Populations have expanded far beyond the ability of those people to feed themselves. In most countries ruled by religious governments, strict laws against all forms of contraception have been passed and enforced.

"Productive land has been turned into wasteland for huge resettlement camps where people from 'those' disliked countries have been incarcerated by people in 'this' country who didn't want them."

He paused to take a drink.

"Over 96 percent of all species that once lived on this planet have either gone extinct or are well on their way.

"Forests and wet lands, critical to this world's ecology, have been stripped bare and drained so that huge boxlike condominium towers could be built to hold the hordes of unskilled and uneducated masses who now rely on welfare vouchers from various governments, who don't even have the actual funds to actually cash those promissory notes.

"In short, folks, this once shining globe we call earth now has the luster of a burned-out light bulb. Our people have tried in a small way to resist the self-destructive actions of others but eventually we came to realize that eight billion people on the other side was simply an insurmountable force.

"We decided we had to leave. And this time we learned from our experience, that it is far preferable to leave when leaving is possible, rather than waiting and hoping that conditions will miraculously change for the better.

"We've had advance operating groups on Mars for some time now. With space ship travel to there possible now in just six days we have been able to use our own ships to quietly move most of our hard assets there already.

"The whole planet of Mars has been declared by the World Government an open territory for homesteading and our people have staked out a nice sized region.

"Our border protection troops, already experienced here on earth with country border control, have established firm border boundaries there, and they are protected. Firmly protected.

"Climate problems have been met by our experienced container specialists, and most people will not even notice any difference in daily weather to what we have here on earth.

"As our policy here on earth has always been to welcome any genuine immigrant to our country who wished to become one of us, so with Mars we will have an open policy.

"Everyone who wants to can move now to the new Martian territory."

Many in the crowd were now crying or laughing or both.

"We figure we can accommodate all who want to go right now with the next four space trips. Ships are being stripped of all non-essential material to hold the maximum number of people. The next departure, scheduled for within two hours, will accommodate all the people here now."

Several older people had stood up and were waving their arms to get attention.

He pointed his arm to indicate they should sit down.

"And for those who don't want to go now, no problem. We have replaced our failing franchise income with the healthy income we're now getting from our recently developed natural gas supplies. These supplies should last 20 years or so.

"Our country here on earth is secure, and will remain so as long as any of us want to stay here.

"We've had many years of experience in keeping out the bad guys who wanted to eliminate us, and that protection will continue until the last one of us is on Mars."

Loud applause and shouting broke out but slowed and stopped when he held up both arms.

"On Mars, our franchise people have already begun a new enterprise. Researchers tell us that within just a few years many of the new general immigrants to Mars—not our people, of course—will be renewing fears and phobias and superstitions imported from earth."

He paused to let the tension build.

"So we have already set up GOD2∞ on Mars.

"That infinity sign, incidentally, is the new trademark sign there, and has been registered with the World Government.

"Initial indications are that it will be just as successful an income producer as GOD® was here on earth.

"Any of you who would like to get into the exciting Mars franchise sales business should contact David Bernstein.

"So we and our descendants should enjoy the same relative prosperity on Mars as we have for many generations here on earth."

He again held both arms aloft to acknowledge the cheers and applause from the crowd.

"And finally," he shouted to overcome the hubbub.

"Finally, folks, our researchers predict that by 2065 this planet earth will be a total write-off.

"Long before then all our people will be on Mars and we can safely watch as earth becomes a footnote mention in future Martian and Universe One history books."

This time the applause started again, built, and continued.

The chairman smiled and joined the applause. His travel bag was already packed and ready to go.

The end (and the beginning?)